The crisp air was filled with sounds—each separate and distinct.

The falling of snow off the bare trees, the swish of the runners and the peal of the sleigh bells.

Jack noticed the red ripeness of her mouth, a ripeness that demanded tasting. There was no sound but the soft plop of snow as it fell from the trees. It was as if they were cocooned in their own little world. Jack fought to keep from taking her in his arms. Once he began kissing her, he knew that he'd be unable to stop.

"We must go back."

Go back? The fizzy bubbles in Emma's veins burst. She slumped against the backboard and braced her feet. She had been sure Jack was going to kiss her. Her whole body ached for the touch of his mouth against hers. Nobody was around. They were safe. No one would ever know.

Suddenly she had to know how he felt about her. Once again the queer reckless feeling filled her. Acting on pure instinct, she leaned toward him.

"Kiss me." She caught his face between her fingers. "Kiss me like you mean it, Jack."

Harle~~~~~~~~~~~~~~~~**ger**
~~~~~~~~~~~~~~~~**nber 2007**

Dear Reader,

Christmas is my favorite time of year. I loved discovering how the modern-day British Christmas tradition has altered and grown from the one celebrated during the first half of the nineteenth century.

The early Victorian period in the northeast of England is absolutely fascinating. It was a time when Britain led the world in civil engineering and design. The mind boggles at what these men accomplished and how their actions changed the course of history.

The High Level Bridge in the story does exist, and is a Grade 1 listed building. Robert Stephenson was the chief engineer, and Thomas Elliot Harrison the assistant. Work was started on the bridge, built for the Newcastle Berwick Railway, in October 1846 and completed in August 1849. Although Queen Victoria offered Robert Stephenson a knighthood when she opened the bridge, he refused. The bridge is currently closed to road traffic, but trains still trundle across it on their way into Newcastle Central Station from London. I trust you will forgive the few alterations I made to the actual history. I am a novelist writing historical romance, rather than a historian writing nonfiction.

I hope you will enjoy reading my tale of Christmas in the industrial north as much as I enjoyed writing it.

Wishing you all the best for the holiday season.

Michelle

MICHELLE STYLES

A CHRISTMAS WEDDING WAGER

HARLEQUIN®

TORONTO • NEW YORK • LONDON
AMSTERDAM • PARIS • SYDNEY • HAMBURG
STOCKHOLM • ATHENS • TOKYO • MILAN • MADRID
PRAGUE • WARSAW • BUDAPEST • AUCKLAND

ISBN-13: 978-0-373-29478-7
ISBN-10:   0-373-29478-6

A CHRISTMAS WEDDING WAGER

DON'T MISS THESE OTHER
NOVELS AVAILABLE NOW:

#875 MASQUERADING MISTRESS—Sophia James

Thornton Lindsay, Duke of Penborne, is astounded when a beautiful stranger comes to London claiming to be his lover. Courtesan or charlatan, could this sensual woman be the one to mend a life he'd thought damaged beyond repair?

Harlequin® Historical is loosening the laces—be sure to look out for our newest, hottest, sexiest miniseries, UNDONE!

#876 THE ANGEL AND THE OUTLAW—Kathryn Albright

A lone lighthouse keeper is a stranger to everyone in the small coastal town of La Playa—and that's the way he wants to keep it. Rachel Houston can't help being drawn to this guarded, gorgeous man and his quiet little girl.

#877 VIRGIN SLAVE, BARBARIAN KING—Louise Allen

It would be all too easy to succumb to Wulfric's quiet strength, and Julia wants him more than she's ever wanted anything. But Wulfric could one day be king, and Julia is a Roman slave. What future can there be for two people from such different worlds?

For my husband, whose support, encouragement and belief in me and my writing have been without measure

Chapter One

November 1846, Newcastle Upon Tyne, England

'It is no good getting your hopes up, Miss Emma, the first survey was clear, like. The Gaffer, your father, would agree with me if he were here,' Mudge the foreman pronounced with a solemn face, his words echoing off the walls of the small office.

Emma Harrison forced air into her lungs and struggled to hang on to her temper despite the overwhelming desire to scream. The last thing she needed was a lecture from Mudge about why the line of the bridge had to remain where it was. She could read a survey as well as any man. Better than most.

'My father agrees with me. I told you this. How many times must I repeat it?' She focused her attention on the plan of the site that hung on the wall.

'Your father ain't been himself lately. Begging your pardon, Miss. Everyone on site knows it.'

Emma forced a smile, ignored the growing pain behind her eyes. Today had started badly, and showed every sign of declining further. Her mind kept circling back to one question—how was she going to ensure that the bridge would be built on time?

A few of the navvies and workmen moved through the site overlooking the Tyne in a dispirited fashion, a full three-quarters less than Saturday. The lantern tower of St Nicholas's Church had been barely visible in the heavy fog on the way in from Jesmond this morning. The works bore little resemblance to the sunlit bustling place of last Saturday, when Jack Stanton had been expected.

Emma drew in her breath with a sudden whoosh. And what if Jack Stanton should appear today? How would he react to the deserted site? She swallowed hard and refused to contemplate the horror that would unfold.

'Be reasonable, like, Miss Emma.'

'I am, Mudge.' Emma tucked a stray strand of hair behind her ear. 'I know the excuses by heart. But it is the Monday after payday. A Saint Monday. The men will return when their pay packets, run out and the publican's pockets are full. I grew up around railway and wagonway projects. It is always like this, always has been.'

Mudge shuffled his feet and muttered another expletive.

She rose and glanced out of the narrow window, wrapping her arms about her waist. The fog had lowered further, making the brazier near the first foundation site glow orange.

'What do you want, miss? What should I tell the men?'

To have this bridge built before my father dies. It is his life's ambition to build the first railway bridge to cross the Tyne. A simple request, but one she didn't dare voice. She had to keep the true extent of her father's illness a secret.

Emma gave a small shrug of her shoulders, and fastened the plaid shawl more securely about her.

'A good run of weather until Christmas, maybe into the

New Year. That the new survey of the riverbed proves true and we are able to get the piers erected in double-quick time.'

'You don't want much, miss.' Mudge scratched his head. 'Shall I add peace and prosperity for all while I'm at it?'

Emma ignored the remark. She refused to allow the foreman to intimidate her. She was no longer eighteen, with only thoughts about her next pair of dancing slippers in her head. She knew how bridges were built. She had learnt.

'Oh, and I forgot—the castle. The keep and the royal apartments are to be retained if possible.'

'Only a woman would be concerned about a pile of old stones. It would be far better if it was knocked down and the stone reused. It was what the first survey said.'

'Nevertheless it is to be retained. The first survey was wrong.'

'Ah, but what about the investors—Robert Stephenson and his new partner…that J.T. Stanton? They're right canny, they are.' Mudge crossed his arms. 'Your father ain't thinking straight if he agrees with you, if you don't mind me saying so. If it were up to me, I'd sell the company. Get out while he still can. Bridge-building is a young man's game.'

Emma bit her lip. She needed Mudge and his ability with the men if she was to have any hope of achieving her father's dream. She was under no illusions about the attitude towards women engineers and women directing important engineering projects. But, equally, she refused to let her father's dream and with it his company vanish simply because he had become too ill to be on site every day.

'If that is all,' Emma said through gritted teeth. 'I will take your report back to my father and return tomorrow with my father's further orders.'

'As you wish, miss. But think on what I say. I never steered you wrong before. There is none that can say that Albert Mudge ain't loyal.'

Emma scooped up the various papers, giving vent to her anger by stuffing them into her satchel. She would prevail. The keep was important.

'Miss, give your father my good wishes. There is nowt—'

'Is anyone here? Or is this shack as deserted as the site outside?' A deep, masculine voice sounded from the front counter.

Emma froze, allowing the papers to drop from her hands and cover the desk in a snowstorm. Seven years, and she knew the voice. It no longer held any warmth or intimacy, but she knew it. Jack Stanton. Fate's little joke. To make the day even worse.

'Allow me. Let me handle this.' Mudge tapped the side of his nose and moved towards the counter.

Emma forced a breath, and resisted the temptation to pat her hair or straighten her gown. She had to trust Mudge on this. Jack Stanton would not come in here. There was no need to encounter him. All she had to do was sit still, safe in her father's room. Unworthy of her, but a necessity.

'I'm expected.' The low, insistent tone echoed through the small study. 'There can be no mistake. You will allow me to pass.'

'Mr Harrison is out, sir. Perhaps if you would care to call again at some mutually convenient time?' Mudge's voice held the right amount of fawning.

Emma gave a short nod. She willed Jack to accept the invitation, to come back at an agreed time when she could be certain of getting her father here.

She eased back in the chair, heard a squeak and winced.

'Mr Harrison will see me. Tell him J.T. Stanton requires an interview. I can hear him moving in the back room.'

'Mr Harrison is unavailable.' Mudge moved to block the doorway with his considerable bulk, shielding her from Jack's sight. 'You will have to call at another time, Mr Stanton, if you wish to speak to him. But I am happy to help you with any enquiries you might have.'

Emma squared her shoulders. She refused to hide in the back room like some frightened rabbit while Mudge showed the site and no doubt put his case to retain the current line of the bridge. She would not be defeated so easily.

Jack Stanton held no terror for her. If she allowed Mudge to continue, her father's secret would be out and the company lost. She knew Jack Stanton's reputation. Almost against her will she had followed his progress as he had risen from her father's very junior civil engineer to one of the most respected and wealthiest railwaymen in the entire Empire. But no one rose that fast and far without being utterly ruthless. She had heard the rumours about how he had fired most of the men building a bridge in Manchester, forcing the remaining to work overtime to get the bridge completed and ensure his railway opened on time.

'Mudge, send Mr Stanton in. I will speak with him.' Emma forced her voice to sound strong. She was no longer eighteen, but twenty-five, a confirmed spinster if ever there was one. Railway millionaire or not, Jack Stanton remained a known quantity. She had ended everything between them. It had been the correct thing to do then. It remained the correct thing. She'd had to put the needs of her family before a fair-weather flirtation, as her mother had called it. If Jack had truly loved her, he would have understood. He hadn't. He had left without a word.

Mudge stared at her, open-mouthed.

'Mr Stanton speaks the truth. His presence is expected, even if it has been delayed.'

'As you wish, Miss Emma.' Mudge removed his bulk from the doorway and made an over-elaborate gesture of welcome. But she could tell from his voice that Mudge was singularly unhappy about the situation. 'Miss Harrison wishes to see you, sir.'

Emma forced her back straight, willing Jack Stanton to have become a bloated man with annoying facial hair and prematurely bald.

The black frock-coated figure stalked in, moving with the grace of an untamed predator. The cut of his coat emphasised his slim waist and broad shoulders. The very picture of the successful businessman, but with none of the flash one might expect from someone as newly wealthy as he.

Emma pressed her lips together. His jet-black hair and eyes were more suited to a hero in a Minerva Press novel or one of the penny-bloods found on railway stalls than to real life.

As with so many other things lately, God had turned a deaf ear to her prayer.

She forced her gaze away from his form and concentrated on the cold gleam in his eye and the faint smile on his full mouth. Arrogant. Self-opinionated. Dangerous.

She extended her hand, forced her heart to forget what he had been like seven years ago. The pain he had caused was a distant memory.

'Mr Stanton. It has been a long time.'

'Miss Harrison.'

He gave a nod but ignored her hand. Emma allowed her hand to drop to her side, wishing she had worn something more fashionable than last year's second best grey, but the grey offered easier movement in the sleeves, and the skirt did not require as many petticoats.

'May I ask what brings you here today?'

'My business is with your father.'

'Your business is with Harrison and Lowe.' She smoothed an errant fold in her skirt. 'We expected you two days ago.'

'I was unavoidably detained. Word was sent, informing your father of my intention to arrive today.'

'Obviously the letter was misplaced.' She waved a hand at

the letters that dotted the desk. She would allow him the fiction of a letter, but she knew there had been none. No doubt he wished to catch them unawares. It was exactly the sort of trick she'd expect from such a man. 'My father is unavailable. Perhaps if you could enlighten me as to why you are here?'

'It was your father who requested the meeting,' he said, with the barest hint of a smile. 'I was hoping you might be able to enlighten me.'

'I hardly think he would. Ground was broken a little over a month ago. My father and Mr Stephenson had several long meetings at that time. Everything was arranged to their satisfaction.'

'I regret I was out of the country then. My boat from Rio was delayed.' His eyes raked her form before coming to rest on her mouth. Emma resisted the urge to straighten her gown. She didn't care what he thought about her. 'By the time I returned, the ground had been broken and the project begun. I trust everything is on time? The Newcastle to Berwick line is open in March and we cannot afford delays.'

Emma gave a slight nod. His inference was quite clear. Had Jack Stanton been here he would never have chosen Harrison and Lowe for the project, despite their long association with the Stephensons. And, given what the papers had said about his recent rise in fortune, she had little doubt that Robert Stephenson would have listened to his newest partner.

She refused to worry about that. She had to make him see that not only would Harrison and Lowe complete the project, as promised, but also that the keep should be saved.

'Then you must be given a tour of the site, and I shall be sure to point out the progress.' Emma forced a smile on her lips. She had not endured the rigours of high society without learning the fine art of dissimulation. 'There is a slight question of how the bridge will go through the castle grounds.

My father commissioned a new survey, and it would appear that we can retain the keep, the very symbol of Newcastle, even if the outer walls have to be destroyed.'

'Now, miss…' Mudge cleared his throat.

'Mudge, I believe you have other duties. I am quite capable of showing Mr Stanton around the site and answering any questions he might have. We are old…friends.'

'*You* show me around, Miss Harrison?' One eyebrow tilted upwards as a half-smile appeared on his lips. 'As delightful as the prospect might be, I hardly wish to trespass.'

'Miss Emma.' Mudge made a small bow, but continued to stand in the centre of the room. 'It is right cold out there. The sleet has started coming down fast, like.'

'I do wish, Mudge.' Emma forced her voice to be calm. She refused to have another screaming match with Mudge. The obstinacy of the man! 'I believe I am the best person to guide Mr Stanton around the site. We have already discussed your jobs for the morning.'

'Very good, Miss Emma.' Mudge continued to stand there.

She looked pointedly at the door and the foreman left, grumbling. Emma hoped that he would force several of the men to make a show of working despite the weather. Jack Stanton had to see that progress, although slow, was being made. He had to. With deft fingers she fastened her bonnet, tying the bow neatly under her chin.

'And now, Mr Stanton—what do you wish to inspect first? The foundations, or the ruins of the castle?'

'I look forward to the tour with anticipation, Miss Harrison. Your dulcet tones will make a change from my usual guides.' Jack held out his arm, which Emma studiously ignored.

Emma heard the slight emphasis on *Miss* and winced. Knew what he must be thinking—Emma Harrison, the woman expected to make a brilliant match, living the life of a spinster. She had made the correct choice. Her mother had needed a nurse in her final days, and now her father needed a companion. She did not need to explain her decisions to anyone, least of all to a man to whom she had only been a passing fancy.

'The foundations it will be. This way, if you please, Mr Stanton.' She tightened the shawl about her body and straightened the folds of her skirt, bracing herself against the sting of the sleet. 'I have no doubt we both wish to spend as short a time as possible on this tour.'

'I am at your disposal, ma'am.' He inclined his head, but the smile did not reach his eyes. 'Can you inform me where your father is?'

'Unavailable.' She pointed towards where a solitary man dug in the mist. 'The sooner we begin this inspection, the sooner it will be over. Harrison and Lowe are the best bridge-builders in the area.'

'So your father always led me to believe.'

Emma attempted to ignore the growing pain behind her eyes. By the end of the tour Jack Stanton would be convinced that Harrison and Lowe could do the job. He had to be.

Jack Stanton followed Emma's slightly swaying hips out of the hut. He had not expected to find her here. As far as he was concerned, Emma Harrison and all she had once stood for belonged to a former life. One he had hoped to blot out for ever. He no longer had need of that dream.

He could well remember the number of beaux she'd had buzzing about her. Margaret Harrison had made that clear. She'd expected her daughter to marry and marry well. Impetuously he had followed his heart and made an offer, counting on her affection for him and his future prospects. She'd refused him, never answered his letter, and he had left. He'd expected, if he heard of her at all, to discover she had married.

Only it would appear she had not. Time had been less than kind to Emma. He tried to reconcile the Emma he remembered with the woman who moved before him, her grey clothes mingling with the mist. Her hair was scraped back from her face into a tight crown of braids and topped by one of the most unflattering bonnets he had ever seen. Her skirt moved through the mud as if it were weighed down with chains. It was not his concern. The past was behind him. He looked forward to a glorious future—building bridges and railways, consolidating his companies and enjoying the fruits of his labour.

First he wanted to discover the mystery of why Edward Harrison had written to him, summoning him here. He had intended on leaving the bridge to Stephenson, simply providing the necessary financing. But Stephenson had agreed with the letter. He needed to go up to Newcastle and determine if all was well.

An icy blast of sleet hit as he exited the meagrely heated hut. Winter in Newcastle instead of the oppressive heat of Brazil. Instinctively he braced himself for the next blast, pulled his top hat down more firmly on his head. Emma had moved on ahead, gesturing, pointing out various spots where the foundations would be laid or where the stone had already been cleared.

The wind whipped her skirts around her ankles but she paid no attention. A sudden gust sent her hurtling forward towards the precipice.

Jack reached out his hands, grabbed her arm, and hauled her back to safety. A stone gave way and tumbled down to the bottom of the castle walls. Up close, he could see her blue-grey eyes were as bright as ever, and her lashes just as long.

They stared at each other for a long moment. Then he let her arm go, stepped away.

'You are safe now,' he said. 'You should be more careful. You would not have landed as lightly as that stone.'

'I know what I am doing.' Her chin had a defiant tilt to it.

'The wind is strong, and in those skirts you are a danger.'

'You can see that this is the best site for the bridge, despite its obvious difficulties, but there is still a question of the exact line.' Emma pointed out across the remains of the castle, moved away from him, ignoring his well-meaning advice. Jack glared at her. 'If the bridge is moved slightly to the left, the keep will be saved.'

She finished with a bright smile, as if she was at a dinner party and had said something witty. God preserve him from interfering women. She obviously had no idea of the time and effort that had gone into the planning of the bridge. And he did not intend to embark on some quixotic crusade simply to satisfy her. 'Both Stephenson and I are of one mind. The early surveys show the current path has much to recommend it.'

'A more recent survey—' Her jaw became set and her lower lip stuck out slightly.

He held up a hand. This farce had gone along enough. Edward Harrison had never allowed his daughters on building sites. The Edward Harrison he remembered had strict notions of propriety. Exactly when had he relaxed them for his younger daughter?

'The early surveys are accurate.' He touched his finger to his hat. 'I could explain, Miss Harrison, but I have no desire to bore you senseless with technical considerations. No doubt you would rather be having a conversation about the weather. Or the latest fashions in London. I fear I am out of step with the social niceties, having recently returned from several months in Brazil.'

'On the contrary, Mr Stanton.' She crossed her arms in front of her, dragging the shawl tighter around her body. 'One of the advantages of becoming a plain, acid-tongued spinster is that one might have interesting conversation rather than simply relating the latest bit of tittle-tattle. We must take our pleasures where we can. I would welcome the discussion.'

'An acid-tongued spinster?' Jack repeated. Spinsterhood was a fate he had never envisaged for Emma Harrison. He well remembered the number of men who had circled around her. She had been the centre of attention at the Assembly Rooms, a bright, vivacious girl with a full dance card. What had happened in the intervening years? How had she come to this? 'They are not words I would associate with you.'

'After my mother's demise, it was a choice between eccentricity or a pale but brave invalid. I believe I chose the more preferable option.' A strange smile played on her lips. 'You fail to disagree with my assertion.'

Jack started, and rearranged his features. He had not realised his thought on the ugliness of her dress and her bonnet was plainly visible on his face. He made a slight bow and sought to redeem the situation. 'I had not realised that being a spinster had much to recommend it.'

'Then you realise very little indeed.' The wind had stained her cheeks and nose a bright pink, a tiny bit of colour in an otherwise dull world. 'I find the building of bridges infinitively preferable to discussions about the latest way to trim a hat, make netting or prick a pincushion.'

'It seems a bit extreme—avoiding matrimony because you harbour a dislike of frivolous conversation.' Jack tightened his grip on his cane. 'I understood matrimony was the goal of every young lady.'

'The reasons for my spinsterhood are not up for discussion,

Mr Stanton. Please know I am content with my decisions.' Her eyes blazed. 'I regret nothing.'

'A wise policy. Would that everyone adopted it.' Jack chose a non-committal response. Where exactly was this conversation leading? What did *Miss* Harrison want? Her words had a different purpose.

'And you? Have you married? Is your house full of frivolous conversation and pricked pincushions?' She gave him a level glance, with a steadiness that he had found entrancing in those long-ago days before he'd learnt about women and their fickle nature.

'Thankfully I have been able to escape the machinations of mothers and their daughters.' Jack pressed his lips together. Her remarks had made it obvious where her hopes lay. He would not have her presuming on the past simply because whatever brilliant hopes she'd had hadn't worked out.

Which was it? A duke or an earl that had not come up to scratch? He had forgotten the name of the man her mother had had such hopes for. And the proud Emma Harrison could not bear to admit she had misjudged the situation.

'But do you not long for domestic bliss, Mr Stanton? Warm carpet slippers by the fire?' That steady pair of blue-grey eyes looked up at him again.

Jack thinned his lips. Was this the reason for Harrison's letter? That he sought to make a match for his younger daughter? If so, he was sadly mistaken. He had no wish to renew his suit. The humiliation had been bad enough the first time.

'At present, my life is such that I enjoy my freedom. No wife would put up with me. I am constantly on the move, going from one project to the next—England, South America and Europe are all one to me.'

Her laugh resembled breaking crystal. 'You see, I was

right. We would have never suited. I have rarely been out of the North East these past seven years.'

'I had forgotten that our names were once bandied together.' He made sure his face betrayed no emotion, but he derived a small amount of pleasure in reminding her of what she had casually thrown away. 'I would hate to think I had anything to do with your unmarried state.'

'Pray do not flatter yourself, Mr Stanton.' Emma drew herself up to her full height. Her hands ached from the cold and the sleet dripped off her bonnet, freezing the tip of her nose.

How dared he imply such a thing?

He made it seem as if she was desperately attempting to discover his marital status and had been pining for him the past seven years. She had refused him and his ungallant offer of marriage. He had not cared for her, only for her fortune and the status such a marriage would bring. Her mother had been right. If he'd cared for her, he would have waited and heard her out. He would have understood what she was trying to explain instead of becoming all correct and formal.

'My decision to remain unwed had nothing to do with you. Why is it whenever anyone sees an unmarried lady they immediately assume she is discontent with her life?'

Jack lifted an eyebrow. 'I must protest. You are putting words into my mouth.'

'You implied. As an old *friend*, I was naturally curious as to what had happened in your life.' Emma crossed her arms. He thought her a desperate hag. What did he expect her to do? Fall down on her knees and beg him to marry her simply because he possessed a fortune and good-looks in abundance? The man was insupportable. If she married at all it would be for love, because a man wanted to share his life with her, not keep her in some little box, surrounded by children and amusements suitable for a lady. 'There is nothing wrong with that. A light enquiry to pass the time.'

'I wished to be certain, that is all. I find it best in these circumstances.'

'You flatter your younger self, sir. I refused proposals before yours and after.' Emma tilted her chin in the air, wishing they were having this conversation when she was dressed in her new blue poplin rather than the grey sack that seemed to be becoming more dowdy by the second.

Jack inclined his head. His lips had become a thin white line. 'Forgive me, Miss Harrison, but what was I to think? You were the one enquiring about my marital status. I have learnt to be cautious about such things. I intended no dishonour.'

'It would serve us all better if you did not jump to conclusions but confined yourself to the facts.' She forced her lips to smile her best social smile and batted her lashes, longing for a fan to flutter.

Jack reached out and caught her by the arm as a white-hot anger surged through him.

How dared she bring up old memories? What had once been between them was in the past. He had made no apologies for how he had behaved. He had made an honourable offer of marriage seven years ago. She had refused. He had not needed telling twice. His nostrils flared.

'You forget yourself, Mr Stanton.'

She gave a brief tug and he let her go. Her hand went immediately to the spot where his fingers had gripped, held it. He pressed his lips together, hating himself, hating his sudden loss of control. It had not happened for years. He took pleasure in looking at things dispassionately. Yet within a few minutes of Emma Harrison's company he had reverted to his gauche youth, when his clothes had been bought ready-made and a ball at Newcastle's Assembly Rooms had appeared an excitingly attractive prospect.

'There is no need to go further. I have seen enough, Miss Harrison,' he said.

He turned his back and rested his hands against the cane, seeking to restore his equilibrium. It had been a mistake to come here.

'You must forgive me, Mr Stanton,' her voice called. She came up by him. An entreating face peeped out from under her ugly bonnet. 'I did warn you that my tongue was razor-sharp and that I have become accustomed to speaking my mind. You were correct. My earlier remarks trespassed on our acquaintance. I did not mean to pry. Nor did I mean to imply anything. Pray forgive me.'

'The fault is entirely mine.' Jack made a bow. 'The journey north appears to have made me ill-tempered and out-of-sorts. I should have recognised it for what it was—a light-hearted remark.'

'Shall we quarrel about that now as well?' She tilted her head and her eyes shone with a hidden mischief.

A brief pang rose in Jack's throat for what could have been. He forced himself to swallow and it was gone. He should not have returned here. On a day like today, too many old memories lapped at his mind, drawing him back to a place he'd been certain he had left far behind.

'I have no wish to quarrel with you, Miss Harrison.'

'Nor I with you, Mr Stanton.' She gave a brief nod. 'I do wish, however, to show you what progress has been made so your journey will not have been in vain. I am sure if my father had known you would be here then he'd have made every effort. As it is, today being the Monday after payday, he followed his normal routine.'

'It has been a most enlightening experience.'

They stood awkwardly. Emma pointed out where the piers should be built. Jack made a few polite comments as the sleet started to drive harder. But he could not rid himself of the feeling that there was mystery here. All was not as Emma Harrison would have it seem.

'Have you seen all that you need to?' The number of men standing forlornly by the brazier had diminished slightly. One or two had started to half-heartedly work.

'I do hope you will keep in mind what I said about the castle. At this stage plans are easily changed, but once we begin to lay the foundations in the river...'

'A building site is much like any other on a Saint Monday. Newcastle does not change.'

'It is good that you are aware of the difficulties we face.'

Jack permitted a smile to touch his lips. He disliked mysteries, but this one appeared easily solved. Her tour, although exact, showed she was hiding something.

Seven years ago Emma and her elder sister had appeared every so often, a tantalising glimpse, but her father had never allowed them to remain on site for long. The mother had seen to that.

This time Emma's words and manner seemed to indicate she knew where every last piece of stone was. Jack's eyes narrowed. At present she appeared to be in charge of the bridge-building. That foreman had deferred to her. The navvies appeared more intent on moving the stone when she was about.

She wielded power here.

An idea so preposterous he nearly laughed. Emma Harrison was a woman.

How would she cope when the foundations needed to be laid in the river? Or when the first iron rails were attached?

He could not see any female up on the scaffolding, making

sure everything went according to plan. Would not *want* to see any woman put herself in that sort of danger.

Such a situation would be disastrous for the bridge and the future of Newcastle as an industrial power. The high-level scheme had to be completed on time. Already Brunel had nearly completed the rail link to Scotland on the western side of Britain. He could not allow it to happen. Newcastle could not fall behind.

'Everything seems to be in good order except for one small detail…your father.'

'My father is absent from the site today, but it has no bearing on the progress.' Her knuckles were white against the tartan of her shawl. 'It is a problem, but there is little to be done. I am hopeful of getting the foundations for all the piers laid before spring. The main construction of the nine piers can then begin in the summer, as scheduled.'

'It is what my company desires as well,' he returned smoothly.

He waited, watching Emma's eyelashes blink rapidly. A snowflake landed on her cheek and hung there sparkling for an instant before melting. Impatient fingers brushed it away but she said nothing.

Jack counted to ten twice. He had given her enough time and opportunity. He was through with her games. During the last seven years he had learnt how to play as well. This time they played according to his rules.

'Precisely how ill is your father, Miss Harrison?'

Chapter Two

Emma blinked as her mind reached for a plausible answer. Something that would explain about her father's illness without telling the whole truth about his condition. She took an involuntary step backwards from the tall figure and mumbled a few polite words about a chill.

'You fail to reply, Miss Harrison.' Jack Stanton pressed remorselessly onwards. His dark eyes ice-cold, boring into her soul. 'Your father has not been here for a while, has he?'

'He was here on Saturday,' Emma said, too quickly and too brightly. She had to remain calm. She took a breath and forced the words to tumble more slowly from her mouth. 'If you had arrived when you were expected, you would have seen him hard at work.'

'And before that?' Jack tapped his cane against his calf. He gave a half-smile. 'Come, come, Miss Harrison, enough of this flim-flam. You have been overseeing the construction for quite some time. You possess a certain familiarity with the site that does not come from casual visits.'

'My father and I have become close since my mother's death.' Emma put her hand to her throat and hoped.

'With the greatest respect, Miss Harrison, you have failed
to answer. The question was straightforward.' His harsh tone
gave the lie to his polite words.

She swallowed hard. She had no intention of revealing any
more private matters. Exactly how much did he know? It had
to be an educated guess, no more. She had been careful.
Mudge was sworn to secrecy. He would not betray her father;
she knew that. She filled her lungs with air. She had to keep
her head and think around the problem.

'He has missed a few days, but I come here every day to
advise Mudge on what needs to be done, following my
father's orders.' She gave a small laugh, a little self-deprecating wave of her hand. 'I am the go-between, as it were. You
know what a stickler my father is. He wants to know everything that happens, even when he is confined to bed.'

'You, Miss Harrison?' Jack's eyes widened. 'What do *you*
know about torque and the positioning of stone? What if you
muddled the message? The consequences could be disastrous.'

'I am my father's daughter. I grew up living and breathing
railways, engines and bridges.' Emma lifted her chin and
stared directly at him, daring him to say differently. It had only
been in the last seven years, to save herself from the tedium
of the sickroom, that she had made any real effort, struggling
at first but determined, and gradually relishing the precise
work, but he did not need to know that.

'That may be so, but what of the men? How do they
respond to a woman issuing orders? How do you command
their respect?'

Did he think her incapable of supervising the men? She
knew as much about building bridges as most men—more,
even. She had helped her father with the early drawings for
this bridge, done the calculations for torque while her father
took to his bed. This was her project and her father's dream.

Possibly her last chance. Her only chance. She took a deep breath. 'The bridge will be completed as per the contract. Harrison and Lowe have never been late before. We have our reputation to think of.'

'That is not an answer.'

'It is the only one required.' She gathered her skirts in her hand. She did not owe this man any explanation. It was obvious he had already made his judgement. Like most men, he believed the female mind incapable of understanding the complex calculations required. Thankfully, she had finally convinced her father otherwise. 'Your concern is about whether or not the firm can do an adequate job. I assure you that Harrison and Lowe will.'

A scream rent the air. Jack's face froze, and Emma felt a pit open in her stomach. The noise was too close, far too close. She heard the sound of people running.

'Someone has been hurt,' Emma said. 'I need to go.'

'A building site is a dangerous place, Miss Stanton.' Jack put out his hand, held her arm. 'I may be of some small use.'

Emma nodded as her mind raced. Where had the scream come from? She tried to reassure herself that no one could be seriously hurt. The men were not working on anything dangerous, not in this fog. But the cries were alarming. Panic never served anyone.

They hurried in the direction of the moan. Mudge was already there, peering over the precipice and shaking his head.

'I don't know how this happened, Miss Emma.'

Emma winced. Near the spot where she had almost fallen earlier there had been a landslip. One of the young lads lay under several stones. His face was ashen and his eyes shut. Part of the castle wall had collapsed on top of him. Her mouth went dry as she saw another stone on the top of the wall tremble.

'We have to get him out of there, Mudge.'

'The wall's about to crumble, Miss Emma!' Mudge shouted. He made a clucking noise in the back of his throat. He shook his head. 'The weather's against us. Better to shore it up first, rather than risk another injury. Nasty piece of work. We shall have to go around from the back. Slowly, like. The sooner this here castle is razed to the ground, the better for the men. It ain't nothing but a death trap.'

Emma's mouth was dry as she peered down, trying to see what line the men should take. Mudge was right. The safest way was to circle around from the back, rather than going straight down the slope. But in the uncertain light it would take hours—hours that the lad might not have.

'We need to get someone down there. To pull him away from the wall. If more stones should fall…' Her voice trailed away.

She looked at Mudge and the other men, but no one met her eye or moved. She willed them to say something. One man shuffled his feet.

'A block and tackle! Now!' Jack barked as he made his way down the slope, half sliding as the soft mud gave under his feet. 'Why weren't the basic safety precautions taken?'

'It is dangerous work, like,' one of the men commented, rubbing the back of his neck but making no move to help him.

'Go and get what Mr Stanton requires,' Emma said firmly. Finally a man set off, trudging through the mud. 'Hurry!'

'What he's doing—it's bloody dangerous,' Mudge moaned. 'We lost one man today. We don't even know if he's alive. I have to think of the others.'

Jack made an exasperated noise and continued downwards, reaching the boy.

'He's alive.' He put his fists on his hips. 'Now, you men will help me to move him from here. I need rope and wood. Working together, we can save his life.'

Emma started to climb down, picking her way through the

rubble. Her foot slipped slightly and she was unable to stifle a small gasp. She froze, her hand digging into the clammy mud.

'You had best stay where you are, Miss Harrison. This is no job for a lady. God help us all if you faint.'

'Mr Stanton, I have never fainted in my life and have no intention of ending that habit,' she said, but she checked her movement and looked for a better route down the steep embankment.

'As you wish.' He shrugged out of his frock coat and stood looking at the fallen lad. 'Once I free him from the stones it should be a straightforward operation. We will lift him out of here.'

'Is he badly injured?' Emma called, fear clawing at her stomach. She disliked the way the stones were lying on the boy's leg. She moved around slightly and saw his distinctive blue shirt. 'That's young Davy Newcomb.'

'It appears to be his leg that is trapped.' Jack bent down and tried to shift the stone with his shoulder, but it didn't budge. Behind him, two more stones crashed down. 'Miss Harrison, you will cause problems. The wall is far from stable.'

Emma reached the bottom and wiped her hands against her skirt. 'You see—nothing to it. I am perfectly safe.'

Jack gave a grunt and his eyes assessed her, but he said nothing. Emma knelt by the boy's side, using her handkerchief to wipe some of the mud from his grey face.

'I'm sorry, Miss Emma.' Davy opened his eyes. 'I took a shortcut, slipped in the mud and fell. Them stones tumbled down on top of me. I didn't mean no harm. I know you said that it weren't safe, like, but it were the quickest way.'

'Hush, hush, young Davy. You need to save your strength,' Emma replied. She held the boy's hand between her gloved ones. The boy nodded and a tear ran down his cheek. 'You are being very brave.'

The men threw down the block and tackle, which Jack caught. Once he had fastened the rope he worked quickly, lifting the stones. Davy Newcomb's leg lay twisted at an odd angle.

'You have been lucky, young man,' Jack said. 'By rights that leg should have been crushed. You may escape with only a bad sprain.'

'That will be something for the doctor to decide,' Emma said. 'As you wish…'

They worked together to lift Davy onto the plank. Jack gave a nod and the men slowly pulled him to safety. Emma gave the lad's fingers one last squeeze before several men hauled him up and out.

'Take him to the hospital,' Emma said, staring at Jack, daring him to say differently. Harrison and Lowe always looked after their men in such cases. It was one of the reasons they commanded their loyalty. 'The company will pay for the setting.'

'Bless you, Miss Harrison,' Davy called.

She turned to face Jack, who was glowering at her, hands balled on his hips.

'I had to help,' she said quietly. 'Someone had to.'

'You should have sent one of the men. You put yourself in danger for no good reason.'

'I saw an easy way down.' Emma dared him to say differently. 'It was important to get his leg freed as quickly as possible.'

She bit back the words condemning Mudge and the other men. He lifted a quizzical eyebrow and his gaze slowly travelled down her body.

'And how do you propose getting back up the slope? In a dress? Weighed down by petticoats?'

'I shall go around the back of the keep. It is an easy enough walk, but straight down was quicker.' Emma adjusted her bonnet so it sat firmly on her head. The sleet appeared to be coming down heavier than ever. She had lost feeling in her fingers. 'You may join me, if you wish. The keep is stunning close up. It is more than the pile of stones Mudge claims.'

'It will give me an opportunity to refresh my memory.' He gave a short laugh. 'You do need to remember, Miss Harrison, this bridge has been a dream of your father's for a very long time. We often used to discuss where it should go.'

Jack put on his frock coat, becoming once again the austere businessman. They walked through the misted grounds of the castle, skirting bits of fallen masonry with the keep rising above them.

'I want to thank you for saving Davy's life,' Emma said.

'I did what any man would have done.'

Emma swallowed hard, but, taking a look at his intent face, decided not to mention that none of the workmen had helped. She bit her lip and concentrated on walking.

'Now you see why the site is a dangerous place…for a woman,' Jack remarked when the office appeared through the mist.

'I always knew it was. I *know* what the risks are. The outer walls are not safe. If you had read the latest survey…'

'I can read, Miss Harrison.' He turned. His eyes became hard. 'Your father and my partners will have to be informed.'

'I fully intend on informing him. No doubt he will write a letter to Robert Stephenson.'

'This accident should never have happened.' Jack Stanton's voice allowed no compromise.

'On that we can both agree.' Emma swallowed hard and looked at her hands.

'How, precisely, Miss Harrison, does Harrison and Lowe intend to prevent more accidents like this one?'

'By making sure the men are supervised correctly.' She waited as the wind lifted her bonnet slightly. She was on firmer ground. She had practised this conversation several times in her head over the last few weeks. If it hadn't been Jack Stanton, it would have been one of the other partners, she tried to reason. They all had links to Newcastle, reasons to travel up from London.

Jack Stanton could not act alone. The other partners liked and trusted her father's judgement. In a few weeks' time, if need be, when her father had improved, she would contact Mr Stephenson and request that he intervene with his partner.

Jack remained silent, regarding her with a steady gaze.

She must not borrow trouble. She had to remain calm and resist the temptation to fill the space with noise.

The sleet swirled around them. Jack eventually cleared his throat.

'What is the precise nature of your father's illness? Your whisper was inaudible earlier. When I worked for your father, he disdained taking to his bed for a mere chill.'

'He will recover in a few days.' She stood, her feet planted firmly, chin held high, meeting his eyes. She was not some young girl who had just put her hair up. She was twenty-five and knew how to speak her mind. He would not intimidate her. 'If you had arrived when you were expected, he would have greeted you.'

'You speak in hope more than expectation.'

Emma gritted her teeth. She refused to reveal her fears, or what the doctor had confided. 'As you have not seen my father in seven years, I assure you that I speak with great authority. The timing of your visit is unfortunate.'

'I arrived when I said I would.'

Emma closed her eyes. She refused to start an argument about that as well. 'Your letter never arrived here.'

'A pity.'

'I trust you have seen enough of the site to form your opinion, Mr Stanton?' Emma tilted her chin and stared directly into his coal-black eyes. 'There is no need for us to stand out in the cold. This conversation, as with our earlier quarrel, has gone on long enough. I wish to visit the hospital before I return home. I want to know the full extent of Davy's injuries before I speak with my father.'

Jack used his gloved fingers to brush a speck of sleet from his frock coat.

'I have business elsewhere. The company is building other bridges. Our rail interests are large and diverse. I am involved with several parliamentary committees on rail safety and other such pressing concerns.'

'That is a pity, as I am sure he would have liked to have seen you. He was quite fond of you…once.'

She heard the sudden intake of breath. Had she dared once too often? But she refused to apologise. His sudden departure seven years ago had cut her father deeply. He had tried to hide it but she knew her father blamed her for losing one of the most promising civil engineers of his generation.

'I can find my own way out, Miss Harrison.' He touched his hat and was gone. 'Give my regards to your father. Once he treated me as a son.'

The mist swallowed the black figure up. Jack Stanton was gone. No doubt to a warm private railway car and a journey back to London. Back to his life.

She was safe. The project was safe. It had to be. And she had come so close to disaster.

Emma stumbled back towards the hut and comfort. She wanted to bury her face in her hands and weep. Why couldn't her tongue be quiet? They had been getting on reasonably well. Then in the space of a few minutes she had brought up the past—twice.

He had never married. No doubt he would. To some young debutante. He had the money and the entrée to society now.

Successful engineers such as Stephenson, Brunel and Jack Stanton were welcomed on the marriage market—the peacetime equivalent of the soldier hero. Men who dared to dream the impossible and make it a reality.

She had made her choice seven years ago. She had chosen duty over emotion. At least their first meeting was over and they knew where each stood. It was as well. She would finish her father's correspondence and then return to her old steady life, secure in the knowledge that her first encounter with Jack Stanton had shown there was nothing between them. He would not seek to return.

Her life would continue much as before. The bridge would get finished and she would find a way to save the keep. Her dream.

The past, in the shape of Jack Stanton or anything else, would vanish. A distant memory. All gone.

Emma Harrison wanted him gone. She had engineered the situation to force him to leave as fast as possible. And he had allowed his pride to come before logic. Something he'd vowed he'd never do.

Jack sat bolt upright and turned to look back at the building site as the bells from St Nicholas's Church tolled two o'clock. The castle's ramparts were shrouded in a thick brooding mist. How many more accidents would happen? She had been lucky that the lad had only suffered a broken leg. The project needed proper supervision. Something Emma Harrison and the foreman appeared incapable of giving.

Emma Harrison was hiding something—something important.

She had not known about her father's letter. She distrusted his reasons for being there. He had to believe her when she said that his reply changing the date and time had not arrived.

But, equally, her actions were not straightforward. She had set a trap for him and he had walked into it.

He passed a hand over his eyes. He had done what he'd sworn he would not do. He allowed himself to become distracted by thoughts of the past. She had inserted the topic about his marital status. He'd reacted, and she had been able to distract him. Once. Then, seeing his reaction, she had done it again after he had saved that lad. Bringing up the past and getting him to leave. She had never fully answered the question about her father's health.

That was not how he played the game. His rules, not hers. Why had her father sent the letter?

Jack attempted to think. There had to be a way around her—a way to satisfy his curiosity.

Monday. A Saint Monday come to that. Edward Harrison was a man who prided himself on his habits—habits of a lifetime.

Jack used his cane to rap the top of the cab.

'I have changed my mind. Not the Forth Street Station. Hood Street. Quickly.'

He settled himself back into the leather seats.

'Now, let us see exactly how you like my rules, Miss Harrison.'

It had to be here.

Emma shuffled through the report for a third time.

The mantel clock ticked slowly, filling the dining room with its monotonous sound. A fire blazed in the grate. Emma infinitely preferred the red warmth of the dining room to the austere whiteness of the drawing room. The recently installed gas lighting gave a yellowish glow to the room.

The papers Emma had brought home from the site lay spread out over the dining table. A few had fluttered down to the floor. She picked another piece up, made a marking, and placed it in another pile. The answer to saving the keep had to be within one of these surveys and the myriad of calculations, but her mind kept wandering back to Jack Stanton and his reason for appearing. Someone must have said something about her father. Jack had never returned to Newcastle before now. She was certain of that.

Several hairpins had come out, and the hair coiled so neatly earlier now tumbled about her shoulders, while her hands were spotted with ink.

Emma gave a quick glance in the pier glass. Definitely not a lady who expected callers.

She made a face. Looking after her father was proving difficult. He was a far worse patient than her mother, who had positively relished being ill and her life as an invalid.

Her father had chosen not to break the habit of a lifetime, despite his assurance to the contrary this morning. He had risen and gone to spend the afternoon at his club. Emma pressed her lips together. She should never have believed his insistence that a site visit was needed. If she had remained here, he would have found it more difficult to disregard the doctor's orders.

However, then she would have never encountered Jack Stanton. Would have never been there to help save Davy Newcomb. A tiny shiver went down her spine.

She needed to decide how to approach Jack Stanton's visit. There would be no need to bother her father with a blow-by-blow account. Whatever repercussions would come by post, she decided. She would take a view if and when they arrived, but he did need to know about the accident. He would have to speak to Mudge.

'Daughter, daughter.' Her father's strident voice echoed down the corridor.

Emma winced. Strident today, and feeble tomorrow. She

had seen the pattern all too often lately. How many cups of punch had he had?

'Papa, where have you been?' Emma rose, and straightened her skirt. She ignored the hairpins flying in all directions. She'd pick them up later. 'I was quite worried.'

Her father came into the room, his black frock coat slightly too large for his frame and his eyes a little watery. 'Monday before St Nicholas's Day. I've been to the club. Do you think I'd miss the final preparations for the dance? I wanted my views known. The punch was far too weak last year.'

'You know what Dr Milburn said, Papa.' Emma signalled to Fackler the butler, who discreetly took her father's coat, and handed him a dressing gown.

'That quack—what does he know?'

'Dr Charles Milburn is a respected member of the Royal College of Physicians, hardly a quack.'

Her father allowed Fackler to help him into the dressing gown. 'I think he comes here to sniff around your skirts, Emma. Now that the widow from Harrogate he was interested in has captured her barrister. You could do far worse than him.'

'Once you wanted a member of the aristocracy for me.'

'That was your mother, daughter.' Her father's eyes crinkled at the corners. 'I was certain that she would not rest until she had made one of her daughters a duchess. She did feel the loss of the title when her father died and it went to her cousin. I wanted you to be happy.'

'I am happy, Father. I chose my lot in life, remember? No regrets.' Emma waved an airy hand. 'Do you not recall the rate of proposals I received…before Mama became ill?'

'Beggars cannot be choosers. You will be twenty-six next birthday. You should make an effort. If not the doctor, there are a number of men at the club. Perhaps a widower with several children.'

Emma gritted her teeth. There was no use in explaining to her father that Dr Milburn smelt of peppermint and had a damp handshake. She thought they had settled the question of Dr Milburn months ago, but obviously not.

'If I married, who would look after you?'

'True, true.' Her father gave a satisfied sigh. 'You do make a good nurse, Emma. Your dear departed mother often said so.'

Emma ignored the comment. She did not wish to dwell on her mother and her saint-like fortitude throughout her illness. Emma knew the truth—the scenes and tantrums. She had nearly gone mad with boredom, being at her mother's beck and call, until she'd discovered her father's engineering manuals and taught herself higher mathematics and technical drawing.

'If you were well enough to go to the club, you should have gone to the site.' She paused, smoothed her skirt. 'Mudge asked after you. There was an accident—Davy Newcomb fell off the castle ramparts.'

'So I understand. But young Davy suffered no worse than a badly sprained leg. A few weeks off and he will be back. The family needs every penny.'

'How? Who told you?'

'You must not imagine you are the only person to tell me news.' Her father looked at her gravely.

'I am not sure I understand.'

'It was Dr Milburn who drove me in his carriage to the club.' Her father tucked his thumbs into his waistcoat. 'I could hardly ask him to take me to the building site. He has a new pair of chestnuts.'

She gave a short laugh and shook her head. 'And now he is not a quack? You suffer from a selective memory, Father.'

Her father gave a pathetic cough. 'You are trying to rob me of one of the few remaining pleasures left to an old man.'

'I speak of responsibilities, not pleasures.'

'If I had had a son…'

Emma rolled her eyes heavenwards. She had heard this lament before. 'You have two daughters. One of whom married a baronet, and the other looks after your household and is also trying to make sure the bridge construction goes smoothly until Dr Milburn pronounces you fit.'

'You will never guess who was at the club.' Her father hooked his fingers into his waistcoat and rocked back on his heels, a self-satisfied smile on his lips.

A strange pricking came at the back of her neck. She could almost believe that if she turned around he'd be there, lounging against the doorframe, an elegant curl to his lip. It had to be.

'Jack Stanton.'

'Jack Stanton.' Her father's smug expression faded. 'How did you guess?'

'He arrived at the site while I was there. I showed off the progress. He led the rescue of young Davy.' Emma wiped her hands against her skirt. 'The entire encounter lasted but a few minutes. I gave your excuses.'

A small white lie, but she refused to worry her father. What trouble could Jack Stanton cause? He wanted the bridge built. Harrison and Lowe had been awarded the tender. The incident with Davy would not happen again. The men had been warned.

'Did you, now?' A twinkle appeared in her father's eye. 'And what do you think of him?'

'What is there to think about? He has done very well for himself.' Emma clamped her mouth tightly shut. She had already waded into trouble earlier today, with her light-hearted remarks to Jack. She had no wish to be mistaken twice.

'Done very well for himself? The man's a railway millionaire. Sought after in London. A peerage in the offing for him and Stephenson if they pull this London to Edinburgh scheme off, by all accounts. I would hate to think what he is worth a year, Fifty-thousand pounds or more. Not bad for a charity boy. Not bad at all.'

'I am very pleased for Jack Stanton. Who would have thought it from what he was like when he worked for you? All tight-collared and ready-made clothes. So serious, and with that strong Geordie accent.'

Emma knew her words held more than an echo of her mother at her most snobbish in them. Far too harsh and judgemental. And Jack's voice only held the slightest echo of a Geordie burr.

'I seem to recall you thought he had fine eyes, or some such nonsense. Your dear mama remarked on it. Then he left abruptly.'

'Papa!' Emma put her hands to her head, dug into her hair, pulling it slightly. She had to remain calm and collected. 'How much punch did you actually drink today? No more of your tomfoolery. Tell me directly, what are you on about?'

Her father nodded. 'Then you will have no objection.'

'Objection to what?' The prickling at the back of her neck had returned with a vengeance. Emma forced her head to keep still. Next she would start believing in ghosts. 'That you snuck out of the house like a schoolboy escaping from lessons? That you have had at least one glass too many of punch? That you will have a bad head in the morning?'

Her father rocked back on his heels, humming a little tune. What mischief had her father done?

'Your father has invited me to lodge with you both.' Jack Stanton stepped coolly into the room.

Chapter Three

Emma stared at Jack in disbelief. She blinked, willing him to be a figment of her imagination. But obstinately he remained, lounging with a lazy grace against the doorframe.

He carried his top hat, and had discarded his cane, but his gaze was as arrogant as ever, looking her up and down, taking in the crumpled nature of her blue gown, the disarray of her hair and finally resting on her ink-stained cheek. He, on the other hand, appeared as immaculate as earlier—the crease in his cream-coloured trousers precision-perfect, and the frock coat barely holding in the breadth of his shoulders.

He had said that he was returning to London but had slunk round to her father's club. Underhanded and devious.

There was no need to wonder any more who had told her father about the accident. Dr Milburn and his pair of new chestnuts, indeed. The only good part was that Jack Stanton had discovered her father in his usual haunt. To think once she had thought him without guile, speaking his mind far too readily.

She forced a smile onto her face. She refused to be the one to renew hostilities.

'Why might you be staying in Newcastle, Mr Stanton? I

thought you had other places to go. Projects to complete. Europe and South America beckoned.'

Jack raised an eyebrow and came farther into the room. 'I wasn't aware that I had given you details of my future plans, Miss Harrison.'

'You led me to believe…'

A faint smile touched his lips. 'You merely assumed. Assumptions can lead to fatal errors. It is best to check the concrete details.'

'Jack has agreed to oversee the bridge in my absence.' Emma's father brought his hands together. 'It is a capital solution to the present problem. He has to stay here with us. I would not hear of it otherwise. He was the hero of the hour, after all, saving young Davy. It could have been much worse, and Mrs Newcomb has suffered much this past year.'

'Your father can be very persuasive.'

Emma watched his lips turn up in a slow, sardonic smile, daring her. She forced her lungs to fill with air and refused to give in to the temptation to scream. There was nothing persuasive about it. He had gone to her father's club with the sole intention of being invited here, with the intention of taking over the project. And he knew she knew it—wanted her to know it.

'I long to hear of the bridges he built in South America,' her father said. 'To think a prodigy of mine should have gone to so many exotic places.'

Emma pinched the bridge of her nose. Very neatly done— the carrot that Jack had dangled in front of her father. No doubt he had implied she had been responsible for Davy's misfortune.

'It means that you will not have to go through the drudgery of going to the site,' her father added.

'It is something I enjoy, Papa.' Emma hated the tightness of her voice.

'Your father agreed with my plan. I will undertake his duties while he recovers. The winter air is not good for a man of his age.' Jack's eyes glittered. 'The railway positively insists on it.'

Emma stuffed her fists into the folds of her skirt. She could see the walls beginning to close in on her again, back to the dreary round of calls and having to make unwanted objects for the drawing room. Exactly how many pincushions did one need? How many pieces of netting?

Worst of all, Jack Stanton would rapidly discover that it was not simply a chill her father suffered from. All she needed was for her father to have one of his bad days. On those days even Dr Milburn's tonic seemed to do no good, and he suffered with a wandering mind, and complaints about an aching stomach. It reminded Emma horribly of her mother's last days. Then it would begin—the offers for Harrison and Lowe, the taking of control and stripping her father of all purpose in life.

She forced her head up, met Jack's dark gaze.

'For how long do you intend overseeing the project?'

'As your father has only suffered a slight chill, I anticipate my tenure will be short-lived. Certainly I shall leave before the Christmas festivities.' Jack watched Emma's hand curl around the piece of paper. She looked less than pleased at the news. Good. He did not intend to have her ruin this project out of some misplaced desire to interfere, or to have something to amuse her otherwise dull days, when she did not have the appropriate training.

'There, you see, daughter. It is all settled. I am hoping to persuade Jack to be the guest of honour at Harrison and Lowe's Goose Feast on Christmas Eve.'

'I am sure you will be well by then, Papa.' Emma forced a smile on her face. She would need a miracle if Jack stayed that long. She noticed the paper she held in her hand had been scrunched tight. She hastily put it down.

Her father passed a hand over his eyes and swayed slightly on his feet. 'If you will both forgive me, I fear the good doctor was correct this time. I have overdone it a little. But the punch was excellent.'

Emma moved to help him, but he waved her away. Soon his unsteady clomp could be heard going down the corridor. Jack made no move to go, but stood looking at her with a deep intensity. Would he demand to know the true nature of her father's condition? Or would he also assume too much punch?

The chiming of the mantelpiece clock made her jump, and seemed to break the spell.

'Goose Feast?' Jack raised an eyebrow. 'Is this something I should know about?'

'Harrison and Lowe give their employees and families a feast at Christmas. We hold it on Christmas Eve, when the Goose Club raffle is drawn,' Emma answered, not bothering to hide the pleasure in her voice. It was a topic she could safely discuss. 'Mr Dickens's recent novel—*A Christmas Carol*—inspired my father.'

'I am sure the company will be happy to help.' Jack gave a short laugh. 'We are as keen to keep Christmas as any. Mr Dickens's novel has not only transformed your father's outlook but an entire nation's. We never celebrated Christmas much when I was growing up, but every year more and more seems to be done.'

'Were you a Mr Scrooge, Mr Stanton?'

'Hardly that. I keep Christmas as well as any man. I was merely making an observation. Tell me more about the feast you propose. Perhaps I might have a suggestion or two.'

'This is something that Harrison and Lowe does on its own.'

Emma pressed her lips together. She knew how it was

done—a little here and a little there, then suddenly the offer was made and all were expected to fall in with the scheme. No, the Goose Feast stayed separate. Harrison and Lowe needed its independence. She knew how these large railway companies worked—impersonal, letting workers go at Christmas to save a few days' wages. Harrison and Lowe cared about its workers.

'I merely wanted to help.'

'The Goose Feast has nothing to do with the bridge project, Mr Stanton.'

'I understand.' Jack made a slight bow, but his eyes remained inscrutable. 'It is well I am overseeing the bridge-building as now you will be able to concentrate on the feast.'

'One could look at it in that light.' She waited for him to make his excuses and leave the room. There was no need for him to pretend a friendship or even a common cause.

He rubbed the back of his neck, started to say something and appeared to change his mind.

'Was there any particular reason that the book struck a chord with your father?' His voice carried less of a commanding note.

'My mother always loved Christmas.' Emma saw no reason to hide the truth. 'She died three years ago, and my father dedicates a toast to her memory each year at the feast. I like to think she would have enjoyed it.'

'I was sorry to hear of her death when your father told me earlier.'

'Why? It was a merciful release.'

Emma moved over towards the mantelpiece. She concentrated on arranging and rearranging the figurines. There was no need to explain any further. She had no wish to revisit the four years before her mother's death. When she had control of her emotions, she turned back. He was watching her with a speculative gaze.

'Having experienced one invalid it made me determined on my present course.'

'You are right. You have turned into an acid-tongued spinster.' His eyes crinkled at the corners. Emma was surprised how much more approachable he had suddenly become.

'I do try to find the positives in my situation. People are so apt to feel sorry for me.'

'And being able to speak your mind is one?'

'I have little time for polite, meaningless phrases.' Emma crossed her arms in front of her. 'It is a relief to be able to speak my mind.'

'You are correct—spinsterhood suits you.' He gave a short laugh. 'I had never noticed before, but you have quite a determined chin.'

Emma swallowed hard, strove to keep it light. 'Mr Stanton, do you delight in provoking me?'

'Provoking you?'

'You seem intent on revisiting our quarrel of this morning.'

'We both want the same thing, Miss Harrison.' He tilted his head to one side, sending a strand of hair flopping over his forehead. 'We were friends.'

'That was a very long time ago.' Emma lowered her eyes.

The silence between them grew. Emma tried to push away the memories of that other time when Jack had taken to calling at the house. She had enjoyed his laugh and his lively way of talking, of making her father's projects seem interesting rather than deadly dull, as she had previously thought.

'I can find other lodgings if my presence discomforts you.'

'I am not discomforted,' Emma said with a quick shake of her head. She was through with him and she had no regrets. Her mother had been right to advise her against him. 'My father appears quite intent on having you to stay. As he said— he does like to discuss civil engineering.'

'And you, Miss Harrison, what do you discuss? What are your preferred topics of conversation?' His voice was low, and designed to soothe. She wondered how many women had fallen for it. 'What do you want to discuss?'

'Something other than bows and ribbons.' She would go for the grand sweep out of the room—something to show him that she was immune to him and his aggravating ways.

'Miss Harrison?' His low voice called her back, held her.

Emma paused, her hand on the doorknob. 'Is there something I have forgotten? The servants will show you and your man where your rooms are.'

'I wanted to reassure you that the foundations will be laid properly.'

'They were always going to be.'

'With you supervising?'

'If necessary. It may surprise you, but I can read a survey. And directing men is no worse than directing servants.'

'Nothing surprises me about you,' he said softly.

Emma rapidly pulled the door shut, certain she heard laughter on the other side.

She shouldn't have run. She had yielded ground to Jack Stanton.

Emma paced about her bedroom, her nightdress swishing about her ankles. Normally she'd be asleep, but every time she shut her eyes she saw Jack's face, with his quizzically lifted eyebrow. She could not be attracted to the man. Her nerves were overwrought, that was all.

Why, when everything was going as she'd planned, did Jack Stanton have to appear?

And what would happen tomorrow when he went to the site? Would Mudge be loyal, or would he take the opportunity to ingratiate himself?

There had to be a way of keeping the state of her father's illness from him. Something.

A low moan broke her thoughts. Emma went still, heard it again. Her father in the grip of one of his nightmares. His stomach must have resumed its cramps. All too often these days he seemed to experience them, and the night sweats. It reminded her so much of her mother's last days.

She grabbed Dr Milburn's medicine and her candle, praying that Jack had not heard.

'Sleep well, Father.' Emma tightened the shawl about her shoulders and closed her father's door with a click. Her eyes ached with tiredness.

She was thankful she had heard her father's moans before he had woken the entire household up. She had given him a dose of his special tonic, despite his complaints about its metallic taste, and he had drifted off to sleep, leaving her free to return to her room.

Her candlestick threw out elongated shadows as her toes sunk into the thick oriental carpet that ran along the corridor.

'Miss Harrison, is something amiss? I heard someone cry out.'

Emma started and gave a small gasp, sending bits of molten wax flying onto the carpet. Jack Harrison stood in the doorway of his room, his hands gripping the doorframe. His white shirt billowed over his form-fitting trousers.

'Have I disturbed you?'

'No, not at all.' The candle lurched more dangerously to the right. Her fingers felt numb. She tried to think, tried to look somewhere other than at the dark hollow of his throat.

'But I did startle you. If you are not careful you will get burnt.'

He reached forward and took the candle from her hand, his

fingers lightly brushing hers. A small shiver went up her arm and she hastily looked away from his intent eyes.

'I was not expecting to see anyone.' Emma hoped her white nightgown would be long enough to hide her feet. Why hadn't she stopped to pull on something more suitable? And why did she always appear at a disadvantage? Her hair was loosely plaited, falling over a shoulder. 'I have quite recovered now.'

'Something is wrong.' His voice surrounded her, low and musical, nearly like a caress, holding her there, pinning her to the spot. 'Confide in me.'

Emma shook her head to clear it. His voice was sending out silken lures, traps for the unwary. She gave a slight shrug. 'There is nothing to confide.'

'There must be a reason for your night-time ramblings.' He looked at her from under hooded eyes, and she reminded herself that he was dangerous, the enemy, the pirate who plundered companies.

'I went to see my father. He called out,' she said, as lightly as she dared.

'Has his chill taken a turn for the worse?'

'His breathing is fine.' Emma's hand played with the end of her plait. 'I suspect he had rather too much punch at the club. I had no wish for him to waken the entire household as he did the last time.'

A crooked smile appeared on Jack's lips. 'Ah, yes, rather a lot of punch was drunk.'

Emma let out a breath. Her shoulders became lighter. He believed her. She ought to go before she revealed anything. Her tongue moistened her lips as she searched her numb mind for the proper phrase. 'If you will excuse me, it is late.'

His eyes travelled up and down her form, lit with something within. 'Very late.'

Emma wanted to tug her shawl tighter around her. This was

Jack Stanton, the man she had refused years ago, the man who wanted to destroy her life. He held no attraction for her, and yet she remembered how gentle his fingers had been when he'd helped her in the castle's grounds. 'I will bid you goodnight.'

His eyes danced. His hand smoothed an errant lock from his forehead. 'I promise to take good care of the site for your father and report back on the progress. There should be no more careless accidents.'

'I thought you would. I have, of course, no interest.' She picked up the candlestick. This time she held it firmly, to prevent the flame from wavering.

'You never were a very good liar, Miss Harrison.' He turned on his heel and went back into his bedroom.

Emma resisted the temptation to scream.

Taking small bites of her toast, and keeping an eye on the breakfast room door, Emma attempted to appear nonchalant. It was just possible that if she encountered Jack she could persuade him to take her to the bridge. Somebody needed to explain the situation to Mudge.

'Are you seeking to waylay me and insist on going to the site?' Jack's sardonic voice asked.

Emma crumbled the bread between her fingers, annoyed that her stratagem had been quickly discerned.

'I had no intention of doing that. I believe Mudge will be capable of answering your questions,' Emma replied through gritted teeth.

'It is good to know you have such faith in the foreman.'

'He has been with my father for six years.'

'But there is something about him that bothers you.' Jack's eyes narrowed. He was a contrast to last night. Last night he had looked untamed, but today he was the picture of the successful businessman. Neither hair nor button was out of place.

His white gloves shone against the cane. And his top hat was a brilliant black. But there was something in the way he walked that hinted at danger, the untamed male animal.

'He is insistent on the current course of the bridge. He thinks trying to save the castle keep is a romantic folly.'

'And is it?'

'I don't believe in romance, Mr Stanton, do you?' Emma looked hard at Jack.

'If I did not believe, I would not be building bridges across impossible chasms,' came the enigmatic reply. 'Sometimes you can do nothing but believe.'

He touched his finger to his hat and was gone.

'Have you met him?' Lucy Charlton asked as Emma came into the young matron's drawing room. She had decided, in the light of the circumstances, she was better off doing the rounds of visiting rather than fuming at home. Luckily it was one of her oldest friend's at home days. Several other women, including Lucy's mother and unmarried sister-in-law, were there, delicately sipping tea, doing fine sewing and eating cakes.

'Met who?' Emma felt a prickling at the back of her neck. 'Who is the new victim of the Newcastle gossip mill to be?'

'Jack Stanton,' Lucy said with a decided snap of her mouth. 'I hear he is up overseeing your father's bridge.'

My bridge, Emma wanted to say. *It is my bridge.* Instead she smiled politely as she sank gracefully down on a sofa. 'He is staying with us. You know how my father likes to talk engineering.'

The women in the drawing room gave a chorus of laughter.

'But tell me about him. Is he as handsome as they say?'

'Forget handsome, is he as rich?' Lucy's young sister-in-law, Lottie, clapped her hands together, her china-blue eyes shining, and her crown of golden ringlets bobbing. 'I heard that he had his carriage and a team of matched greys sent up from London by train this morning. More than twenty thousand per year—can you imagine?'

A frisson of excitement ran through the company, and the other women began asking questions all at once. Pincushions, fans and cups were tossed aside as the room hummed with excitement.

'Let Emma speak,' Lucy said with a smile. 'Sometimes, Lottie, I think Henry is correct when he says that you have fewer manners than a baboon.'

Lottie subsided with a practised pout. 'But I only want to know.'

'He is from Newcastle. He used to work for my father. He left about seven years ago, and returned yesterday.' Emma accepted a cup of tea and delicately sipped it, wondering how she would turn the conversation away from Jack. She had no wish to think about the man.

'Emma Harrison, you must know.' Lottie leant forward. 'Tell me every little detail. After all, you were consigned to the shelf long ago—you must know what he was like when he lived here. Mama does not remember a thing, a solitary thing. I need to know. Twenty thousand. Can it be true? Can a man earn that much?'

'I am the same age as Lucy.' Emma regarded Lottie with a steady eye. She refused to allow Lottie's little remarks to annoy her.

'But she is married with two young children. That hardly signifies.' Lottie gave a deprecating wave of her hand. Her lips curved upwards in a mischievous smile. 'Emma is a living relic of a bygone era.'

Emma forced her face to remain bland as the rest of the room gasped.

'Now, Lottie, hush, and stop being rude.' Lucy turned her

placid face to Emma. 'Emma, dear, do not mind Lottie. She is a little thoughtless and over-excited this morning.'

'I do not mind Lottie at all,' Emma returned with a smile. 'I have no intention of minding Lottie. She exercises enough minds as it is.'

Harmony was restored as the room burst out in laughter. Even Lottie joined in after she'd puzzled out the pun.

'Now, shall we talk about our dresses for the ball?' Lucy said, clearing her throat. 'I thought the cream silk would be best for Lottie, to show off her complexion.'

'But it has too much lace.' Lottie made a little moue with her mouth. 'I wish it to be much more décolleté. I am sure to be wildly in demand, but I shall save a dance for dear Mr Stanton.'

She lowered her eyes and fluttered her lashes to the sighs of others in the room. Emma contented herself with raising an eyebrow as Lucy led the conversation firmly on to other topics.

The talk ebbed and flowed about her, but Emma's mind kept returning to Jack Stanton and the St Nicholas Ball. She could not go to this ball and see the women fawning over Jack Stanton as if he were some prize to be won. Emma tapped her finger against one of Lucy's pincushions and smiled. She had the perfect excuse—her father's health.

'Mr Stanton, there is a problem.' Mudge came into the office and stood twisting his cap. 'One of them stone blocks you wanted set up has fallen. Right on top of some tools. It looks as if you will have to let the men go early. It is far too late to do anything about it now.'

Jack lifted an eyebrow. He had expected something like this. If not today, then tomorrow. The men planned on testing him, to see what sort of overseer he would be: whether he knew his job or was simply a man parroting words without any feel for how a bridge was built. He shrugged out of his frock coat and checked his pocket watch. 'There remain at least two hours of good daylight. I believe the problem will be easily solved before then.'

Mudge's mouth dropped open. 'Are you sure you want to do that, sir?'

'I am positive.' Jack looked directly at the burly foreman. 'I think it is about time the men see what I am capable of.'

'You're the gaffer…' Mudge bowed.

'Lead the way.'

Jack regarded the block stone, artfully arranged to look as if it had fallen, but it was too neat and precise. The problem was not difficult, but tricky enough that if a man did not know his engineering he could make a mess of it. Jack smiled inwardly. No doubt Mudge thought he was being very clever— testing the new supervisor. There were two ways to handle this.

Jack picked up a sledgehammer, feeling its balance, and regarded the poorly placed stone. Behind him, he could hear bets being put on. The men never changed. They needed to be shown that he meant business. He lifted the hammer, brought it down with a crack, felt the shudder of the impact, and cleaved the stone in two. It broke beautifully. He closed his eyes in relief and blessed his first foreman for forcing him to learn.

Mudge and the men looked at him open-mouthed. No doubt they had expected him to call for a block and tackle. Or take the wrong approach.

'Once again, the most direct route works,' Jack said, dusting his hands off. 'The tools are accessible.'

'Yes, sir.'

He could see the respect in the men's eyes grow. They were builders. They understood.

He walked back towards the office, then paused, turned around and faced the men. 'I want all the tools and other items that have gone missing on the site while Miss Harrison was in charge returned. No questions will be asked, but I want them back, or unfortunately jobs will be lost.'

He saw the looks of astonishment on their faces, as well as the reddened cheeks, and knew his words had hit their mark. This site would be run properly until such a time as Edward Harrison was able to resume his role.

'You overdid it yesterday.' Emma came in to her father's study to discover him wrapped in blankets with an ice pack on his head. 'Several cups of punch too many.'

'Such a way to greet your dear papa.' Her father removed the ice pack and looked at her with bloodshot eyes. 'Why does the number of glasses of punch I can drink and rise the next morning with a clear head appear to decrease with age? Must the servants' footstep be quite so deafening?'

'Why did you invite Jack Stanton to stay with us? To oversee the bridge?' Emma asked quietly. 'I thought we had agreed.'

'It will be until I get over this cold.' Her father held out his hand. 'After what happened to young Davy, how could I do otherwise? I felt for his mother. It has been barely a year since his father died. Terrible business, that.'

'He's back home now, with his mother and grandmother. Dr Milburn sent word with his account this morning. I thought to visit them.'

'You are a good woman, Emma. Your dear mama would be proud of you.' Her father gave a cough. 'She would be the first to admit that she was wrong about Jack Stanton. She used to say that he would never do anything with his life, and look at what he has accomplished.'

'Papa—'

'You may do all the warning you like, Emma Harrison, but remember I know Jack Stanton wants this bridge built as badly as I do—as we both do.'

'As does Robert Stephenson.' Emma crossed her arms and stared at her father. 'Mr Stephenson would come up and oversee, I am sure, if you asked.'

'Stephenson has other bridges to build. This one needs to be iron and stone. It cannot be simply iron. Stanton is the only one who can supervise the men. I trained him. I trust him.'

What about me? You trained me. Emma longed to shout, but one look at her father's face showed that he would not take kindly to the suggestion.

Her father cleared his throat. 'Now, let us forget bridges and talk about something much more pleasant—the Assembly Rooms' St Nicholas Ball. What is the latest news from the social round?'

'Absolutely not! I forbid it!' Emma crossed her arms and prepared for battle. 'You had a bad night last night. Going to a ball will do you no good at all.'

'But you were excited about the prospect yesterday morning. I distinctly recall hearing about a rose silk dress.'

'That does not signify.' Emma forced her face to remain expressionless. 'You know what the night air does to your chest.'

'Mrs Charlton will be ecstatic. She has been trying to claim a place for Lottie in the top quadrille set for months.'

Emma rolled her eyes. 'You know my feelings about that woman and her odious daughter, Father. I only see Lucy because she is one of my oldest friends and they do not often visit, preferring to leave their cards.'

'But you have seen them recently.' Her father looked at her with a shrewd expression on his face.

'I saw Lucy this morning, and Lottie was there, crowing about her most recent triumphs.' Emma held up her hand, stopping her father's speech. 'But even the thought of denying Lottie does not make me relent. We are not going.'

'It is you who doesn't want to go.' Her father signalled for his coffee to be poured. 'It is a revenge for me inviting Jack Stanton here. You are doing this to be deliberately awkward.'

Emma took a sip of her tea. 'I think only of your health. Last night you were once again in the grip of a nightmare. And you refused to take your tonic. You are being ridiculous.'

'Am I?' Her father reached over and gave her hand a pat. 'I know you well, my daughter.'

'As do I know you, Father. It is my final word.'

'Ah, Stanton,' Edward Harrison said, not bothering to rise from his armchair, where he sat wrapped in shawls and a blanket. 'What is the news of the progress? Are you satisfied?'

'It is as your daughter predicted—your men have returned and are hard at work.' Jack came into Edward Harrison's study. He had spent most of the day at the site. The foreman had nearly fallen over himself in his efforts to be helpful, dropping hints about the state of Harrison's health, but never actually saying anything. His actions only confirmed Jack's suspicions. 'Mudge informs me there is a second survey of the riverbed.'

'You will have to ask my daughter where it is.' Harrison raised a hand, and then allowed it to drop back onto the blanket. 'She does all the organising these days. A remarkably good organiser, Emma. Ask her where anything is, and she knows.'

The last person Jack wanted to think about was Emma. Last night in the corridor he had been struck by her vulnerability. She was not only nursing her father, but also trying to do a man's job.

'I was most impressed with the willingness of your men to work.'

'Once their pay packet ran out.'

Jack laughed, but then sobered. The lines of tiredness were etched on Edward Harrison's face.

He wondered that he had missed them when he'd encountered him at the club. Harrison had not aged well. And, despite Emma's declaration, he knew a woman could not run an engineering firm. Not one as young as Emma.

'Harrison and Lowe has an excellent reputation. If you wish to sell your controlling stake, the company would be delighted to look into the purchase. On favourable terms.'

He closed his mouth and resisted the temptation to say anything more. He who spoke first lost. The clock on the mantelpiece ticked loudly. Jack resisted the impulse to fill the silence, but allowed it to grow until his nerves screamed. He could see from the way Harrison's hand twitched that he felt it, too. Jack willed him to give in, to say yes.

'At the present time I have no desire to sell.' Harrison gave a cough and rearranged his blankets.

'The offer is there, should you require it.' Jack made a show of examining his cuffs. He had done the decent thing. Surely Harrison had to realise the offer was fair, more than fair? Once the news of his illness got out, the vultures would begin to circle.

'I understand, and I will remember it when the time comes, but it has not come yet.' Harrison leant forward, his eyes bright. 'Tell me, what do you think of my youngest daughter?'

'Miss Harrison? We have barely spoken today.' Jack narrowed his eyes. Was this going to be it? A not-so-subtle attempt at matchmaking? He had avoided such lures before. Not even for the prize of Harrison and Lowe would he give up his freedom. There were certain limits.

'May I speak plainly?' Harrison cleared his throat and glanced over his shoulder before continuing. 'I need your assistance in a small matter. It concerns my future and the future of Harrison and Lowe.'

'Please do. I am delighted to be taken into your confidence.' Jack closed the study door with a click and settled himself in the armchair opposite. Harrison had piqued his interest. He was intent on some scheme, and if he humoured him he might be able to get him to seriously entertain the offer.

'My daughter suffers a misguided notion that because she runs my house she can order me about. She has taken it into her head that I am far sicker than I am.' Harrison gave a wan smile. 'In short, she fusses and forbids me small pleasures.'

'This has nothing to do with me. I make it a policy never to get involved in domestic disputes.' Jack started to stand up. He could easily see what had happened. Emma had acquired a taste of power when her father was ill, and now she wished to extend it over his business. She had become a harridan. 'As an unmarried man, I have little expertise in such matters.'

'A pity.' Harrison made a temple with his fingers and peered out over it. 'I regret that until this matter is solved it will fully occupy my mind. I would like to think about your kind offer, but…'

'Tell me about your troubles, and perhaps we can come up with a solution.' Jack settled back in the chair. He would hear Edward Harrison out and then politely decline. Emma was somebody else's problem. Not his.

'She refuses to allow me to go to the Assembly Rooms for the St Nicholas Ball. I may no longer cut quite the figure at the quadrille that I once did, but it does my heart good to see the pretty young things in their dresses.' Edward Harrison gave a discreet wink. 'There is a widow…'

'I wish you good hunting, but I fail to see what this matter has to do with me. Inform your daughter that you are going and have done with it.' Jack held up his hands. Harrison should take a stronger line. If he truly wanted to go to this dance he should go, and suffer the consequences. He allowed Emma far too much freedom.

'It is not that easy. Emma…well, I have no wish to quarrel with her. She has taken to avoiding such things.'

'Your daughter has sound reasons. I find such things a bit of a bore myself.' Jack permitted a tiny smile to cross his face.

'Yes, but before my wife became ill Emma loved such pursuits. All gone now. I am not sure she even remembers how to dance.' Harrison shook his head and gave a heartfelt sigh. 'Sometimes she takes her duty far too seriously. And I fear she does not entirely approve of the widow.'

Jack tightened his hold on his cane. No doubt the widow in question did not come from the appropriate background and therefore was deemed unworthy. Emma had been well indoctrinated by her mother.

She needed to learn a lesson. Fast. She could not simply go on organising people's lives to suit her whims. Mudge had complained about her meddling this morning. Now it was her father's turn. The woman had to be stopped.

'You want my help so that you may attend this ball and speak to your widow without your daughter knowing? Aiding your suit,' Jack said, carefully watching Edward's features.

'You understand my meaning, Jack.' Harrison took on the expression of a sly fox.

Jack nodded. He understood the code. If he did as Harrison asked and persuaded Emma to attend the dance so that Harrison could pursue his widow, Harrison would seriously consider his offer for the company. The situation might be turned to his advantage. He would enjoy administering a lesson that Emma Harrison badly needed to learn.

'I will do what I can, but it must be Miss Harrison who decides.'

'And, Jack, I never forget a favour.'

'I am counting on that.'

Chapter Four

Emma chewed on the end of her fountain pen and counted for the third time the number of geese they would need for the Goose Club's raffle at the end of the feast. It was always a difficult moment, and she had no wish to get it wrong. The memory of Mrs Mudge's outrage last Christmas, when they'd been one goose short, still rankled.

The problem was that her mind seemed to be wandering today. The lines of figures swam in front of her, twisting and merging into Jack Stanton's saturnine features. Was it her imagination, or did his dark hair curl slightly at his collar? And what would it be like to be held in those long-fingered hands as they waltzed? If they waltzed. She cursed the gossip from Lucy's at home for unsettling her. She had no interest in him, refused to, and there was not the slightest possibility of her going to the dance.

'Miss Harrison, when you have a moment?'

Jack strode purposefully into the morning room without a courtesy knock. His dark eyes flashed as he surveyed the room with all the arrogance of a lion surveying his domain.

The morning room became much too small. He was far too

close, and far too masculine for such a feminine room, with its bows and fussy coverings left over from her mother's reign.

'Is there something I can help you with, Mr Stanton?' Emma kept her voice chilled.

'I do hope so. It is a small matter, and will only take a moment of your time.'

She calmly put down her pen and rose. She straightened the folds of her dress. She could do this—act in a perfectly natural manner. Her breathlessness had nothing to do with him, and everything to do with lack of sleep. She banished the giggling gossips from her mind.

'Did you find everything to your satisfaction with the bridge?'

'The bridge is progressing admirably.'

'Then is there something wrong with your accommodation? I am sure Fackler will be pleased to sort it out.' Emma raised her hand to summon the butler.

'The room is comfortable, and your staff have been welcoming to my valet.'

'But there is something wrong.' Emma kept her head held high.

'A dance is to be held at the Assembly Rooms to raise funds for the St Nicholas Church.' Jack's voice flowed over her, enveloped her senses in its warmth.

'This is the fifth year that such a dance has been held.' Emma tilted her head, trying to assess where the conversation was leading. She would have to work the conversation back round to the bridge. She put her hand on her well-thumbed copy of the latest survey. 'It is quite the thing. Assembly Rooms balls are held in high esteem. Their reputation has only grown since Strauss appeared with his orchestra eight years ago.'

She hated the way her voice caught on the last words. There should be no reason why Jack would remember the first waltz they had shared. The first time he had gone to such an occasion.

She had buried it deep within, half-forgotten until an inconvenient time like today, when the memory sprang full-blown upon her. It was even more poignant than the memory of the last waltz they had shared—the one directly before he'd proposed to her. She regarded the scattered papers.

'Yes, you danced every waltz that night. Always a different partner, always in demand.' There was more than a touch of irony to his look. 'The veritable belle of the ball.'

'I used to live for dancing. Mama despaired about how many slippers I wore out.'

'Indeed.' His eyes narrowed.

'Oh, yes.' Emma gave a little fluttering laugh. 'She used to make a joke of it. How I would need a wealthy husband who could keep me in slippers. Utter nonsense, but Mama was like that.'

'Have you worn out many slippers lately?'

'The state of one's shoes is not something a lady discusses with a gentleman.' Emma tilted her chin in the air.

'We both know my origins, Miss Harrison.' Jack's voice dropped several degrees in temperature. 'Charity boys, even those who have made their fortunes, are rarely considered gentlemen in the best circles.'

Emma pressed her lips together and silently cursed her wayward tongue. His origins were no mystery—father dead at nine, grammar school, and then articled to her father. Everything Jack Stanton had he had worked for. He had acquired the polish of a gentleman, rather than being born to it.

'I attend dances regularly,' Emma said brightly, and knew her words were no more than a polite lie. She did go to the dances. However these days she spent far more time watching her father play cards or chatting to Lucy and the other young matrons than dancing.

Jack drew his upper lip between his teeth. 'And yet I did not discover your name on the list for the St Nicholas Ball.'

Emma released her breath. He seemed content to allow the subject to be changed. 'Is that important?'

'It is a popular dance—the best attended of the year, according to my sources.' A faint smile touched his lips. 'I understand the punch is superb.'

'I don't normally drink punch. Strong spirits are the bane of many an existence.'

'That is too bad. But it is no reason for you to forbid those who enjoy such things.'

The fog in her brain cleared as if it had never been. This had nothing to do with Jack wanting to waltz with her and everything to do with her father's desire to go.

Her father.

Her father had enlisted Jack's aid. Emma crossed her arms. He was not going to get around her that easily. She had made her mind up. It was for her father's own good. The state of his health had to be kept a secret. Dr Milburn had warned her shocks must be avoided at all costs.

'Have you been speaking to my father?' she asked, watching for any sign.

'He mentioned it, and how much he looks forward to it each year.' Jack took a step forward, so close that if she reached out her hand slightly it would brush his. The thought shocked her to the core. She forced her hand to remain in her lap.

'Then you will know that I have forbidden his attendance.' Emma kept her eyes trained on the overly emotional biblical scene that hung on the wall just behind Jack's right shoulder.

She should have known her father would try something like this. She had to keep calm. She had no wish to relive the humiliation from Lucy's at home. She willed him to leave the room before her words tumbled out and she revealed her true reason for forbidding her father. Even the thought of doing so made her cringe. Pointedly she rustled her papers and bent her head.

'Why, Miss Harrison?' A quizzical frown appeared between Jack's eyebrows. 'Your father has suffered from a chill. Why are you trying to deny him his pleasure? I saw how much he was looking forward to it at the club the other day.'

'I have no wish for the chill to turn into something worse!' Emma fumbled with her fountain pen, dropped it and watched it roll, coming to rest on the toe of Jack's highly polished shoe. Jack reached down, held it in mid-air as if undecided. The anticipation of his fingers brushing hers filled her. Emma knew her cheeks had become flushed, her throat dry. It was some sort of ailment, this inexplicable attraction towards him.

She forced her shoulders to relax, but a small stab of disappointment filled her when he placed the pen on the table and stepped back, his eyes watching her much as a cat might watch a mouse.

'Then you believe he is in danger of becoming seriously ill?'

'Nothing of the sort. I refuse to allow him to jeopardise his recovery. Papa is no longer as young as he used to be. I have lost one parent and have no desire to lose another.'

He raised an eyebrow. 'Your father does not appear in any danger of dying.'

'Not today!' Emma exclaimed, then paused and regained control of her emotions. She had to hope that Jack would overlook the outburst. 'But I have seen what over-exertion can do.'

'Miss Harrison, if he is that weak perhaps he should consider selling his company.'

Emma drew in her breath sharply. She had to keep her head. She had given too much away already. Selling the company to someone with a reputation for making money like Jack Stanton was the last thing she wanted to happen. One hint of her father's long-term health and the price would drop. And would he want to keep on all the men? Some of the families had been with Harrison and Lowe since her grandfather's day.

'That is not what I said.' She forced her voice to sound firm and confident, a contrast to the mass of butterflies and aches in her stomach. 'I wish for my father to return to full health as quickly as possible. The night air will be no good for his lungs.'

'Neither will the river's damp,' Jack countered remorselessly.

'Bridges are my father's life, Mr Stanton.' Emma was unable to conceal the catch in her throat.

'I realise that,' he said quietly.

'I have work on the Goose Feast to do, Mr Stanton.' Emma pointedly picked up her pen again, willing him to go. 'If you only came as an emissary from my father, perhaps you would be good enough to go back and tell him that his stratagem will not work. I am absolutely immovable on the point.'

She nodded towards the door. Jack would now do the polite thing and depart. She waited. He did not move. Instead he settled himself in the armchair and picked up the latest edition of the *Newcastle Courant* and noisily began turning the pages. She sat down at her desk and bent her head.

'Mr Stanton, if you please, I am trying to work.'

Jack Stanton's eyes twinkled as he put the news sheet down. 'Do you mean that as a challenge? Is that why you are holding that paper up like a shield? What are you frightened of, Miss Harrison?'

'I am not frightened of anything.' Emma dropped the paper back on the desk with a thump. She placed her hands in her lap and grasped them together to prevent her from making wild hand gestures.

'I think, Miss Harrison, it is not your father you are worried about, but yourself.' Jack Stanton leant forward as his eyes assessed her. He lowered his voice. 'Could it be that the latest dances scare you? Has the once sought-after Miss Harrison not yet learned to polka? Are you afraid of losing your hard-won dignity? The polka, Miss Harrison, combines all the intimacy of a waltz with the vibrancy of the Irish jig, or so my dancing master assured me when I learnt the steps two years ago.'

Emma rolled her eyes heavenwards. She had to remain aloof, control her temper. 'Polkaing reached Newcastle several years ago, and I do know the steps. As in London, it is wildly popular.'

'Show me.' Jack placed the news sheet down and rose. 'Will you do me the honour, Miss Harrison?'

Emma's mouth dropped open. She looked over to where Jack stood with his hands outstretched. Her mouth went dry. What would it be like to be enfolded in those strong arms again?

'This room is not big enough for a demonstration.' Emma narrowed her eyes.

'Take the risk, Miss Harrison.' He came forward with out-stretched hands. 'The only thing that will happen is a few pieces of knocked furniture. Inanimate objects, easily repaired.'

'Mr Stanton, the space is limited.' Emma tried to ignore the tiny thrill that ran through her. Her breath caught slightly in her throat as she remembered his hand brushing against hers last night. 'I hate to think of my mother's ornaments suffer-ing damage. They are a lasting reminder of her.'

'What a pity. But if there was enough space, would you polka with me?' A shadow of a smile touched his lips. 'Speaking hypothetically.'

'Yes, I see no reason in theory why I should not polka with you. The experience could be quite amusing.' Emma lifted her chin. 'It is nonsense to speculate on such things. It can't be done.'

'All we would have to do is move the tables and chairs. Put a few Dresden shepherdesses beyond reach.' Jack tapped a finger against his cheek. 'There will be space, Miss Harrison.'

He began to move the small table where several Dresden figurines stood, blank-faced and garishly dressed. Her mother's choice, rather than hers. Emma watched, horrified. He intended to make her dance. They would be alone in the room with his hand on her waist, her hand on his shoulder. Heat infused her cheeks.

'Mr Stanton, I must protest. There is no music. Cease this foolishness.'

'I will hum.' Jack start to move about the room, holding out his arms. 'A partner would make this much easier, Miss Harrison.'

'Stop, stop!' Emma shook her head and tried to contain the laughter that threatened to bubble out over her. 'Do you always talk such nonsense, Mr Stanton?'

'Only when it is required.' His eyes sobered as he came to a standstill, no more than a breath away from her. So close she could see the gold stud that held his collar together. 'If not dancing, tell me what you are afraid of. Why are you not going?'

'Why should I be afraid of attending such a thing?' Emma looked away from his deeply penetrating eyes. 'I am as disappointed as my father. My ball dress was ordered months ago. Rose silk with Belgian lace. Quite the thing. Some might even say daring.'

'And you a confirmed spinster.'

'Spinsters dance, Mr Stanton.' Emma swallowed hard. There was no need to say the only people who might consider the neckline daring were aged spinsters. 'I was quite looking forward to it, but then my father became ill. There are certain sacrifices that one has to be prepared to make. But I am unclear if you understand that.'

'As both my parents died when I was young, perhaps I do not understand the nature of sacrifice—is that what you are saying?' Jack's eyes narrowed. 'I can assure you, Miss

Harrison, that you are mistaken. I do understand why people feel compelled to look after others.'

'You are putting words into my mouth!'

'Forgive me.' Jack made a sketch of a bow, and the corners of his mouth relaxed slightly. 'I merely wanted to know why you did not want an evening's entertainment. As I recall, the Assembly Rooms held a great attraction once. A parent's health would not have concerned you.'

'Such attractions die when one encounters real life.' Emma gave a little wave of her hand. 'I grew up, Mr Stanton, and realised there was more to life than dancing, society dinners and frivolity. As I said before, my interests now lie in other areas.'

'And real life was…?'

'My mother became ill. I discovered other things interested me far more than dancing slippers.' Emma stood up. She gave her most chilling nod, indicated the door. 'Mr Stanton, this conversation is pointless.'

'Hardly that.' Jack cleared his throat and a superior expression appeared on his face. 'You have yet to say one word that proves to me you are not scared of going to the dance. It is more for your convenience than your father's that you have chosen not to go. You are afraid to polka. You are afraid people might whisper that the incomparable Miss Harrison is on the shelf.'

'I care about my father.'

'Then why have you forbidden him the dance?' Jack ticked off the points on his fingers. 'He is not ill enough to warrant the sale of the business, and you say you are not frightened of dancing, but you decline to prove it. We are at an impasse.'

'You have not told me how your visit to the bridge went.' Emma looked at Jack. The shadows from the gaslight heightened his features. Maybe he was right, and she was using it as an excuse. Her dreams had been full of him last night, standing there, smiling his sardonic smile. She had no wish to feel his arms about her. Not here, in this enclosed space. Her breath was coming a bit too quickly.

'But I have told your father.' A smile transformed his face from planes and shadows. 'I refuse the distraction, Miss Harrison. I am wise to your games. But, as you seem intent on playing, can I suggest an amusing alternative?'

Amusing alternative? Emma swallowed hard. The conversation's direction was clear.

'I suppose the price of obtaining information about the bridge is my guarantee that I will go to the dance and demonstrate I can polka?' she said, refusing to prolong his teasing.

'We begin to understand each other, Miss Harrison. A polka for information. A fair exchange.'

'You leave me little choice.' Emma's throat tightened around the last words.

'It is not a death sentence, Miss Harrison. You used to enjoy the reels, as I recall.' His eyes narrowed. 'But you have not said you will go. One thing I learnt quite early on in my career is to have all the terms of the contract spelt out. It makes it easier for both parties.'

'You have my agreement. I will go, and if there is a polka I will dance.' Emma faltered and tried again, this time with a much firmer voice as she banished all memories. 'Does that satisfy you?'

'For the moment.'

Emma passed a hand over her face as she got a sinking feeling in her stomach. What had she agreed to? She could always find an excuse not to go later, but now she wanted to know. What had he found out at the site? 'Now will you tell me what happened at the bridge?'

Jack's black eyes danced with mischief. 'There is very little to say. Mudge has been most accommodating, and work is progressing.'

'Your words are bland and give precious little away.' Emma crossed her arms. 'I have given you my promise. It is time for you to honour yours.'

'Miss Harrison, this is a most inappropriate conversation to be having with you. I am shocked at your suggestion.' Jack gave a slight bow. 'Shall we wait until after your polka?'

Weak-willed and weak-minded, Emma decided as the carriage stopped in front of the building site.

That was what she was.

Allowing Jack Stanton to manipulate her into agreeing to go to the Assembly Rooms was a mistake of the highest order. She should have stuck to her plan, refused to be manipulated by either her father or Jack. As it was, she would have to face Lottie Charlton and her minions, and hear the giggling gossips.

She could visit the building site whenever she wished. Jack Stanton could not stop her. He would not dare.

Several of the workmen turned and stared at her, almost as if they had never seen her before. A hush fell over the site and all eyes seemed to follow her every movement. Emma hesitated, straightened her jacket and bonnet, and proceeded to the office with firm footsteps.

'Miss Emma,' Mudge said, his eyes widening.

'I have come about—' Emma began.

'I will take care of Miss Harrison.' Jack's smooth voice interrupted her words. Without saying a word, Mudge bowed and left the room. Emma blinked. The foreman had never moved with that much speed before.

Jack came forward into the small foyer. He was dressed in his shirtsleeves, his collar open at the neck and a towel looped around his neck. It looked as if he had been doing physical labour, working with the men. Not what she'd expected at all.

Emma swallowed hard and tried to regain control of her

pulse. Her head seemed very light, and all she could concentrate on was that little patch of skin at the base of his throat, glistening slightly. She had thought her dreams last night were bad, but the reality of him was overpowering. She ran her tongue over her lips and struggled to focus elsewhere.

'This is a closed site, Miss Harrison.'

'I am the daughter of Edward Harrison.' Emma tilted her chin upwards and waited.

'There are no exceptions. The work is not at a point that I want the public to gaze and gape. It is far too dangerous. You know what happened to young Davy. One misstep and he fell.'

'I have been to see Davy. He is one of the reasons I am here,' Emma said quietly, thinking about the terrible scene of poverty she had come from. Davy Newcomb had been released from hospital. His leg was not broken, merely sprained, but the Newcombs depended on Davy's wages to make ends meet. That much had been clear from the way Mrs Newcomb would not meet her eyes. She had wanted to do something for them. But Mrs Newcomb had refused. She have never taken charity and was not about to start. Emma had left, feeling dissatisfied.

'How is the lad?'

'He will recover, given time. It could have been so much worse. He knows what he did wrong.'

'I am glad to hear that.' Jack gave a nod. 'Hopefully he will learn from this not to take short cuts.'

'Davy is bright. He planned on going to grammar school.' Emma gave a sigh. 'It is just unfortunate his father died earlier this year. His mother depends on him and his wage. He seems to have given up all idea of learning.'

'It is hard, but it can be done if one has the discipline. The Institute of Mechanical Engineering offers night classes and other opportunities for self-improvement.'

'Hopefully Davy will become inspired, but I am more worried about his family. They need every penny. I have told his mother that Davy's position is safe until such a time as he is strong enough to return.'

Jack crossed his arms. 'What is your business, and why couldn't it wait until I returned to your father's?'

'It is not you I wanted to speak to.' Emma clung onto the remnants of her temper. He should show more concern about Davy. He had saved the boy. She looked up at the grey sky, drew a deep breath. Davy was not his employee. Thankfully. And she had to concentrate on why she was here. She had to discover if what he'd told her father was the truth or simply a polite lie. Mudge would know.

'Then who?'

'Mudge.'

'You will not find him easier to get round, I assure you,' Jack stated. 'Mudge knows who he answers to. Your father is pleased with the progress so far.'

Emma looked over Jack's shoulder rather than meet his smouldering gaze. Her eyes widened as she saw the pile of tools. The levels that had vanished last week were back, as were a variety of shovels. There was no need to ask who had caused their return, or why. The men were probably frightened of him.

'Are you always this tyrannical, Mr Stanton?'

'When the occasion demands…' A faint half-smile played on his lips.

'Very well.' Emma withdrew a sheaf of papers from her reticule. 'I came to see Mudge about the final Goose Club list.'

'The Goose Club?' Jack's eyes widened. 'What does Mudge have to do with this Goose Club of yours?'

'Mudge, as foreman, collects the monies from the men throughout the year. He keeps an up-to-date list. Somehow I only have last year's.' The answer tripped off Emma's tongue. She had been under no illusion that Jack would be easy to get round, but she did want to see what was happening—and gauge how long she had to convince her father and Jack to move the piers. Speaking to Mudge was the best way, as her father had refused to divulge the information, telling her she had to go and speak with Jack.

'You should have given me the message this morning.' Jack regarded Emma, standing before him. Her blue poplin morning dress increased the blueness of her eyes. Her cape and matching hat, with its feathers curling towards her ripe mouth, completed the picture. Her acquiescence last night had been too quick, too sharp. He had anticipated some sort of re-arguard action, and Miss Harrison failed to disappoint.

'I did not see you this morning. I only realised the final list was missing when I went through the accounts.' Emma held up the paper with a smile. 'The geese are drawn at the feast. We are missing final payment from six of the members, including Davy Newcomb. But he has paid. I checked with his mother.'

'Do you need the list today?' Jack asked between gritted teeth. This was a ploy of Emma's to get her own way. He had no doubt that she planned to interfere and cause problems. It had taken most of yesterday to undo the damage that Mudge had implied her orders had caused. Her eyes widened, and she looked very innocent, but her expression did not fool Jack. She intended her visit for other purposes. And he had little doubt what would happen in her wake. He had already spent more hours than he cared clearing up oversights and errors. Had he not appeared when he had, the bridge would have been seriously delayed and possibly unsafe.

Jack stepped forward and took the piece of paper from her. The names were neatly written out. She had a fair hand. He had to admit that.

'It is the second of December. The feast is the twenty-fourth. It does take time with ordering. I want plump geese.'

'And while Mudge is checking on the details…?' Jack placed the piece of paper down on the front counter. He could see a certain logic in her statement, but he still did not trust her.

'I had planned to see what was happening with the foundations.' Emma gave a slight shrug and her bonnet shadowed her face. 'There is no harm in that.'

'You cannot think I have so easily forgotten our bargain, Miss Harrison.'

'But we also agreed that I was to look after the feast.' She leant forward. 'The problem with the list is new and unforeseen. Nothing to do with our wager.'

Jack's lips tightened to a thin line. The woman was impossible. It was no wonder she had never married. No man would want such a wife. 'We are at an impasse. Mudge is busy at present. We have begun investigating the castle walls.'

'No, not an impasse.' She gave a small laugh, but her eyes showed shock. 'Hardy that. I am happy to wait while Mudge finds me the correct list.'

'I cannot let you do that. It would be too much of an imposition.' Jack put out a hand, caught her elbow and propelled her towards the door. Emma dug in her heels and, short of carrying her, Jack saw that she was not going to move.

'Are you trying to get rid of me, Mr Stanton?'

'I am trying to do my job in the best way I know how to, and that includes not having any interference from unqualified people. Building a bridge takes more than placing a few piers in the ground and a plank or two over that. Once this bridge is built, it should last.'

'I am familiar with the plans,' Emma said through gritted teeth, hating that he had seen through her.

'Then you will know the hard work and the many mathematical calculations that have gone into perfecting it.'

Emma wrenched her elbow away from him. Glared at the infuriating man before her. He was exactly like all the other men of her acquaintance. She wondered what she had ever seen in him. 'What are you saying? Do you think women are not capable of making complex calculations?'

Jack ran his hand through his hair, making it stand up on end. 'I am certain some women are capable of doing the mathematics.'

'And you think I am not.' Emma continued remorselessly on. 'You think I am only capable of being a decorative object!'

She hated the way her voice rose. She glared at him and struggled to regain her temper.

Jack looked away first.

'Bridge-building is not a hobby for bored women,' he said at long last, turning back to face her. His voice held that very calm and reasonable note, the one that made her want to scream. 'You could do more harm than good by inferring with things that are beyond your comprehension. There must be a thousand worthy causes that need your attention.'

'Is this what you think my interest in the bridge is—interference?'

'Miss Harrison, we have an agreement. You have yet to fulfil your part of it. Until that time I would suggest you let me get on with my job.'

Emma rolled her eyes heavenwards and clung onto the last remnants of her temper. 'The reason I came is important as well.'

'And you will have your precious list, and the correct number of geese you need. Order several more than you need. I am quite willing to foot the bill. Problem solved.' Jack smiled, the sort of smile that lit his eyes and no doubt had the power to make women go weak at the knees. 'Now, if you will let me get on with my work…'

Emma stiffened her back. 'You are leaving me no option.'

'I am not.'

He escorted her back to her carriage and saw that she was comfortably settled, tucking the carriage robe around her. Altogether the solicitous gentleman, despite his attire. 'If you will excuse me, I have a bridge to build. No doubt you will have some social calls to make.'

'As a matter of fact, I do.'

Emma pressed her head against the seat and closed her eyes. The memory of his fingers brushing hers lingered, grew. She did not want to like Jack Stanton. She wanted to hate him. But she found herself growing increasingly attracted to him.

Chapter Five

Jack paused in the doorway of the dining room. The gaslight lit a charming domestic scene. Emma was curled up on a sofa, reading, while her hand absently stroked a black cat. It was perfect. Almost too perfect. Jack felt a pang in his insides. He tried to hang on to the illusion for a while longer. He had forgotten how much he had once longed for a family, and how cruelly she had snatched the hope away. He forced himself to remember that as well.

'Miss Harrison.' Jack gave an indulgent smile. No doubt she was reading a Minerva Press novel. He could see a half-sewn pair of slippers lying abandoned next to her.

She glanced up and stuffed the book behind a cushion. Her hands went to her hair, automatically adjusting the pins.

'Mr Stanton, I didn't hear you come in.'

'I am sorry to interrupt such a charming tableau. Pray continue with your reading.'

Jack thrust his hands into his jacket pockets. There was no reason to keep thinking about this woman. She wasn't even pretty—not in the conventional sense, not any more. Her nose was too long, and her cheeks far too pale for the china doll prettiness favoured by society. Her eyes had taken on a serious glint, and there was determination in her chin, but once he started to look at her he found it difficult to draw his eyes away. All day he'd found his mind wandering back to her, wondering what her next move would be.

'Did you wish to speak to me about something?' She tilted her head to one side. 'Another attempt to induce me to polka? Or is it something more ridiculous?'

With a start he realised he was staring at the shape of her lips. Quickly he crossed over to the fire and gave the coals a stir. The fire leapt back into flame, consuming the coals with orange tongues. Bright, brilliant, but over in an instant.

The thought shook him. He had sworn never to have anything more to do with this woman after the way she had treated him. But that was in the past. He had put the past behind him, so why had he returned to her?

'That list you gave me this morning—I presume it was in your own hand?' he said, when he had regained control.

'It was.' A frown had appeared between her brows. 'Mudge will find the correct list, I am sure, and your company will not have to provide the extra geese…if that is what concerns you.'

'Which you have ordered?' Jack said.

'It had to be done.' She raised her chin and the blue flecks in her eyes fairly danced. 'I asked for the largest they had.'

'I feared you might have done so.'

'You are not telling me that you now wish you had never made the promise?' She tilted her head.

'I always keep my promises, Miss Harrison, foolish or otherwise. And I fail to see how anyone could consider giving a few geese at Christmastime foolish. But I thought to order turkeys. They are larger birds, and their meat goes further.'

'That is true, but it is too late. The order has gone in and I would be loath to change it.'

'But I did not come to speak of this.'

'If you did not come to tell me about the Goose Club, why have you invaded my bower?'

Jack waited. Now that he looked closely he could see the piles of notes, and a pen. Miss Harrison had not been reading a Minerva Press novel. She had been doing calculations. Something about the bridge concerned her.

'You have a distinctive way of forming your "e"s.'

'I had an eccentric governess. She taught me a little of this and that, but nothing of any real substance.' Emma gave a brief self-deprecating laugh. 'It was not until my mother became ill that I really learnt to apply myself.'

'It can be tedious being at the beck and call of an invalid when one is used to going out in society.'

'I managed.' Emma held her breath. She had no wish to explain about the relief she'd felt when she did not have to make meaningless small talk any more or strike attitudes, a living picture to be admired.

'You did one or two of the sketches for the bridge.' Jack looked at her, daring her to deny it.

'I may have done. My father wanted to see if I could draw properly,' Emma replied cautiously. She watched his face for any sign that he had guessed what she had done, any opening so she could explain without accusing her father. 'My drawing has always been a great comfort to me.'

If he suspected the main design had been done by her, rather than her father, she could well imagine the eruption. He would insist on the whole design being redone, rather than simply moving the line. She had to face facts. If she wanted this bridge built, she would have to keep silent, downplay her role. The design was correct. It was the position that was wrong.

'They are very charmingly executed. I notice yours have the keep in the background.'

'I think it is important to retain the past.' Emma met his deep black eyes, eyes that assessed but showed little warmth. Tried to ignore the sudden butterflies in her stomach. 'The castle is central to the city. It is where it gets its name.'

'The castle belongs to the city's past.' Jack banged his hands together. 'It is the city's future I am concerned with. If the bridge becomes too expensive to build, Newcastle will cease to have its position as one of the premier cities in the Empire, if not the world. How then will the citizens of New-castle fare? The workers and their families?'

'But…' Emma tried to think of an argument that would sway him. He had to understand that tradition was important to people.

'You should not have false hope, Miss Harrison.' Jack tucked his thumbs into his waistcoat. 'The ground farther down the bank is poor. Your father's precise calculations have shown that. It can't be done. Not without causing the foundations to go down much deeper.'

'It can't be done?' The corners of her mouth quirked upwards. 'I thought the motto of the modern British engineer was it *can* be done.'

'One cannot fight the laws of nature.'

'It is impossible to work outside the laws of nature. Even a woman like myself knows that.' Emma fought to keep the exasperation from her voice. 'It is just…'

'Just what?'

Emma regarded her hands. How could she confess that she was certain some of her father's calculations were wrong, dangerously wrong? She had worried before, but after what she had read today she knew. She wanted a little more time to recheck. But how could she have missed it before? How could her father have made those errors? 'A few more experiments have been made, a new survey…it leads to slightly different conclusions.'

'A survey you ordered? When your father was laid low by his chill?'

'Yes.' Emma kept her head upright. There was no need to explain about her discovery that several of her father's calculations were wrong. He had transposed several of the numbers. An honest error, but one that needed correcting. 'I thought it prudent.'

She waited for his answer. This was probably her one chance to get him to see about the bridge. And once she had done that she would have no need to go to the dance. Her lips curved up into a tiny smile.

'Miss Harrison, this is the most inappropriate conversation.' The corner of Jack's mouth twitched.

'Inappropriate? Why?'

'You very nearly had me discussing the bridge.'

'Is there something wrong with that?' Her eyelashes fluttered. 'It is something we are both interested in.'

'You forget our contract—we have yet to dance, to polka. You have but to say the word and we could dance in this very room.' He tilted his head, his eyes assessing her. 'No, Miss Harrison, I fear you think me only funning you.'

Emma struggled to keep a straight face. 'Are you not?'

'I am deadly serious about it. I never neglect a contract.'

'Are we not to speak until then? Or only discuss the weather?' She lifted a hand. 'I do not need to tell you how much speaking about the weather bores me.'

'What do you wish to speak about?'

'Your travels.' She gave a decisive nod. She would work the conversation around to the bridge. 'Tell me about Brazil and your work there.'

He laughed, the sort of deep, rumbling laugh that flowed over her, enveloping her in its rich enjoyment of life. 'I can tell you about the places I have visited, but not about the bridges or how they relate to the one I am currently constructing. Tell me, what is it about going to the ball that you fear most? Why do you seek to hide?'

'I don't fear anything.' Emma curled her hand. She lied. She feared Jack Stanton and his ability to see through her. She feared the stories she had heard of his business practices. How had he made so much money, so quickly? She had a duty and responsibility towards her father's employees. She could not simply lose her reason because he was near.

'Papa, I want to speak with you.' Emma paused in the doorway of her father's study. She had gone over and over in her mind how best to approach this. Dr Milburn had been quite insistent the last time her father had had a fit—nothing was to be said to upset or alarm him. He took such pride in his work and his accuracy. The shock could kill him.

A large snore emanated from under the red handkerchief.

'You must wake up, Papa. It is important.'

Her father sat up, blinked his eyes open. 'Huh? What? Oh, it's you, Emma. What domestic crisis are you going to tell me about now?'

Emma took a deep breath and plunged ahead. She had to keep calm. She would even say that it was her fault, take the blame. He had to understand the importance of what she had discovered.

'Papa, it is about the calculations for the bridge. I couldn't understand why the two surveys were so different, but I think I have uncovered the reason.'

'Say no more, daughter.' Her father held up his hand. 'Stanton has already told me about your agreement. I am not going to aid and abet you. All the calculations in the first survey are accurate. If Stanton is half the engineer I think he is, he will recheck the calculations. But, daughter, he will find them accurate. My calculations always are.'

'Papa, I only came to ask…'

'Mudge discovered the list, if that is what you wanted to know. Came to me about it earlier, with his cap in his hands. Mrs Mudge had put it in a disused teapot and forgotten it.' Her father raised his paper. 'All this fuss about a pair of geese.'

'It was more than that, and you know it. It is the principle of the thing. I had no wish for the Goose Club to be a disaster like last year.'

Her father ran a finger around his collar. 'There were reasons for that.'

'And I swore this year would go smoothly. Jack Stanton refused to let me speak to Mudge! He threw me off the site.' Emma struggled to take a breath, and waited for her father to agree with her.

'The plain fact of the matter is that you can't stand to lose.' Her father put his hands behind his head and leant back. 'And you know Jack Stanton has bested you. Well, my girl, I have held the lines too slack since your mother died. And it is about time somebody took you in hand—stopped you from becoming like my great-aunt Agatha, who kept cats and painted rather poor watercolours of dreary landscapes.'

'I have never been tempted in any way to be like Great-Aunt Agatha.' Emma looked at her father in horror, remembering the eccentric woman who had smelt distinctly musty and had had a booming voice. She rushed to the pier glass and regarded her face. It was still hers, and not Great-Aunt Agatha's hooked nose and squint eyes. 'You must not say such things.'

'I see I have found your weak spot—Great-Aunt Agatha.' Her father chuckled and turned the page of his news sheet. 'I shall have to remember that.'

'But, Papa, this is serious.' Emma turned from the glass. She clasped her hands together. She had to make one last effort. 'The line of the bridge will have to be moved. It is imperative that it is moved. You must let me show you why.'

'Emma, we have been over this before. I know how much time you spent, and what a help you have been, but Jack Stanton is here now. If there is an error, which I highly doubt, he will find it. I trained him to the highest standards. There is no one I trust more to do a proper job.' He made a chopping motion with his hand. 'The only way you will be able to discuss the bridge is to go to the St Nicholas Ball.'

Emma pressed her hands to her face. She would have no option but to go to the ball and face Lottie Charlton and her cronies. Mentally she lowered the neckline of her ballgown. An inch and a half would serve better. A living relic, indeed.

Several hours of boredom was worth it if she achieved her goal in the end.

Jack was right—she could not change the laws of nature, but she could work within them. She would go to the ball and triumph. And then Jack would have to listen to the reason why the line of the bridge must be moved. It would be done without revealing the state of her father's health or who was to blame.

Butterflies attacked Emma's stomach, swooping and swirling. It was one thing to plot and plan, and quite another thing to execute. She could not help wondering if perhaps she had made the neckline of her ballgown a fraction too daring. And while the new hairstyle was certainly becoming, did it make her seem altogether too frivolous?

The urge to demand the carriage turn around and go back to the house filled her.

'Is there some problem, Miss Harrison? You look perturbed.'

'Nothing.' Emma shook her head a little more vigorously

than strictly required. Her earrings swung against her jaw. She would not concede victory to Jack Stanton. She needed to hear what was happening with the bridge, particularly as her father had taken to dropping small hints about the progress and then refusing to yield any more information. She believed he took a great deal of pleasure in doing so. 'I wondered how long until the carriage arrived at the Assembly Rooms.'

'We have joined the queue. It won't be long now.' Her father stuck his head out of the window. 'I can see the Charltons have two new bays. And whatever is Fanshaw doing with a livery painted on the side? You would think he would know by now.'

'Hush, Father. You sound as bad as Mama.'

'Nobody could be as bad as that.' Her father gave an indulgent smile. 'Poor woman, she was absolutely obsessed with social position. But she had a full life. Unlike Great-Aunt Agatha.'

'Please, Father, no homilies about marriage. Not tonight.'

Emma gave a hurried glance over to Jack, who appeared to take no notice of the exchange but directed his studious gaze out of the window.

The faint strains of a waltz emerged from the Assembly Rooms as the carriage finally reached the covered entrance. Its fabled chandeliers blazed, making a welcome pool of light in the dark. Emma shifted away from Jack. The close confines of his carriage, and her father's insistence, meant they had shared the same seat.

Emma swore her father's eyes twinkled as he alighted. His intent became clear. Matchmaking. Her father had used her interest against her. She had played directly into his hands. She should have guessed. But Jack had no interest in her. He had set up this silly contract simply to force her to go to the ball, to please her father and to teach her a lesson about interference.

'You will survive the dance. I promised you that.' Jack's hand briefly touched hers as she alighted from the carriage. The kid gloves he wore were neither shining white nor faded, but had an expensive sheen to them. In fact everything about Jack tonight, from the cut of his evening clothes to the gold stickpin in the centre of his stock, proclaimed that here was a successful man, a man of great wealth and taste.

'I planned on it. Like you, I do try to keep my promises, even if they are foolishly given.' Emma inclined her head. 'Did you think I would find an excuse?'

'The thought had crossed my mind—several times. But you appear determined to discover what is happening with the bridge.'

'The company belongs to my family. I have an interest.' Emma concentrated on rearranging her cloak.

'You should leave such things to the experts.'

'You mean to you,' she said quickly.

'And your father.' He nodded towards where her father was greeting several of the town worthies. 'He is well respected.'

'And you think I should have no interest in such matters?'

'What I think has very little relevance, as I did make a promise. Had I really wanted to keep such things a secret, I would never have made the promise.'

'Then this was purely an exercise to get me to go to the dance.'

'To get you over your fear.' He gave a wide smile 'The prospect of the evening seems to have improved your father no end. He seems as giddy as a schoolboy.'

She had to admit, from the way her father jumped down from the carriage, he was far more sprightly than she had thought. However, he had taken to refusing his tonic, complaining that his stomach cramps were always worse after it than before. And goodness knew when his other symptoms would return. It was only a matter of time. She had to face facts. Dr Milburn had been quite clear on that. She had to be practical, but she also had to ensure Harrison and Lowe would survive.

'As I said—it was a chill. He is inclined to overdo things at times. Mama used to complain about it regularly.'

'The evening will do your father good. There, now, you can relax. He has made it to the door. He is safe from the night air.'

Emma pressed her lips together. Jack was making it sound as if she acted like her father's gaoler, or an overly-protective nanny. 'I have no wish for the chill to return. It was…frightening to see my father in bed.'

'You will be gratified to know that he has decided to be sensible and allow me to oversee the bridge until at least Christmas.'

'But I understood you had a number of projects…' Emma said with dismay. She had hoped she'd be able to persuade her father without involving Jack. She was not sure if she was ready to explain that it had been her father who had made the mistakes. She had clung to the hope that Jack would tire of this game and depart, now that her father appeared to be getting better.

'None as pressing as this one. I am not satisfied with the riverbed. The second survey—' He stopped, and his lips turned up. 'Ah, but I shall say no more until after I have seen you polka.'

'You enjoy teasing me. We are here now.'

'But a contract is a contract, Miss Harrison.'

'I shall hold you to your promise,' Emma said, and allowed the maid to take her cloak and muff. Her hands smoothed the rose silk, making sure it fell smoothly.

Jack's eyes suddenly darkened as the full glory of her ballgown was revealed. The rose silk and Belgian lace set off her complexion nicely, she thought, and the spaniel curls at the side of her head made the planes of her face seem less angular, younger somehow, but she had definitely lowered the neckline a little too much. She resisted the urge to pull it higher.

She lowered her lashes and quickly scanned the list of dances. 'There is a polka first. Or one immediately after supper.'

'I had wondered if you would mention it.' Jack took the printed sheet from her. 'Normally a lady waits to be asked.'

'We have an agreement. Unless you mean for me to dance with someone else?'

'How did our contract go?' His voice rippled over her, holding her in its warmth. 'Remind me of the exact terms. Did we specify who you were to dance with?'

'I…I can't remember.' Emma hated that her voice faltered, that her mind appeared to be more intent on the shape of his mouth than on the terms of their agreement. She straightened her shoulders. It was humiliating to think that he did not really want to dance with her. He knew that they had agreed on a polka, and that was the first dance. It only stood to reason. Maybe he wanted to wait until the one after supper, see her sit on the sidelines, waiting to be asked? Emma forced her spine upright. This was not going to be the first time she had spent most of a dance seated.

'My father has entered into the spirit. He refuses to divulge any information.'

'I believe he can sense an opportunity.' Jack's hand touched the small of her back, guiding her forward and up the stairs. 'You are now here, but can you polka properly? I have no wish to cause you embarrassment. Or would you prefer a waltz?'

A waltz. Emma moved away from his hand. He had no idea what the two words did to her insides, making her remember what it had been like all those years ago here. They had waltzed then. He had been light on his feet, and a warm cocoon had surrounded her. What would it be like to waltz with him now? Emma's mouth went dry. She thought she had buried such thoughts a long time ago.

She noticed Jack was watching her with speculation in his eyes. He had probably forgotten. Emma straightened her skirt, lifted her chin, and became determined to look forward. 'I can polka, Mr Stanton. I am quite determined to polka.'

Emma did not want to think about how many times she had practised the steps in her bedroom this afternoon. She'd been determined not to make a fool of herself. And now it appeared that Jack had simply used it as a way to get her to attend the dance. She need not have bothered.

A tiny smile appeared on Jack's face. 'I never doubted that for an instant.'

'Ah, Miss Harrison, what an unexpected pleasure.' Dr Milburn's strident tones echoed around her, causing her to jump. 'Is your father here as well? He looked peaked the last time we spoke. I fear it can be but a matter of time before we are called to increase the amount of tonic your father takes.'

Emma winced and turned from Jack's suddenly narrowed gaze. She should have planned for Dr Milburn. She could only hope that he did not mention her father's illness.

'My father has disappeared into the throng, yes.' She waved a vague hand towards the ballroom. 'He has probably gone to the gaming tables. You know his addiction to whist.'

'You are taking a risk, Miss Harrison, a definite risk.' Dr Milburn shook his head, his blond locks slightly swaying. 'I trust you made sure he was well wrapped up before you both ventured forth?'

His eyes lowered to her neckline. Emma felt her flesh crawl. She wished she had brought lace with her, but to retreat now would be to admit she had made a mistake.

'My father has improved a good deal recently.' Emma raised her chin, and ignored the tiny pain in the back of her eyes.

'I put it down to stimulating dinner conversation myself,' Jack remarked, straightening his cuffs and moving so that he had subtly placed his body between Emma and Dr Milburn.

Dr Milburn looked him up and down with a raised eyebrow. 'And you are?'

'Jack Stanton. I believe we knew each other in our younger years at school. You are Charles Milburn.'

'Ah, yes, I can place the features. You were a charity case. I heard you were working for Harrison and Lowe again.' Dr Milburn's voice was cold. 'I suppose it explains why Miss Harrison has arrived with you.'

'Mr Stanton is one of the foremost civil engineers of our day, Dr Milburn.' Emma kept her voice steady.

'Indeed, Miss Emma.' Dr Milburn gave a cough. 'I must have heard the latest gossip wrong. I could have sworn that he had returned to his old post.'

Emma bit her lip. The insult to Jack was unmistakable. She could tell from his stance that the barbed comment had hit home. After all he had achieved, he remained vulnerable.

'Mr Stanton is looking after the project while my father recovers,' Emma said. 'He is Robert Stephenson's new partner, and has been entertaining my father and me with his tales of railways in far-flung places.'

She waited, and saw Jack's shoulders relax slightly, and Dr Milburn's frown increase.

'Hopefully you are making sure he takes his tonic, Miss Harrison. You must not underestimate its importance for a man in your father's condition. I have seen so many like him—fine one day, and the next they are at death's door. I am sure it is not a fate you wish on your father.' Dr Milburn drawled the words.

'No, indeed.' Emma cringed. The last thing she needed was Dr Milburn dropping hints about her father's health in the presence of the man most likely to exploit the information. And she had to remember that Jack was the enemy, not Dr Milburn.

'Edward Harrison needs medicine for a chill?' Jack asked. 'What is wrong with him?'

'I recommend all my elderly patients take my tonic.' Dr Milburn puffed up. 'It does wonders for them. I am sure it helped prolong the late Mrs Harrison's life.'

'My father has a very independent mind.'

'I know, but I am counting on you, Miss Harrison. You will save a dance for me, won't you?'

'But not a polka. She is already spoken for with that dance,' Jack said smoothly, but his eyes were cold.

'Perhaps the Sir Roger de Coverley. It is a fine dance, very respectable.' Dr Milburn indicated that he considered the polka to be beneath him. 'The committee have decreed, in accordance with tradition, that the reel will be the last dance. A festive way to end this holiday ball.'

Emma glanced from Jack to Dr Milburn. Jack Stanton appeared close to creating a scene. What had happened between these two in the past? She hid a smile. Dancing with Dr Milburn would show Jack that she was not without partners.

'Yes, I believe I am not engaged for that one.'

'I look forward to it with great eagerness, Miss Emma.' Dr Milburn made a bow and was gone.

Emma breathed a sigh of relief. Nothing untoward had happened. She started to go towards the chandelier room, but Jack's fingers held her elbow. She turned to see his intent face—black hair framing even darker eyes.

'How long has Charles Milburn been your father's doctor?'

'For the last five years or so. He was wonderfully kind when Mama was dying.' Emma tilted her head. 'Dr Milburn serves as Papa's personal physician and the company's doctor.'

'We knew each other at school.' Jack forced his jaw to

relax, forced his mind not to revisit the petty cruelties Milburn had inflicted on those unable or unwilling to stand up for themselves. 'I had always wondered who Milburn reminded me of, and now I know.'

'Who?' Emma tilted her head, and her curls touched the white column of her throat.

'A man I was unfortunately acquainted with in Brazil.' Jack chose his words with care.

'And this person was not someone you were overly fond of?'

'He was a conman and murderer,' Jack stated, and watched Emma pale.

'Dr Milburn kept my mother alive.' Emma's voice became chilled. 'Mama lived for his visits. He has been helpful with my father, who is not the best of patients. People change. You have.'

'As you say, people change.'

'Father would have a match between Dr Milburn and me, but I suspects he says it in fun.' Emma gave a little laugh. She could hardly confide her unease to Jack. Dr Milburn was fine as her father's physician, but as a husband—never! 'He knows I am determined on my spinsterhood.'

Jack's eyes travelled down her face, finally resting on her neckline. A bold, caressing gaze that caused a strange warmth to grow inside her. Emma resisted the urge to pull her neckline higher. 'In that dress, you look anything but a spinster.'

'I shall take that as a compliment.' Emma looked at him from under her eyelashes.

'It was an observation, Miss Harrison. Pray do not mistake the two.'

Several men claimed Jack's attention before Emma had time to give a suitable retort. She glared at his back.

Chapter Six

'Emma Harrison!' Lucy's laughing voice called out from the increasing throng of people. 'Of all the things!'

Emma spotted her friend, sitting with the other young matrons as the dancers swirled around them. The room baked in the glow of the crystal chandeliers. The committee had ensured the rooms were festooned with greenery, giving it a very festive look.

'Is there something wrong?' Emma asked, as she noticed Lucy's brows puckering.

'I haven't seen you wear a dress like that in years…not since…well, since your mother became seriously ill,' Lucy replied, holding out her hand. 'Are you going back on the marriage mart? Giving up on your determination to lead the solitary life?'

Emma shook her head. 'I made an unwise bargain.'

'A bargain? Do tell me more.' Lucy patted the seat beside her and Emma sank gratefully down. She had forgotten how many petticoats a ballgown required, and how much the weight increased. 'If you look now, you will see that my sister-in-law is seething.'

'Why?' Emma looked with interest to where Lottie Charlton stood, listening to Dr Milburn. 'She does appear to have swallowed a rather nasty plum. Perhaps she is not enamoured of Dr Milburn's conversation.'

'You upstaged her entrance. Lottie had consigned you to the shelf, and you—you have leapt off it in spectacular style tonight. That dress, Emma!'

'I have done nothing of the sort.' Emma gestured with her fan towards the increasing crowd of men who surrounded Lottie. The petite blonde was half hiding her face behind a fan, and laughing flirtatiously at something Jack said. Emma ignored the stab of jealousy. 'She is quite the picture. You can see from here the officers lining up to beg her acquaintance from one of the stewards. You will see. I shall have my normal place at your side for most of the dances while she is the reigning belle.'

'Reigning belle she may be, but Lottie is also a minx. She has enticed Mr Higgins to put mistletoe up, and is determined to catch your Jack Stanton under it.' Lucy nodded to where the kissing ball presided in the centre of the room. 'It's also hidden in the garlands. She will come to no good one of these days, and be married off to the wrong man.'

'He is not *my* Jack Stanton,' Emma retorted, and then worried that she had said the words too quickly. She should have concentrated on Lottie's misdemeanours—a much more suitable subject, and having little or no peril.

'You arrived with him, and there's a sort of glow about you tonight that I haven't seen in many years.' Lucy folded her hands in her lap and gave a very superior smile. 'It makes you look years younger, less like a dried-up prune.'

She ignored the glow, and the prune comment. Lucy had obviously mistaken strain and heat from the chandeliers for something else. And her clothes were suited to the purpose.

'Only because Jack Stanton forced my hand,' Emma said between gritted teeth.

She restrained her fingers from fiddling with the pearl button of her glove. *A lady does not fidget*—words her mother had tirelessly repeated rose up again. Her life now was very different from one that her mother would have considered proper.

'Forced you?' Lucy put her hand over her mouth, but Emma saw the amused glint in her eyes. 'I find it hard to believe that any man could force you to do anything. You have grown formidable, Emma.'

'You have been a friend for a long time, Lucy, and I shall allow that remark to pass.' Emma lifted her fan to hide her expression. It was all right for Lucy to talk. She had chosen Henry Charlton six years ago, after she had been out for a while but before her star had started to wane. It was not a love-match, but one in which Lucy professed herself content. 'But even old friends should not presume to take liberties.'

'Stuff and nonsense, Emma, we have been friends for ever.' Lucy laid a gloved hand on Emma's arm. 'What I worry about is what will happen if your father remarries.'

'I don't think that is a possibility.' Emma gave an arch laugh and hoped. She had not confided in Lucy about her father's illness and her fears.

'You do need to think about it.' Lucy's hand tightened. 'He is not that old, and he is possessed of reasonable fortune. See how that farmer's widow from the Tyne Valley circles.'

Emma shifted uncomfortably as a cold chill passed down her. She had been in charge of the house ever since her mother became ill—seven long years. If her father did remarry she would be delighted for him, but the house would cease to be her domain. 'I can always be a companion.'

'Emma, you are not one of life's companions—ready to

fetch and carry, read aloud dull religious tracts and do endless tatting and netting.'

'You didn't think I would make a good nurse either,' Emma reminded her. 'You made many dire predictions and told me that I would abandon Mama and wed before the year was up.'

'Sometimes I think you persisted simply because you delight in proving everyone wrong.' Lucy's brown eyes twinkled. 'I have known you for a long time, Emma Harrison.'

No, I persisted because my heart ached. Emma caught her lip between her teeth. Where had that thought come from? She banished it. She was happy and content with her life. Her sole concern was her father, and keeping him alive. 'There may be something in that, Lucy.'

'Miss Harrison.' Jack's warm voice washed over her. 'Here I discover you. You appeared to have been swallowed up by the crush.'

'I did not know you needed to discover me.' Emma slowly lowered her fan, placed it in her lap, but her insides trembled. She had hoped that Jack would be content with her simply appearing at the ball. 'I thought I was visible from all angles.'

'Have you forgotten? We are to polka.' His manner was light but his eyes were cold. 'The first dance is the polka. I do not see any point in wasting more time. And you do not appear engaged for the dance.'

Emma's heart sank. Now that it came to it, she was less than certain that she could do it. She knew the steps. But to be out in the middle amongst all those people—people who could remember when she'd been the belle of the ball instead of being led out onto the floor for the Sir Roger de Coverley at the very end. 'I had thought I would have longer.'

'Longer? Longer to get up your nerve, or to find an excuse as to why you are suddenly afflicted with pains in your legs and cannot dance?'

'Emma, you never said that Mr Stanton had asked you to partner him for a dance. You silly puss.' Lucy's eyes twinkled with mischief. 'And here I thought you were to keep me company until Dr Milburn claimed you. Pray, take her away, sir. She does precious little dancing these days, not like when we were young. I should like to see her polka.'

'She *claims* to know the steps, but I have my doubts.' Jack's gaze challenged her.

'You doubt my word, but I am no liar, Mr Stanton. I do know the steps.'

'She is shocking, isn't she?' Lucy put her finger to her lips. 'I trust she will not tread on your toes.'

'I have never trodden on anyone's toes.' Emma put her hand on one hip. 'Really, Lucy!'

'Emma is far more interested these days in silly calculations about wind speeds and tides,' Lucy continued, as if Emma had not spoken. 'For ever going on about them. I mean, who would be interested in such things as a topic of polite conversation?'

Emma's breath stopped in her throat. She was torn between the desire to shake Lucy and the pride she took in her own ability.

'Indeed? I had not realised her interest in civil engineering extended as far as that.'

'Oh, yes. You should see her designs for the new bridge. I saw the early sketches, and then how—'

'Lucy Charlton, you are allowing your tongue to run away with you,' Emma said quickly. 'Sometimes I don't think you know what you are saying.'

'But I do know what you are trying to do, Emma Harrison! And I quite agree with Mr Stanton that you should not be allowed to sit on the sidelines when other lesser dancers take to the floor.'

Lucy's elbow dug into Emma's back, forcing her to stand. Emma shot a black look at her friend.

'Tell him,' she said in an urgent undertone. 'Tell him you were teasing me.'

'I am funning, Mr Stanton.' Lucy fluttered her fan. 'She has been sitting here tapping her foot to the music. She is the same old Emma Harrison that she was years ago. You have come to her rescue not a moment too soon. She was using her hand to stifle a yawn.'

'And I thought you enjoyed my company, Lucy,' Emma protested, but she gave her friend a grateful look. She had to tread very carefully where Jack was concerned.

'Miss Harrison.' Jack held out his hand. "The dance is about to start. Try to look as if it is not a death sentence.'

'A death sentence? Hardly that, Mr Stanton!' Emma struggled to contain her nervousness. Mentally she rehearsed the steps again. She only hoped the tempo would not be too fast.

'Your face seems to have paled significantly.'

'I stood up too quickly.' Emma forced her lungs to fill. 'My stays…'

'Yes, of course. That would explain it.'

'Shall we go?' Emma held up her fingertips.

'Have no fear, I shall endeavour to entertain you with quips about wind speeds and the height of floods, as your friend suggested.'

'I don't think this is quite the appropriate place for an in-depth discussion.' Emma straightened her shoulders.

'No? You should have thought about that before you agreed to our little contract.'

'You don't mean to cheat, Mr Stanton, do you?' A cold shiver ran down Emma's spine. She might as well cause a scandal and abandon him on the dance floor if all the information he was prepared to give her would be contained in the length of the dance. She needed longer, but she would begin her explanation now, while she had the chance. 'I desire a full account of what has been happening. I had grown quite used to it. The bridge-building has become an obsession with me. Lucy was right about that. I'd like to speak with you about the line of the bridge and the new survey. I believe I have discovered why it is different from the earlier one.'

'You should know, Miss Harrison, that I never cheat where business or ladies are concerned. And I never combine the two.' He gave a half-smile. 'I only thought to tease you a little, but I see now you resist such things. Shall we indulge in a light flirtation instead?'

'I think we should polka,' Emma said firmly. The last thing she wanted was a flirtation with Jack. She had to remember that he was the man most likely to ruin her world.

'As you wish…'

Emma gulped, lightly placed her fingers in his and allowed herself to be led out onto the floor with the other couples. She ignored the viperous glance that Lottie gave her. Jack put his hand on her waist and gave a nod. The music rose up and surrounded them.

'Heel and toe and away we go,' Jack said, before they began.

'Excuse me?' Emma resisted the impulse to laugh.

'It is the way I was taught the polka. The little rhyme helps. You had a worried frown on your face. Are you sure you have danced the polka before?'

'I know the theory.'

'There is a world of difference between theory and practice, Miss Harrison. Both in the fields of dance and civil engineering.'

Emma stumbled a few steps, but then found her rhythm. Unlike the smoother and slower waltz, which attracted all sorts of participants, the polka was mostly confined to the younger generation. Jack proved an able partner, guiding her around the floor with expertise, but not so good that he danced like a dancing master. Emma began to relax, and began to notice little things—the way his hand rested lightly against her back, the slight curl of his hair, his crisp masculine scent, and most of all the shape of his lips.

Emma missed a step and stumbled against him, her body colliding with the starched white linen that covered his broad chest. Her breath hissed through her lips. Jack smoothly manoeuvred them so it appeared as if her stumble had been planned. Emma regained her footing and they galloped around the room once more.

'I'm sorry,' she mumbled, and felt heat surge through her cheeks, praying that he would think it was from the exertion of the dance.

'It was undoubtedly the floor's fault, as someone once said to me.' The words were quietly spoken.

'They have not improved it in eight years,' she said, her breath catching in her throat. All too clearly she remembered when they had first waltzed as Strauss played, and she had said those very words to him. It had been the start of her awareness of him. Then, about a year later, he had asked and not waited for her answer.

'No, obviously not.'

She glanced up and saw his dark eyes had softened slightly, and his face had become serious. She had forgotten the exact curve of his lips. What would they feel like? Soft or firm?

"The music has stopped.' She withdrew her hand, but her feet refused to move. 'You must have other partners waiting. A waltz is next.'

A strange smile crept over his face. 'Miss Harrison, it is an intriguing place that you have ended the dance at.'

Her gaze travelled upwards and saw what they had stopped under. Mistletoe. Lottie's little mischief-making. She should have thought and found a way to steer clear of it.

His finger lifted her chin and his eyes searched her face, coming to rest on her mouth. 'The prospect is tempting, but not here, I think. It wouldn't be a good idea. It is far too public.'

'No, it wouldn't.' Emma agreed with his assessment, despite the faint ache of her lips. Already several of the old ladies were turning their gimlet eyes towards them, pince-nez poised for a better look. The room would buzz with gossip if he brushed her lips. But then if he left her standing there without even a peck on the cheek the room would echo to whispers that he had spurned her. Silently she cursed Lottie Charlton for her little innovation. 'I can see my father signalling…'

'Are you trying to run away, Miss Harrison?' His hand tightened on hers, turned it over. Capturing her. 'You need to pay a forfeit.'

'Not at all. I had not intended to stop here. It was happenstance.' The words were a mere breath. Her lips tingled as if he had actually touched them, instead of simply fixing them with a gaze.

'Some might say otherwise.'

He raised her hand and lowered his head. She fixed her gaze on the curls at the base of his neck, tried to ignore the sudden warmth flooding through her.

'Please,' she whispered, hardly knowing what she was asking for.

'I am always happy to oblige.'

His mouth touched the inside of her wrist, where her glove gaped slightly, touched naked flesh, lingered, and somehow it was much more intimate than she'd thought possible. And over in a breath.

'Until the next time.'

'The next time?' Emma whispered, looking up at Jack.

If he danced with her again tonight the gossips would be linking their names together. Her limbs trembled. She wasn't sure she was ready for that. What was past was past. She was no longer the girl of seven years ago. She no longer laughed as much, and she certainly knew pain and hardship far more than she had done.

Who did Jack see when he looked at her?

'Is there to be a next time?' She had meant the words to be sarcastic, but they came out plaintive, like a child asking for a sweet.

He gave a nod. 'And a waltz, I think, rather than a polka. Your servant, Miss Harrison.'

Emma put her hand to her cheek, felt the coolness of the kid leather against the flame. The mark of his lips seemed to be imprinted on the inside of her wrist. Such a simple act, but it had appeared to be far more intimate than a brush of lips against her brow. She watched his broad-shouldered figure disappear into the crowd.

'Stanton—here I discover you. I thought you would have been at the gaming tables.'

Edward Harrison's voice interrupted Jack's thoughts as he watched Emma taking part in a country dance. Her skirts swayed and he caught a glimpse of a slender ankle, saw Milburn looking as well, and fought against the urge to slam his fist into the doctor's smug face. He pointedly turned away from the dance floor.

'I make it a point never to gamble. I prefer to take calculated risks.'

'Which explains how you have acquired so much money so rapidly and seemingly effortlessly.' Harrison held out a cup of steaming punch. 'You predicted the phenomenal growth in the railways. I wish I had taken your advice then. You were right.'

'I like to think so.' Jack took a small sip of the lamb's wool punch—so called because the mashed roasted apples floating on the surface bore a marked resemblance to newborn lambs' fleece. The heady combination of steaming brown ale, sweet white wine, cinnamon, ginger and nutmeg always reminded him of the Christmas season.

'I know so, Stanton. I know so indeed. Who would ever have imagined that railways would become such a necessary part of the Empire in such a short span of time?'

'Harrison, did you find your widow?' Jack nodded towards where several older women sat, gossiping, at the edge of the floor. 'Does the course of romance run smoothly?'

'She is in a tolerable frame of mind.' Harrison rocked back on his heels. 'It was lovely to see you circling the room with Emma. Your dancing has improved over the years. I remember how you once used a surveyor's level to practise your waltzing.'

Jack gave a tight smile. This ball appeared to be dredging up old memories, feelings he'd thought long-dead. The hours he had put in practising bore little relation to the actual feel of Emma Harrison in his arms. Then. Or now.

'Thank you, the pleasure was all mine.' Jack inclined his head, pulling his mind away from the past. 'Your daughter is very light on her feet.'

'I had hopes for you and my daughter once.' Harrison waved his hand in the air.

'That was a long time ago,' Jack replied carefully. He had not expected to feel anything when he took Emma in his arms, but his body had responded to her nearness. He had wondered what her lips tasted like. Ripe cherries? Syllabub? It was as if the years had melted away, and yet he knew he was not the callow youth he had been.

'I would like to inspect the works tomorrow—see what is going on,' Harrison said, bringing Jack back to the present with a crash.

'That can be arranged, I am sure. I look forward to showing you around. There are a few questions I have about some of the calculations.'

'They are all accurate on the first survey. I checked them myself.' Harrison's mouth turned down. 'I may be getting on in years, but my mind works admirably, Stanton.'

'I like to double-check, Harrison. I hope you don't mind. I am only following your teaching.' Jack regarded Harrison with a steady gaze. There was more to this situation than he had first thought. 'If I am working on a bridge, I want it to last.'

'And, Stanton, I think we can bring my daughter along— if she isn't too tired from her dancing.' Harrison gave a proud smile. 'Now, if you will excuse me, I must go and entertain my widow. She is to partner me at whist.'

Harrison sauntered away, and linked arms with a woman only a few years older than Emma. The woman gave a huge sigh and fluttered her eyelashes. Harrison turned a light shade of pink.

Jack narrowed his eyes. Emma might feel safe and secure in her position as her father's hostess, but what would happen when he remarried, as he appeared intent on doing? He doubted she would like a position as a companion, serving at the beck and call of an aged relative. He found he could take no pleasure in the thought.

There was something alive and vital in Emma that called him tonight.

One of the dancers knocked against the greenery, sending a sprig of mistletoe tumbling to the ground. Jack reached down, picked it up, intending to return it to its place. His gaze narrowed as Emma circled past in the arms of one of Her Majesty's soldiers. Her skirts swayed in time to the music. She appeared to be every inch the social butterfly, but he knew that was a lie. There was a new seriousness about her, something that had not been there before.

Their eyes met, held for a brief heartbeat. She was the first to look away.

'So, Emma, your father wants me to take you to the bridge, rather than discuss the situation with you in the drawing room. Did you enlist his aid? And who are you trying to protect?' Jack said softly, as he twirled the sprig between his fingers. 'How far are you prepared to go to realise your desire?'

Chapter Seven

The chandelier candles had burnt low, and the ballroom was bathed in a golden glow. The wooden floor had become splattered with candle wax. A molten drop narrowly missed Emma's shoulder as she circled around the dance floor with one of Lottie's officers.

'Miss Harrison, you are not attending,' the Major said.

'I am sorry. I will endeavour to be a more gracious partner.' Emma gave a quick smile and forced herself to stop looking for Jack's broad shoulders.

Every time she went out on the floor she looked for him. He was different from the man she had so very nearly given her heart to seven years ago. Outwardly he looked similar, but she sensed an intense drive, a desire that had not been there before. He had pursued his dream and won.

What was worse, she knew that, given the choice between dancing with him again and finding out about the bridge, she would be tempted to forget her duty and choose the dance.

'Miss Harrison, I believe I have the pleasure of the next dance.' Dr Milburn's voice interrupted her thoughts and she found her nostrils assaulted by peppermint. Dr Milburn's cod-like features swam into view.

'Dr Milburn, I had not realised the end of the ball had arrived.' She held out a slipper and gave a rueful smile. 'I fear the worst for this pair. I have hardly been able to sit since the polka.'

'I noticed you were much in demand.' The doctor inclined his head.

'It makes a change. I had quite forgotten what it was like to dance all night.'

Dr Milburn frowned. 'You know, I worry that your father is involved with Jack Stanton.'

'My father has known him a long time,' Emma said carefully. 'He gave Mr Stanton his initial training.'

'We were boys together.' Dr Milburn gave a braying laugh. 'He was a charity pupil and had much to say for himself. Breeding will out.'

There was something unpleasant in Dr Milburn's tone. Emma took a deep breath. What was Dr Milburn implying— that Jack was not entitled to his money because he had been a charity case? That he had somehow acquired it illegally? Her mind shied away from the thought. Impossible.

'He has done well from the railways.' Emma crossed her arms. 'All of them have—Brunel, Stephenson, and the rest.'

A look of annoyance crossed the doctor's face. 'You know in my charity work I go to the homes of workers. Poor places they are. Foul. Sometimes I wonder about this Industrial Revolution they are always going on about. Is it making the world a better place?'

'What does this have to do with Jack Stanton?'

Dr Milburn gave a shrug. 'I hate to think of what must have happened to those poor devils he bought out. How do they feel about his wealth? And the women he has romanced but not married? You must be careful, Miss Harrison.'

'I believe I understand the measure of the man. He is overseeing the bridge—that is all.' Her wrist tingled slightly where Jack's lips had brushed it. 'I have no interest in the man.'

'I am relieved to hear it.' Dr Milburn made another bow. 'I believe the reel is about to begin. Shall we?'

Emma let him lead her out on the floor. As they lined up, ready to begin, she saw Jack in the next line. Jack's eyes were on her, cold and hard, speculating. Something she had never noticed before. A shiver ran down her spine. What did he have planned for her? Was Dr Milburn right about his business practices?

'Miss Emma, the dance has begun,' Dr Milburn complained.

Emma looked down at the floor, trying to pay attention to her dance steps and banish all imaginings from her clearly over-taxed brain.

'I shall now retire to my room a happy man,' Emma's father pronounced when they arrived back at the house. 'I am not getting younger, but these balls do my heart good.'

Emma made a move to follow her father up the stairs. Her feet ached, and she was certain a blister was developing on the base of her right foot, but a happy glow filled her. She had forgotten dancing could be this much fun.

'A word, Miss Harrison, if you please.' Jack gestured towards the drawing room.

Emma swallowed the quick retort. Her body quivered as if his hand had brushed hers. She forced the tiredness down. Surely Jack could not want to have a discussion about the bridge at this hour? She had counted on it being tomorrow morning. As it was, she had probably had one cup of punch too many. It was the only thing that could account for this lighter-than-air feeling. In the morning she expected to feel every inch of her twenty-five years again.

The embers of the fire gave out a golden orange glow, giving the normally sedate room a mysterious allure.

'Is there something wrong?' Emma asked as she moved about the room, straightening all the cushions. Her heart thudded in her ears as Jack shut the door with a click.

'I have been remiss.'

'Remiss?' Emma's hand froze, hanging suspended in mid-air, hovering over a cushion. 'You have been most pleasant all evening. I can find no fault with your behaviour. You even shepherded old Mrs Armstrong into supper. Goodness knows that was above and beyond the call of duty. She assumes everyone is deaf and in need of an ear trumpet.'

'She is pleasant enough, but my choice of dinner companion is not what I want to speak about.' The darkness of Jack's hair contrasted sharply with the whiteness of his shirt-front, giving him a dangerous look.

'The bridge? You wish to discuss the bridge now?' Emma held out a cushion as her mind struggled. She was over-tired from dancing and would have to guard her tongue. Where to begin? How to begin?

He took the cushion from her and replaced it on the sofa. The air was suddenly tinged by his very masculine citrus scent, holding her, enveloping her. Within the space of a heartbeat the room had shrunk. Emma's tongue wet her dry lips as her pulse began to race. They were alone, and it was unlike the last time they had been alone. Then, the servants had been about; now the house was hushed. Above her, she could hear the distant sounds of her father getting ready for bed.

'I promised you another dance—a waltz, I believe—but I became entangled in other matters.' The fire cast shadows over his face, concealing his expression. 'And you…were busy.'

'After our polka I was not a wallflower.' Emma's voice sounded breathless. She concentrated on the mantelpiece clock, ignoring the way her body became alert, as if it expected something to happen—wanted something to happen.

'I dislike saying something and not doing it.' Jack took a step closer. If she reached out a hand she'd encounter his shirt-front. Her palm itched to touch, and she barely restrained it.

'There is not another ball between now and Christmas. Put it out of your mind. I have.' Emma knew it was a lie. All the time she had waltzed with the other men she had thought about what it had been like to be in Jack's arms. How safe and familiar it had felt, like returning home. She struggled for control. 'Shall we speak about the bridge? It is another promise you made. I am eager to hear your progress.'

'If a polka was worth a discussion, might a waltz be worth a site visit to see how things are actually progressing?' His voice dropped an octave, became thick rich velvet that stroked her skin.

She struggled to remember what was important.

'It might be. But we are discussing theory only, Mr Stanton. I told you there was no ball between now and Christmas.' A pang of disappointment ran through Emma. Against all reason, she wanted to be in his arms again. The reason did not matter.

'What if I hum?' He held out his hands. His eyes were shadowed. 'Would you dance with me? Here, now, in the firelight?'

She attempted to draw a breath, but her stays were pulled far too tightly. To dance here... A tingle of excitement rippled down her spine.

'You are teasing me, Mr Stanton. Waltzing in the drawing room? Without music?' Emma tried a laugh, but it died in her throat as she saw his expression. The light from the dimmed gas gave him a dangerous look, his face all planes and shadows. And his evening dress did nothing to tame him. If anything, it showed that the merest veneer of civilisation covered him.

'I have never been more serious.' He moved over to the fireplace.

Emma stared at him, took an involuntary step forward, gave an imperceptible nod.

Tomorrow she would be sensible. Tonight she wanted to feel his arms about her waist. She had drunk a cup too many, and even her blood seemed to be tingling.

'Once around the room and that is all.'

'As my lady commands.' He put one hand on her waist, and the other clasped her free hand. Emma's fingers trembled as they touched his shoulder, felt the muscles rippling underneath.

He began to hum loudly, a definite waltz, a Strauss waltz like the one that they had first danced to all those years ago. Was it deliberately chosen? Or simply the one waltz tune he knew? Emma hesitated, longed to ask but decided against it. She had no desire to alert him to the fact that she remembered. She dreaded to think what construction he might put on that piece of intelligence.

At his look, she joined in. Her hum matched his. He nodded, and his hand rested more firmly on her waist, pulled her body closer to his. His hand seemed to burn through her dress.

They circled the room once. Their feet slowed, the humming faded. Stopped.

Her gaze tumbled into his, caught, held. Emma knew she should step back. Propriety demanded it. But her limbs were powerless to move.

She wanted to stay where she was—in his arms. Safe. The desire to lay her head against his chest and hear the steady thump of his heart threatened to overwhelm her. She made one last effort towards sanity. Pushed back against the circle of his arms.

'I should go.' She looked towards the closed door. It seemed an age away. She had no idea how she would make it there without stumbling. Her legs seemed to be made of jelly.

He made no reply, but his mouth swooped down and captured hers. Lips touching lips. His hand came and cupped the back of her head. It seemed as if her entire world had come down to this one thing—the pressure of his mouth against hers.

Firm, but gentle.

A warm ripple coursed through her. She had been kissed before, quick pecks, and once someone had kissed her full on her lips. But nothing like this lingering possession of her mouth, this kiss that threatened to unravel her senses. She should move back, but her spine appeared to have melted. She wanted the moment never to end. The kiss changed, became more seeking, more urgent, devoured her lips as his arms tightened and drew her closer, crushing her against his hard body.

The clock chimed, striking midnight, and Emma jumped away from Jack. Her face showed panic, but her lips were a little too full, too red. He made no move to keep her there.

He had meant to test her, to see how far she'd go and to pull back at the last possible moment. Then this had happened. He had tasted her lips, felt them curve underneath his, yield, and it had taken all his self-control not to go beyond that. Even now his hands itched to reach out and press her warm body back against his.

'Forgive me, Miss Harrison—the mistletoe.' His breathing was laboured, as if he had run a long distance. He forced his lungs to fill with air, his hands to remain by his sides, his head upright.

'There is no mistletoe here.' She crossed her arms and narrowed her eyes.

He raised an eyebrow. 'You surprise me with the boldness of your assertion, Miss Harrison. There is a sprig in your hair.'

Her cheeks flamed red as her hands explored the knot at the back of her head. 'Where? How did I not notice? Do you know how long it has been there? Imagine what the gossips will be saying!'

'Not so very long.' Jack reached out and plucked the sprig from where he had placed it as they were dancing. A mild deception, but surely better than the accusing stare. And her lips had tantalised him all night. 'You should be more observant.'

He kept his face perfectly solemn and waited.

The corners of her lips twitched.

'I am sure that wasn't there before.' Her eyes danced as a tiny bubble of laughter escaped. 'I am positive. It couldn't have been. Lucy Charlton would have said something when we parted. You put it there.'

His laughter echoed hers.

'Are you accusing me?' He raised an eyebrow and dared her to carry the flirtation further.

'Maybe.' She lowered her lashes and developed a sudden interest in the pattern of the Turkey carpet.

He hesitated, waiting.

The ticks of the clock grew louder, reverberating through his body. He forced his hands to freeze. Years ago they had once shared a flirtation, and he had rushed things. And had lost her.

He refused to lose again.

Jack shut his eyes. Seven years ago he had vowed to start afresh, not to look backwards. He should not break his resolution simply because the woman he had held in his arms was Emma Harrison.

'Then perhaps I did have something to do with it. Now, say you forgive me.'

Her cheeks flushed, and her mouth became redder. A small sigh escaped, but the carpet still held her interest.

He waited, wanted her to offer her lips again, wanted to plunder her mouth. He had felt her quivering response.

Her small white teeth caught her bottom lip and she turned her head. 'There is nothing to forgive.' She gave a small trill of laughter and trailed her hand along the mantelpiece. 'As you said, it was the mistletoe's fault. It could have happened to anyone.'

Her eyelashes swept down, forming black smudges on her cheeks, making her look like she'd used to. Jack's hand curled at his side.

He had to remember what she was capable of—how he had poured out his heart to her in that letter and she had cut him dead, never answering, never acknowledging it. He had used her silence as a spur to make something of his life rather than settling as a junior civil engineer.

With the death of one dream came another.

But there was something different about Emma. Something that called to him, urged caution. All was not as it seemed.

'Why did you dance with me?'

'I told you that I was very interested in the bridge. I wanted…wanted to go on a site visit.' She tilted her head to one side. 'You did promise.'

'And why is that?'

The words seemed to resonate throughout the room. Emma could hear the warning behind them. Danger. She had nearly forgotten who Jack Stanton was, and how much depended on him not guessing the truth about the bridge and its design. She had to find a way to alert him to the errors in the calculations without explaining about her father.

She had to think about more than the way his arms had felt against her, or how she'd wanted to lay her face against his chest and confess her fears about her father, about her future. She could not explain. Not even now, after they had shared a kiss. Especially after they had shared a kiss.

A kiss.

No one had walked in on them, but the possibility had been there. What would her father have said? Would he have forced the issue? The worst thing was that she wanted to feel the pressure of Jack Stanton's lips again, be encircled in his arms. She wanted all this.

'Tell me, Miss Harrison.' His words coaxed her, but she saw his intent expression. 'Tell me, Emma.'

'Because—' Emma bit back the words to explain about the mistaken calculations. Now was not the time to discuss such matters. She wanted to enjoy the romance of the night. 'Because I like to take an interest in the things my father does. It gives us something to discuss besides the weather.'

Even as she said the words she knew how false they must ring. She covered her mouth with her hands and hoped.

Jack's face hardened. He reached over and lit three candles, making the room suddenly bright. 'Hopefully one day, Emma, you will trust me enough to tell the truth.'

'And hopefully one day you won't need to cheat. Mistletoe in my hair, indeed. To think I trusted you. You are worse than a rake.' She drew herself up, picked up a candle to light her way, and gave a nod. 'I expect the site visit tomorrow morning.'

'But—'

'You should have read the fine print of our contract, Mr Stanton,' she said firmly. 'Goodnight. Annie, my maid, will be expecting me. I have no wish to keep her waiting.'

She hurried out of the room before her legs gave way. Before she begged him to let her stay.

Jack let her go, despite the temptation to haul her back and kiss her again, to properly taste her mouth. He was sure she would return.

Her footsteps echoed as she mounted the stairs quickly.

He poured a brandy out of the decanter, held it up to the light, swirled it and saw the colour of her hair in the glass. He downed the liquid in one great gulp.

'The game is not over yet, Miss Emma Harrison.'

Chapter Eight

'Emma, I must say I think the way your hair is done today suits you,' her father remarked the next morning, as Emma sat nibbling at her bread and butter. 'Much better than the old way, which made you look as if you were attempting to become a younger version of Great-Aunt Agatha. The resemblance is not quite as marked today.'

Emma bit back the words to inform her father that she would wear her hair how she pleased, and that she had never, ever looked like Great-Aunt Agatha in her life. She had decided to agree with Annie and keep the spaniel curls at the sides of her head. They did soften her profile. Emma glanced at the small marble mantel clock, and then back at her father.

'Father, what are you doing down so early? It is barely even light.'

He was dressed in his frock coat, and his large gold pocket watch gleamed from his waistcoat. She had not seen him dressed like this since the Saturday before last, when they had expected Jack to arrive. Then it had been only at her insistence, and they had arrived at the site in time for the eleven o'clock break, not before.

Her father calmly settled himself at the breakfast table, signalling for his breakfast and coffee. Fackler moved silently and swiftly, arranging her father's napkin and getting the food he required almost before he asked for it.

Emma reached behind her and pulled out his tonic, but he waved it away.

'I want all my wits about me today.' He wrinkled his nose. 'The taste bothers me, and it makes my head pound. You worry too much.'

'You don't want to have another attack.' Emma tightened her grip on the bottle. She hated to think what would happen if her father did have a full-blown attack while Jack was here.

'You let me be the judge of my health, daughter. I have everything under control. I know the risks. I have done the calculations. Sometimes it would seem that you credit me with little sense, Emma.'

'That is an unfair accusation.'

'The truth is never an accusation.' Her father's blue eyes met hers in a steady gaze. 'Now, the day's a-wasting. Where is that young Stanton?'

'Why, Father? What are you planning with Mr Stanton?'

Emma tried hard not to smile at the description of Jack as young. She could well remember when her father had used to call him that. He used to speak of him regularly at the dinner table until her mother had clicked her tongue and moved the conversation away from business.

Jack was not 'young' Stanton, not any more. Just as she had grown and changed, so had he. He had become more dangerous, sophisticated and…desirable. He was a mature man. There was nothing boyish about him.

Her hand trembled as she set the coffee down, sending the liquid spilling over the edge.

'A surprise is planned.' Her father rubbed his hands together.

'You are definitely up to something. I can see the gleam in your eye.' Emma leant forward. 'Confide in me, Father, you know you want to. What mischief?'

'No mischief. You are going to inspect the bridge today, and I am coming with you.' Her father began attacking his eggs with great vigour.

'Yes, I know I am going. That is hardly news.' Emma stopped and her eyes narrowed. She stared hard at her father. 'How did you know I was going to the bridge? When did you see Mr Stanton?'

Her breath caught in her throat as tiny wings of tension filled her. Jack had gone to see her father this morning. But about what? She tried to calm the sudden butterflies. It was all too quick and new.

Her father gestured with his bread and butter. 'I had a little word with Stanton at the Assembly Rooms last evening. Thought it would be a capital idea. You have been moping about the place long enough. Have no idea why you have taken to that bridge, but you have. And that's all there is to it. It must be in the blood. Never thought I'd see a female interested in such things. Your mother's eyelids grew heavy with the merest mention of a mathematical formula.'

'But you enjoyed her conversations and amusements. You encouraged her.'

'She was right. I did spend far too much time speaking about work. It astonishes me that my youngest daughter should share the same sort of passion. You had a fit of the blue devils last week when I refused to tell you about the progress.'

'I do not mope,' Emma retorted quickly, before her throat became tight. She'd had no idea her father was that perceptive. She'd have to be far more careful about choosing her words. How she explained the mistake—particularly if he was not taking his tonic. 'I have been seeing to the preparations for the feast, filling the boxes for the poor and making sure my ballgown was fit to be seen. I have had a thousand and one things to do.'

'I knew how much you had been missing it. Stanton agreed with me when I spoke with him at the ball. You were dancing with some soldier.'

Emma stared at her father as her mind went back over what had happened last night. Her mouth became dry and the coffee tasted like ashes. Jack had known! He had already agreed. He had manipulated her into the dance and the kiss! The kiss that she had wanted to go on and on need never have happened.

And, what was worse, it was she who had initiated the kiss. She had been the one to lift her mouth, to have her feet stop, and to stare up into his deep dark gaze and will him to lower his mouth.

A shiver ran down her back. She should feel ashamed, but she didn't. The kiss had been something special, something time out of mind. But it would not be repeated. Ever.

It need not have happened. If she had but known. Jack had toyed with her. He had always intended on taking her to see the bridge. Shame washed over her.

'You? You arranged this day?' She banged her fist on the table, giving vent to her frustration. 'How could you do such a thing without consulting me?'

'What was it that you said? I swear my hearing gets worse and worse. Soon I shall need an ear trumpet.' Her father put his hand over hers. 'I shall go on my own. You need not worry about coming up with an appropriate excuse. Jack Stanton will understand. Your interest in the bridge was short-lived. You have found something new to occupy your time.'

'You deliberately mistake me, Papa. I do want to go,' Emma said quickly. 'It will be the highlight of my morning.

I am happy that you feel well enough to go. Dr Milburn's tonic must be working its usual miracles.'

'That's my girl.' Her father tapped the side of his nose. 'I haven't been taking the tonic. That's why I waved it away this morning. Didn't want Stanton to see how ill and namby-pamby I had become.'

Emma's answer was stopped by Jack's arrival into the breakfast room. Not a hair was out of place, and his cream-coloured trousers had perfect creases in them. Everything about him proclaimed gentlemanly elegance, but her mind kept remembering the way his mouth had felt against hers. The way he had held her. The way he had tricked her.

She twisted the napkin in her lap between her fingers and willed herself to forget. He had used her. She had to hang onto the thought. His sole interest was the business. He did not care about Harrison and Lowe and its employees. All he saw in her was a means to an end.

'Everyone is up,' he remarked, and his dark eyes shone with a hidden fire. 'Are you intent on coming to the bridge this morning? It can be postponed if you desire.'

'Yes, we are. I am determined to see the bridge today, and my father is as well.' The words came out more forcefully than she'd intended. Jack raised an eyebrow.

'I had never intended it would be anything but a chaperoned excursion. I am well aware of your dedication to the social niceties, Miss Harrison.' There was a hint of mocking laughter in his words.

'Yes, even though I am on the shelf, I do find it easier to conform to social convention.' Emma pressed her lips together and attempted to look stern. 'There has never been any whiff of scandal in this family. My mother raised my sister and me properly.'

'I am pleased to hear it,' Jack said, his dark gaze directly on her mouth. His velvet voice flowed over her, reminding her of their dance and subsequent kiss. 'I am sure you will enjoy the outing.'

Emma frowned, then pulled herself together. She had to remember what he was, and how he had tricked her last night.

'That remains to be seen,' she returned tartly.

Jack and her father exchanged glances. Emma narrowed her eyes. Her father was up to no good. It wasn't matchmaking. She did not think he would be underhanded enough to try that. Not after what had happened seven years ago.

She simply did not know what her father was up to this time, and it bothered her. If Jack Stanton was involved, she doubted that it would be to her advantage.

The building site sparkled in the sunlight. Heavy overnight frost lay thick, covering everything. The puddles were lightly crusted with ice and crunched slightly when she stepped on one. Two of the young lads were playing at sliding along the length of the site, but with one look from Jack they stopped their game, picked up some stone and began working again.

Emma snuggled her hands deeper in her muff as she watched the plume of air rise like a cloud around Jack, obscuring his features.

During the carriage ride she had done everything possible to keep her skirts from touching him. He had seemed to take a delight in provoking her, moving his foot ever so slightly towards her when the carriage rounded a bend. And still she couldn't stop thinking of that kiss!

'The site appears to be covered in ice,' she said, to cover her dismay.

'I have no wish for you to fall.'

'I am quite steady on my feet.' She managed a smile. 'All my partners' toes remained unbruised last night.'

'You may be an excellent dancer, but black ice is another matter. Caution is called for.' An amused smile touched the corners of his lips as he put his hand under her elbow to guide her around an icy patch.

Emma pressed her lips together. He had deceived her last night. The decision to bring her here had been decided long before they spoke in the drawing room, long before his hands touched her waist, long before… She wrenched her mind away. 'I am not made of porcelain, Mr Stanton. I can stand on my own two feet.'

'You appear perturbed this morning, Miss Emma.'

The amusement in his eyes deepened. His fingers remained hovering just below her elbow, tantalisingly close. Her whole arm quivered with anticipation. Then she saw her father's eyes gleam, and a tiny smile appear on his lips. A rush of ice water went through her veins and Emma forced her body to move away from him. Jack's actions were for her father's benefit. He had engineered the whole situation. He had enlisted Jack's aid, but surely he had to see that Jack was playing a game of his own. Now Jack had to realise that she understood the rules, understood what he was trying to achieve.

'You tricked me!' she said, when her father had disappeared from earshot. 'You had every intention of taking me here today. There was no need to waltz. No need at all.'

'It was you who insisted. I merely enquired. And very enjoyable it was, too.'

'I? You—!' Emma stopped, raised her eyes heavenwards as rushing heat washed over her.

'You react very well to teasing, Miss *Emma*.' His eyes danced with hidden lights. 'You always did.'

Her breath was drawn in with a hiss as she noticed the change in address. Not Miss Harrison, but Miss Emma. The way he'd used to say it all those years ago, with an emphasis on the 'Emma'. She had to admit she rather liked the sound of her name on his lips, but that was beside the point. He was using her Christian name.

'Normally a gentleman asks a lady's leave before addressing her so familiarly.'

'We have already agreed that I am no gentleman. My birth precludes that.' His eyes hardened. 'You would do well to remember that, particularly in drawing rooms at night.'

'What are you, Jack Stanton?' Emma asked slowly.

'A civil engineer who happens to be a very good businessman and who also happens to be taking you around his latest project.'

'It is my father's project,' Emma said, her heart beating fast. He had been here little more than a week, and already the bridge belonged to him. She could see it in the way the materials were stacked, and the way men saluted him. Soon he would be using his business practices and methods, rather than the ones her father always used.

'What do you mean by that statement?' His eyes narrowed.

'Harrison and Lowe are building this bridge,' she said, crossing her arms and staring directly at him.

'Harrison and Lowe are building the bridge for Robert Stephenson and Company, so it belongs to both of us.' He made a bow and gestured towards the river, where bright sunshine glinted. 'I am determined to show you what I have accomplished. I think you will notice a change even in the short time. I hope you will approve.'

'It is not up to me to approve or disapprove.'

'But it would make things much easier if you did,' Jack said quietly. If he was to discover the truth, Emma would have to trust him. She would have to help him understand why her father had made elemental errors. He wanted her to see that it was in her and her father's best interests to help him gain control of the company. Harrison had a reputation to protect, and he had a bridge to build.

'It is my father you should be showing around.'

'You are his daughter.'

Rather than continue to meet Jack's penetrating stare, Emma's gaze swept around the site. Despite the cold, there were a good number of men here, working away. She gasped slightly as she saw Davy Newcomb clumping across the yard. The young boy gave a cheerful wave.

'What is he doing here?' Emma turned to Jack in astonishment as Dr Milburn's warning crowded back into her brain. She had been so caught up in last night that she had nearly forgotten who Jack was, and how he'd earned his reputation. 'Surely he is injured?'

'I have found him work to do.' Jack gave a slight shrug, as if the boy's condition mattered little. 'This site has no place for slackers or layabouts.'

Emma struggled to control the indignation growing in her breast. Davy Newcomb should not be here. It was wrong of Jack to force him to work. Did Jack consider this appropriate business practice? Forcing injured men to work or become unemployed? 'But he sprained his leg. He should be resting. You should not have had him back here. He is in danger.'

'His family cannot afford for him to rest. He is the only breadwinner, although his mother does take in laundry.' Jack stared at her, his dark eyes hardening. 'What would you have me do—make sure his family starve at this time of year? You surprise me, Miss Harrison, with your unchristian spirit.'

'That is not what I said.' Emma put her hands on her hips, preparing to argue. She did not want to think about his sudden reversion to the more formal use of her name. All she knew was that Jack Stanton was in the wrong. Davy Newcomb should not be here. He was a danger to himself and to the other men. 'It is not the way my father runs his business.'

'I am in charge here, until your father recovers enough to take back the reins. Permit me to run this building site as I see fit.' Jack turned on his heel and strode away towards the office.

'But…but…you have to understand about the men's good will,' Emma said to his uncompromising back. She gritted her teeth. High-handed. Arrogant. And totally sure of himself.

He had to see that having the lad back was folly of the worst sort. Bad for morale. Bad for Davy Newcomb. Bad for Harrison and Lowe. Emma bit her lip, torn between following him and continuing her protest and finding out the truth. There was a chance that she could undo the damage he had inadvertently caused.

'I will speak to him and let him know that his position is safe. Let him know how Harrison and Lowe truly treats its employees,' Emma called after him.

Jack stopped and slowly turned. His face was hewn from granite and his eyes were cold. 'As you wish.'

Emma hurried over to where Davy had stopped to readjust his crutch as he balanced a sheaf of papers in one hand. 'Are you all right, Davy? Is your leg healing?'

'Yes, Miss Harrison, I fare well enough with this here crutch.' The boy pushed his cap back and gave her a cheeky grin. 'I don't aim to fall down no more cliffs, ma'am, if that was what you were worried about. Right brave I thought you were, to climb down as well as the gaffer. 'Course I didn't know he was the gaffer then, like.'

'Your leg, does it pain you much? Particularly after working here?'

'Could be better, could be worse,' Davy replied with a shrug.

'But why are you here? Surely you should be at home, recovering?'

'The gaffer has given me some jobs to do. Important ones they are, too!' The note of pride in Davy's voice was unmistakable. He shifted his weight and stood a little taller. 'He came by the house t'other day and had a little chat with me mam. Told her what a fine young man I was shaping up to be.'

Emma glanced over towards Jack, who was busy issuing orders to some of the men. Her fist clenched around her reticule. He had taken it upon himself to go see Davy and his family. It was not the way her father ran his business.

'You should be at home,' she tried again. 'Your leg needs to heal properly before you come back to work. You and your mother must not worry, Davy. There will be a place for you here when your leg is better. The Newcombs have worked for Harrison and Lowe for as long as I can remember. First your grandfather, then your father, and now you.'

'Miss, please don't send me away.' Davy caught her sleeve and looked up at her with pleading eyes. 'We need the money, like, and it is far warmer in the office than it is at home.'

'I am sure the company can arrange something.' Emma smoothed her skirts. 'My father is here today. I will have a quiet word with him. You will not starve.'

'The Newcombs don't accept charity.' Davy drew himself up to his full height. 'I knows you mean well and all, miss, but the gaffer and I have it sorted.'

Davy clumped away down the hill. Emma watched him go with mixed emotions. Had she made a mistake? Had she been too quick to judge? She pressed her fingertips into the bridge of her nose, trying to think. She needed to have answers, and fast.

'Did you learn anything from your conversation with Davy?' Jack said as she went into the back office. He did not move from his place behind her father's desk. His eyes could have been smooth black marble, and his voice held a distinct chill to it.

'We have been having a discussion. The lad is as obstinate as you.'

'I shall take that as a compliment.'

Emma crossed her arms, stared back at him. She would get
to the truth of the matter. 'Why is he here? The boy is injured.
He should be home, resting!'

'Have you tried to make him rest? Do you know why he
is here? Do you care about that? Or did you simply leap to
conclusions and find me guilty? Pretty little assumptions that
fit neatly into your view of the world.' He placed both hands
on the desk and stood up. His eyes burnt. Emma took a step
backwards as she became aware of the anger he was holding
back. 'Let me know when you are ready to listen, and then
maybe we can speak.'

'No... I....' Emma put her hand to her throat as she remembered Davy's words—he would not accept charity. She
had gone about this all wrong. She dropped her gaze and concentrated on her glove's pearl button. She swallowed hard,
aware his burning gaze was on her. 'I am sorry. You are right.
I have no idea why Davy Newcomb is working here today.
But he should not be here. It is not the way my father's
company does business.'

'Emma Harrison, you are the most infuriating woman!'

'I know. I have to be.' She put her hands on her hips. 'My
father's workers matter to me. They are part of the family. We
have a duty towards them. I have no wish for that boy to be
crippled for life. He has a mother and siblings to support.'

Suddenly his face softened; the lines became less harsh.
'Miss Harrison, can we talk about this sensibly? Shouting like
fishwives will do neither of us any good.'

She tilted her head to one side. A fishwife! Was that how he
saw her? 'No, you are right. I have no wish to be regarded as
someone vulgar. No doubt Mudge and my father can hear us.'

'I suspect they can hear you down on the quayside with great ease.' A smile broke over his face. 'And me as well.'

Her breath caught in her throat. No man had the right to look that handsome or be that infuriating. She had to meet him halfway. She had to show him that she could listen. It was her only hope of getting him to understand about the necessity of changing the bridge's line.

'I will listen,' she said quietly. 'I am ready to hear your explanation.'

Jack pressed his palms against the desk. When he spoke, he spoke clearly, emphasising each word as one would to a child.

'Davy Newcomb is here because he wants to be here. It is his choice, freely made.'

'But he is in pain. He cannot serve as an apprentice with a hurt leg. You should never have allowed it.'

'We came to a mutually beneficial arrangement.' A very superior expression crossed his face. 'It has solved several problems.'

'But he can't work. You are asking the poor lad to fail, and if he fails he will find it difficult to get other work.' Emma struggled to keep her voice calm. She had to put her objections in a manner that Jack would understand. 'The company cannot afford to carry someone who does not work properly. He will be a danger to himself and to others on the site.'

'And I say he can work!' Jack struck the desk with his open palm. 'Allow me to decide who is and who is not a danger on this site. I run this site my way.'

She swallowed hard. She'd have to leave the argument for later, but she knew she was right. Davy should be at home, resting. 'I will *naturally* have to defer to you. You are currently in charge here.'

'You will.' His eyes softened. 'If it makes you feel better, Davy has left Harrison and Lowe's employ.'

Emma stared at him, uncomprehending. 'He is here on site, working.'

'He works for me and me alone.'

Chapter Nine

'I am not sure I understand,' Emma said carefully as she stared at Jack. One part of her mind took in the small details, like how his long fingers rested against the desk, the slight curl of his black hair and the intent expression of his eyes, while the other part kept turning over and over the information. He had given Davy Newcomb a job. A job! 'He already has a job. He works for Harrison and Lowe as an apprentice.'

'No, he doesn't.' Jack stood up. He hooked his fingers into the pocket of his waistcoat. 'As you rightly said, Harrison and Lowe has no position for someone who is injured. He would be a danger to the others.'

The ribbons that tied Emma's bonnet threatened to choke her. He had dismissed Davy, and then hired him. Why? It made no sense. She wanted to hate Jack, but Davy was here, and clearly loving what he was doing. 'Why should you want to employ him? You already have a valet.'

'He is not my valet. Nor is he my personal servant.'

'Then what is he?'

'My personal assistant.'

'You have taken Davy on as your personal assistant?'

'I need assistance here. Little jobs. Jobs that require a quick mind and willing hands. It seemed the perfect solution to the problem.' His lips curved upwards. 'To both our problems. I went to see him the day you came to the site about the goose list. You were right that day. I should have gone before.'

Emma flattened her hands against her skirts as her insides twisted. She had done him a grave injustice. His solution for Davy Newcomb was extremely practical. The boy and his family would not accept charity, and yet he could not do heavy building work. Sensible. Practical. 'I misjudged your intention, Mr Stanton, and I deeply regret my earlier words. They were thoughtless. Please forgive me.'

'Sometimes the solution to a problem comes in unexpected ways.' He held out his hand, a strong hand, with tapering fingers. 'Shall we start again, Miss Harrison? Shall we be friends? Work together instead of against each other?'

'Start again?' She put her fingertips against his, felt his fingers curl around hers for a brief instant before she withdrew. Friends. That was all, and she would have to remember that. "I think I can agree to that. I welcome your friendship.'

He gave a smile. 'It is good to know that you have decided to trust me and my judgement.'

Her insides squirmed. If she truly trusted him she'd tell him about the mistakes in the calculations, and her father's illness, but to do that would mean exposing everything. How would he react? What damage would it do to her father's reputation? Dr Milburn's warning about Jack's underhanded business practices still resounded in her ears. Could she really trust Jack Stanton to behave honourably when serious business was involved? She'd wait and see if there was an opening, a way she could explain. See how their friendship grew.

'What exactly are Davy's duties?' she asked with a bright

smile, changing the subject. Once she knew more, she could decide. 'He appeared laden down with equipment and charts.'

'There are measurements that need to be done. Experiments I want rechecked. Davy is ideally placed to do them. He is bright, and willing to work.' He nodded towards Davy, who had reappeared with several different instruments. 'If he proves as able as I think, I am quite willing to help him train as a mechanical engineer. The Empire needs more. Progress demands it.'

'Why do you need to do experiments?' Emma forced her voice to stay calm.

'I have found it best to make sure of everything. Both Brunel and I agree on the matter. Attention to detail ensures the success of a project.'

Emma's breath stopped. Was this a solution to her problem? Could she explain where her father had gone wrong without seeming to criticise him? Ask that Jack repeat the experiments, repeat the calculations?

'I…that is…my father undertook a series of experiments before the bridge was designed. Wind speeds, flooding, and looking at the bedrock.' She hesitated, wrinkling her nose. There had to be a way of explaining this. 'It is possible that one or two needed more data. My father was ill earlier in the year…'

Jack schooled his features. Emma had helped with the experiments. That piece of information did not surprise him in the least, particularly not after what he had read. The question was, who had made the errors? They were simple, and easily made, but the fact remained that Edward Harrison should have caught them. Unless… He dismissed the idea as preposterous. Had Harrison been the one to make the mistake, and was Emma covering for him?

It would appear Emma Harrison had definitely developed an interest in civil engineering. She knew the correct terminology, and the bridge design did show her distinctive handwriting.

'I was not happy with everything I read,' he said carefully. 'It would appear a few mistakes were made. Perhaps not enough attention was paid…'

'The greatest care and attention was paid to the experiments.' She tilted her chin upwards, the blue in her eyes deepened to a flame. 'It is the way my father has always done things.'

'I am not accusing your father of anything.' Jack held up his hand, stopping her words. She had raised her defences. He would have to find another way to get to the truth. 'Through long experience I have learnt to conduct my own, rather than rely on another's interpretation of the facts. Mistakes happen when one least expects it. Numbers can get transposed.'

She started, and her eyes became wary. She trailed the toe of her shoe along the dusty floor. 'It could happen.'

'I think it might have here, but I have to be certain. Much depends on getting the location right. I have decided to take the cautious approach. The current weather has given us time.'

'You are going ahead with the present course, then?' Her voice was quite small.

'Yes, for the moment. But you were right to ask for another survey. It does show that the ground might be better if the line was moved away from the castle keep. A few simple calculation errors in the original document.'

Jack watched Emma's face become animated. It was as if he had given her a diamond bracelet. Or a load had rolled off her back. He had not been able to sleep last night, and he had read the report. He had also seen the neat notations Emma had made in the margins. Those calculations were accurate, unlike the ones he had questions about.

Exactly who had made those first calculations? It seemed incredible that the Edward Harrison he knew would make such a basic error.

'Do you mean that?'

'Nothing is certain.' Jack ran his hand through his hair. More than ever he wanted to make her smile like that again, but this time at him, because of him, not because of the bridge.

'But you will retain the keep? It is important. It is a symbol, and symbols matter.' She had pressed her hands under her chin, and her eyes were shining.

'I cannot promise anything, but the river appears slightly narrower, and it is possible that we could have seven piers in the water instead of the nine that your father originally planned. Nine is just too many. It will add to the cost enormously.'

'I see.' Emma spoke around a tight lump in her throat. She should be happy that Jack was even considering moving the bridge. But he was also changing the design, and it appeared that he planned on being here much longer than she had first anticipated. Was this something else that he'd forgotten to tell her?

Exactly what did her father and Jack have planned? She should be furious, but her heart was rejoicing. She wanted to spend time with Jack. After last night, when she had danced in Jack's arms and then his lips had touched hers, it seemed as if the world had become a different place, bright—sparkling with the possibility of adventure.

She had lived too long in her own safe world, with limited horizons. Suddenly her future horizons appeared vast and enticing. She concentrated on filling her lungs with air. She had to be cautious and not say too much. The last thing she wanted was to reveal everything, to ruin everything.

She had to remember that Jack Stanton had the potential to be her enemy. She had been wrong about Davy, but she had no firm idea about his intentions towards Harrison and Lowe. One wrong word, one slip, and she knew the vultures would start to circle. How many companies had he swallowed on the way to his fortune? But he was moving the line of the bridge.

'Seven arches instead of nine, but the design would

remain the same?' she said, struggling to keep the excitement from her voice.

'It is a good solid design, despite the unusual combination of iron and concrete.'

'It is important to get this bridge right.'

'I plan on having it standing…' Jack paused and his smile broadened '…for at least the next one hundred and sixty years.'

'One hundred and sixty years?'

'Yes. Think of what someone might think in 2007 as their train passes over this bridge.'

Emma stared across the grey water moving under the low-level bridge. She tried to see her bridge and think what Newcastle might look like then. She screwed up her eyes and shook her head.

'I can't think that far ahead. It is beyond my capability to think that far in the future.'

'Think of your great-great-grandchildren riding on a train crossing the bridge.' He leant forward, pointed, his eyes alight with a hidden fire. 'Can you see it now, Miss Emma? The lit carriages? The girl with her nose in a book? What do you think she is thinking about? Do you think she even wonders how the bridge got here, or suspects you might have had something to do with it?'

Emma looked, but all she noticed was how close Jack was, and the shape of his mouth. One kiss stolen and she was thinking about more. She had to stop building bridges in clouds. Bridges needed firm ground and strong foundations. With Jack, here and now, she felt as if she were about to slip over a precipice.

'I am unmarried,' Emma replied quickly. She was a spinster. There would be no children, let alone great-great-grandchildren. The thought depressed her. She had wanted children once.

'Miracles do sometimes happen.'

'Not those sorts of miracles, Mr Stanton.'

Emma toyed with her glove. If she allowed herself, she would start to build iron bridges in the air. Marriage was something she had given up hope of long ago, when she had decided it was far more important for her mother to spend her last years being looked after by someone who loved her. And by the time she had died Emma had become aware that such opportunities had passed her by. Men were interested in younger, prettier women, not women who read books on civil engineering and were inclined to speak their mind.

'Are you not being hard on your prospects? You may meet someone one of these days. Such a thing is not beyond the realms of possibility.'

'As I have said before, Mr Stanton, I enjoy being a spinster. It gives me freedom.' Emma raised her chin and directly met his gaze. 'I am not looking for anything beyond friendship.'

'Who are you trying to convince, Miss Harrison?'

The wind ruffled his hair slightly, sending it across his forehead. Emma's fingers itched to touch it. She forced her body to turn. She gazed out at the swiftly moving river.

'You are relying on Davy's help,' Emma said firmly. 'Are you sure he can do this with his leg?'

'He has a very quick mind. I think he will make a first-rate civil engineer if he gets the schooling he needs.' Jack put his hands on his hips. 'I intend to impress on him the benefits of education, night school. He can work and learn.'

'Are you planning on remaining in Newcastle for a long time, then?' Emma disliked the way her insides trembled. She was torn. She wanted him to stay, but not at the risk of losing her father's company.

'Somebody has to oversee the bridge and co-ordinate the building of the central railway station,' came the enigmatic reply.

'But my father will be well soon.'

'I do hope so.'

Emma watched a plume of breath come from Jack's mouth. 'I have some books—old schoolbooks. I could give them to Davy. They are cluttering up the schoolroom my sister and I used.'

'He will refuse anything that gives the slightest impression of charity. It would have to be skilfully done, but it is a good thought.'

Emma bit her lip as she watched Davy determinedly cross the yard. 'What do you suggest? I would like to do something for him, to encourage him.'

Jack was silent for a moment. The sun sparkled off the white frost, dazzling her eyes. Emma pulled her bonnet more firmly on her head.

'Are you familiar with German Christmas trees?' he asked at last.

'Yes, they have reached Newcastle—just.' Emma gave a small laugh. 'My father and I put one on the table in the drawing room last Christmas Eve. I have ordered one from the confectioner's already for this year. It is to have oranges, lemons and sugar-iced grapes on it. But what do Christmas trees have to do with Davy not accepting charity?'

'A party I attended at the London Mission Hall last year had an exhibition of German Christmas trees—trees of love. At the end of the party the presents adorning the trees, and one or two below, were handed out.'

'It is just perfect.' Emma clapped her hands together, her mind quickly turning the idea over. She could almost see the scene before her. 'Why hadn't I thought of it? I can remember reading about it in the *Illustrated London News*. Is there time? The feast is less than two weeks away.'

'If you will find the presents, I believe I can find the tree.

And I think a tree as large as the hall at the Institute of Mechanical Engineers can take, rather than a series of small pinetops. Shall we do it, Miss Emma? Will you work with me on this project?'

'Consider it done.' Emma's mind raced. She tried to list everything that needed to be done. She had been wrong. He had changed. It was such a lovely thought to do that for Davy and the others. It would allow them to accept a bit of charity. 'I will get a list from Mrs Mudge and Mrs Newcomb. They will have an idea about what the children might need.'

'It would not have to be elaborate. Nuts and fruit go down well.'

'And I can ask my father to play Old Christmas now that he is more fully recovered. He can hand the presents out. There is a green robe somewhere in the attic, and I can easily find a Yule log to strap to his back. I am sure Mrs Newcomb can fashion him a holly crown.'

'I can see your father as Old Christmas somehow. His hair is the right colour, and he is thin enough.'

'I can't think why I did not think of this before. It will make a capital end to the feast.' Emma clasped her hands together, resisting the urge to throw her arms about him.

'Sometimes we need others' help to achieve our dreams.'

Emma stared at him. His eyes glittered with banked fire, though his hand was loosely wrapped around the ebony head of his cane. The words had a deeper meaning. Did he understand about the bridge?

'This was supposed to be a tour of the site.' Her voice sounded strained to her ears, and her insides trembled.

'Why don't I show you some of the experiments? Unless you find such things deadly dull?'

'I would like that.'

* * *

Jack's fingers brushed her elbow as she scrambled down the bank. A bolt of heat seemed to pass from him to her. Emma went still, concentrated on breathing. The wind blew the ribbons from her bonnet across her face. She pushed them away, and nearly turned into him. She could see his pearl collar stud. She became aware that they were alone here, without her father. The shouts of the workmen were distant sounds. Her lips ached.

A seagull rose from the river and the spell was broken. She hurried down to the river on her own.

In the cold, the river moved sluggishly, and a faint layer of ice was apparent in the shallows. Emma's eyes widened at the array of instruments. Some of the experiments she had not even considered necessary, but once Jack explained the reasoning, she knew they had to be done. She asked a few questions, and heard the growing note of respect in Jack's voice.

'Some people consider a bridge to be stationary,' Jack said. 'But it is not. Bridges are constantly moving. They need to be able to withstand the stress of changing forces.'

'I know that.'

'There is a world of difference between the practical and the theory. What works in theory may not work in practice.'

'Are you trying to tell me something?' Emma went over and righted one of the sticks being used to measure the height of flooding.

'Making an observation, that is all.'

'I do understand the practical side of bridge-building,' Emma replied.

'You say you do, but I wonder…'

'You wonder what?'

His eyes flashed with hidden fire, and a mischievous dimple appeared at the corner of his mouth. Emma realised with a start that she had forgotten about the dimple, and the way it showed when he was very pleased about something. 'Would you like to go to the theatre with me?'

'What does the theatre have to do with bridge-building?' Emma's voice sounded breathless. She glanced over her shoulder and saw that they were quite alone by the river. The shouts and cries of the men were distant noise.

'There is an educational pantomime at the Theatre Royal, looking at several bridges and points through history as well as other sights for the amusement of onlookers. We could discuss them.'

'You wish to take me on my own?' Emma said the words slowly. The treat was tempting, but impossible. Surely Jack knew that. They were not even courting, let alone engaged. There was no understanding between them. Exactly what was her father playing at? Having failed with Dr Milburn, was he trying his matchmaking skills again? The temptation was there, but the obstacles were insurmountable.

'I have discussed it with your father. A party will be going. Your friend Lucy Charlton and her husband are included. You will be properly chaperoned.'

'I had no idea you were that well acquainted with Henry Charlton.'

'He has a business that he wishes me to invest in. For old times' sake I have agreed to listen, to hear what he says.'

'But you have your doubts.' She could well remember the drawling tones of Henry when he had first encountered Jack, and the way he had once humiliated Jack over his ready-made suits and strong Newcastle accent. She had been surprised when Lucy had married Henry, but—as Lucy said—she had chosen security and contentment over happiness.

'Why would you say that?' Jack's eyes had taken on a granite look.

'You were hardly friends. It surprises me that he seeks to draw on past acquaintance in that way.'

'I thought you had forgotten everything that happened seven years ago.' He tilted his head to one side. 'I had barely any recollection of him.'

'I had put it from my mind, but I do remember the way Henry Charlton behaved. It bothered me how some of them treated you. I never liked him very well after that. It is only because I am so fond of Lucy that we remain friends.'

'I cannot change the past, Miss Harrison. But I can change the future. It is the future that concerns me, not the past. I will invest if the business plan shows promise.'

And where do I belong? Emma longed to ask. *What we shared last night—was that linked to the past or the future?*

Instead she swallowed hard and pressed her gloved fingers together. She had to contain her emotions. She had to look at this dispassionately, as no doubt he was.

'You have discussed this trip and the pantomime with my father and others. Is there anything else you have committed me to that I should know about?'

'I am not in the habit of betraying confidences, Emma. Perhaps you can enlighten me. What else should I be planning to do?' His eyes twinkled with some unseen mischief. 'Put mistletoe in your hair? Forgive me, Emma, but I don't think you would take kindly to that happening to you twice.'

'I have no idea.' Emma clutched her reticule more tightly and resolutely turned her gaze from his mouth. Even the mere mention of the kiss caused a ripple of warmth to infuse her body. 'I shall have to see if my father is too ill…'

'Your father has recovered quickly for a man of his age and disposition.'

'He loves speaking about engineering. I am sure your being here has helped with his recovery.'

'His enthusiasm is infectious. I know I caught it from him many years ago,' Jack replied. 'Now, will you give me your answer? Will you cement our new-found friendship with a trip to the pantomime?'

Friendship. She could trust him with a trip to the panto-mime. Emma closed her eyes. But she could not explain about her father and his attacks. Jack still saw him as strong and vigorous. She wanted to trust him, but first she wanted to be sure her instinct was correct. He was very different from the man she had known seven years ago. She had to think about people other than herself. It could wait a little while yet. 'That is the reason you are asking me—friendship?'

'What other reason could there be?' His eyes searched her face, stopped at her mouth. 'I wish this war between us to end.'

'Hardly a war.'

'You appear intent on seeing the worst in me.'

'Not the worst.' Emma tightened her hand around her muff. 'I have apologised about jumping to the wrong conclusions about Davy.'

'If you have no objections to my personage and my offer of friendship, why don't you want to go?'

She was very neatly trapped. Keeping her father's illness a secret was far more important than wondering why Jack had invited her. Emma inclined her head. 'In the spirit of friend-ship and new starts, I will go. You have given me the as-surance that I will be properly chaperoned, and it has been a while since I have seen a pantomime at Christmas.'

The dimple reappeared by Jack's mouth. 'Look on it as an educational experience, Miss Emma. A way to improve your mind. You might learn something.'

'Father, what game are you playing?' Emma asked Edward Harrison the minute they climbed in the carriage and the wheels started turning. 'Why did you leave me alone with Jack Stanton? Surely Mudge did not need you for that long? This is not another of your matchmaking schemes, is it? I have told you before, I am quite happy with my life.'

'I have no idea what you are talking about.' Her father turned his mild blue eyes towards her. 'Daughter, did you not enjoy your tour? You were gone a long time with Jack Stanton, and I waited for you, not the other way around.'

'We were looking at his experiments.' Emma laid the muff on her lap. 'He is not satisfied with some of the calculations and wants to do them himself. They may take some time.'

'He wants a reason to stay in Newcastle.' There was a smug curve to her father's lips. 'He knows I always take great care over my calculations. They have never been wrong before.'

'I fear you are right, Father. I worry that he wants to take over the bridge construction.' She had said the words, and now she waited for her father's denial.

'There are worse men I could think of,' her father replied, with maddening complacency. 'But I do not believe that is his intention at all.'

'Then what is it?'

'He means to court you, Emma.'

Emma stared in disbelief at her father, willing his eyes to twinkle or the ghost of a smile to appear. Something, anything to show he was in jest. Surely he could not have forgotten about what had happened all those years ago? But his face stayed serious.

'You must not say such things, even in jest. It is impossible. Everything is finished between Jack Stanton and I. It finished years ago.'

She willed her father to believe her. Jack Stanton was not interested in her. He had kissed her last night to prove a point. And he was inviting her to the pantomime because he thought she spent far too much time alone and was frightened of facing society, having suffered from a humiliation.

'This is no joke, nor a merry jape to make the journey home pass quicker, daughter.' Her father's hand enfolded hers. 'I am perfectly in earnest. Do you think I would have left you alone with him last night or today if I'd had the slightest suspicion that his intentions were less than honourable?'

'But he has no intentions. Business occupies his every waking thought.' Emma withdrew her hand, slid it into her muff and clenched her fist. 'Sometimes I wonder if your illness clouds your mind. Soon you will swear you hear wedding bells, when all the sound will be is the bells in St Nicholas's lantern chiming the dinner hour.'

'Daughter, what a thing to say! I can read the signs very well indeed. My mind is as strong as ever it was. You are being purposefully blind.'

Emma tried to ignore the trembling in her stomach. She had to make her father see. He should not harbour such fantasies. She was very glad he had no idea what had passed between Jack and her last night. Luckily it had not gone further.

'Mama's mind wandered at the end.'

'Shall we leave your mother alone? Her affliction was her own, and quite different from the mild chill I suffered.' Her father rapped his cane on the carriage floor. 'No, I am as sound as I ever was, and you, my daughter, are being stubborn.'

Emma looked out of the carriage window at the scene unfolding—the children sliding on the ice, the women hurrying with parcels, the men striding along. A few of the broadsheet salesmen had started their Christmas patter songs. A lump grew in her throat and she swallowed hard, forcing it down. Certain things had to be said before her father utterly ruined her life.

'Have you forgotten, Papa, Jack Stanton left seven years ago without a word?'

'Daughter—' Her father cleared his throat several times.

'Surely I meant more to him than a half-hearted proposal.' Emma turned her gaze back to the scene outside the carriage. 'It was you and Mama who counselled me to wait and see, saying that if he was serious he would send word. He never sent a letter, never gave me the chance to explain about Mama's illness.'

Her father's eyes slid away from her, and he developed a sudden interest in the carriage seat. 'Your dear mama did it for the best, Emma. Sometimes, though, I have lain and wondered what if—particularly in these later years, when you have developed such a gift for engineering. It is too bad that you were not born a man, my daughter. What a civil engineer you would have made!'

'What did my mother do?' Emma bit out each word, and resisted the urge to shake him. She would not be distracted by his civil engineering remarks. She had to know what her mother had done! How had she discouraged her unsuitable suitor? Was there far more to what had happened seven years ago than she first thought?

'Such things are best not spoken of. One never criticises the dead, Emma. Remember that.' He reached out his hand, but Emma ignored his fingers. 'What happened is water under the bridge or grains of sand between the fingers. One can never turn back the hands of time.'

'What did she do? You must tell me!' Emma clasped her hands together in her lap. She wanted to shake her father, to get him to tell her what her mother had done.

'Emma Harrison, keep your voice down. Both the driver and the footman will hear!'

Emma closed her eyes and concentrated on her breathing. By the time she felt she could speak without raising her voice the carriage had arrived back in Jesmond, and Fackler had come out to greet them. She waited until her father had sat down in front of the drawing room fire. She began to pace.

'Emma, you seem disturbed.' Her father held out his hand. 'Did you see something amiss at the site? I must confess Jack Stanton keeps it in better order than ever I dared hope.'

'What did Mama do, Father? You will not fob me off by speaking about the bridge. I know you too well.' Emma stood in front of him and placed her hands on her hips. 'I have a right to know.'

'Her sole thought was your future happiness.' Her father did not meet her eyes. 'She had no inkling, of course, about who Jack Stanton would become. Neither of us did. She thought him a fine enough young man, but beneath her daughter. You have to remember that Claire had just married a baronet. She had high hopes for you—very high hopes. A member of the aristocracy, or failing that someone who had land and wealth. Someone who would keep our youngest in the style she should have been. Someone to appreciate you.'

'She thought of no one but herself.' Emma put her muff down on the small table. She tried to control the cold anger that flooded over her. Her father might like to pretend, but she had known her mother's faults. She had still loved her, but had known what she was like. 'You know how selfish she was, how ambitious. It was never for me or Claire, but for her own position. She wanted a title. She never forgave you for being a second son.'

'You should not speak of your mother in that way! She loved you, and wanted the best for you. Her daughters meant everything for her. The sacrifices she made…' Her father's eyes held a slight glint of tears. 'She had her faults, but she loved you.'

'We both know what a snob she was, Papa.' The words came tumbling out of a place deep within Emma, a place she had thought hidden well, but once she had begun she had to continue. 'Why try to deny it? She may have loved Claire and me, but ultimately she wanted that title. She never asked me what I wanted.'

'It is the job of parents to make sure their offspring marry the correct people—people they would be suitable for, not ones for whom they have a passing fancy.'

Emma breathed deeply. Perhaps her father was speaking the truth. She knew her parents' marriage had been a love-match, but one that had not lived up to her mother's expectations.

'Tell me what she did, Papa. Why do you feel guilty? You know I loved my mother, but I wasn't blind to her faults. And I loved her all the more because of them.'

'I grow weary, Emma.' Her father passed a hand over his brow. 'I fear this morning's inspection took a great deal out of me. You were right earlier. I was foolish to abandon the tonic.'

'I shall get some right away.' Emma rang for the butler, obtained the tonic, and poured out the correct dose. 'You must be careful, Father. You must do as Dr Milburn says.'

'You are a good daughter, Emma.' He patted her hand. 'We shall speak no more of this. Your mother did what she felt she had to do.'

Emma gritted her teeth and allowed the conversation to drift. There had to be another way of finding out why her father felt guilty. It was something to do with Jack's proposal of seven years ago.

Chapter Ten

After her father had settled down with the day's papers, his tonic and a glass of sherry, Emma left him in the drawing room and hurried into the morning room, where her mother's old desk stood. She tapped her fingers against the rosewood. Her father was definitely hiding something—something that her mother had done.

She had gone through her mother's letters when she died, and there had been nothing about Jack Stanton there. She would have remembered. Her mother had been meticulous about noting everything down, keeping a log of correspondence. But her father felt guilty about something—guilt that Jack's return had sparked.

Had Jack sent something? A letter explaining why he'd left without waiting for her final answer, perhaps? It could explain so many things.

She made a wry face. If he had, it had vanished a long time ago. A small fire crackled in the fireplace, sending out a little bit of warmth. It would not yield up any secrets. She hated to think how long ago the ashes from any letter would have been taken out.

A surge of anger swept through her. What right had her mother had to make that sort of decision? Emma had been eighteen when Jack had made his offer. She should have trusted her.

Emma pressed her hands against her forehead. She had chosen the course of duty. Chosen it before Jack had asked. Her mother had been ill, deathly ill. They had only expected her to last a few months, but she had lingered for years. Her mother had had the right to expect a nurse, someone who loved her, and Claire had already been married.

Jack had simply not waited for an explanation, just stormed off. And if he hadn't been able to bear to wait for that, would he have waited for her? The 'few months' her mother had had left had turned into years. Long years where she had learnt the value of using her mind and thinking—something her mother had encouraged her to do, as it kept her near at hand. She might have resented her mother, and her demands, but they had grown closer, and in the end her mother had approved of her chosen path.

Emma slapped her hand against the smooth wood of the desk. She lived in the real world—one not populated by romantic imaginings but punctuated by precise calculations.

Her hand had hit a tiny carved rosebud on the back of the desk, and Emma was sure she'd heard a distinct click. She opened the top and looked. A panel was slightly pushed out. She started to push it back, and then paused, got out a paper-knife, and pulled.

A bundle of papers fell out, tied in a blue ribbon. Like a ghost, the faint lavender scent of her mother's perfume wafted through the room, tickling her nose and making her recall the sound of her mother's laughter and her lightning-quick wit. Emma's heart constricted at the unexpectedness of the memory.

Emma's hand trembled, and she concentrated on the letters.

She sorted through them quickly, searching for Jack's signature. Then smiled at her own actions. What had she expected? A letter like in some penny-blood? They were all simple correspondence between Mama and her best friend. But why had she shoved them in the secret compartment? What secret had she wanted to hide from Emma?

Emma rescanned the letters—mostly domestic happenings and crises that had once seemed insurmountable and insoluble. A single sheet of paper was dated from seven years ago. The writing was crossed to save money. Emma turned the paper to read the continuation of the letter.

Her eye stopped, and she reread the next to last paragraph.

You did the right thing, Margaret, with that letter—what the heart doesn't know, the heart doesn't grieve over. Emma will get over Jack Stanton in a few months' time. You did what you had to, my dear. Be proud of it. Your daughter will thank you, given time.

Emma rechecked the date. It was a few weeks after Jack's proposal, after she had asked for time to consider. She had had no other serious offer at the time. Jack must have sent a letter, and her mother had intercepted it.

For a long time, Emma sat stunned. Then she noticed the cold creeping up her fingers as the fire burnt down to a pile of ash and the daylight started to fade.

Jack obviously thought she had received his letter and decided not to reply.

Emma looked at the wavering words again. What could she say? She had no idea what she would have done if she *had* received the letter. Had her mother even broken the seal, or had she simply recognised the handwriting and burnt the letter?

There was little point in asking her father. She did not

want to risk another scene. She had no desire to bring on an attack, have her father gasping for breath and Dr Milburn called to administer his pills. No, she refused to take the risk.

There was no point wasting time wondering what might have been. Because it wasn't—never could be. She had to live in the present, not dwell in the past.

Emma pressed her hands to her forehead. She had to consider that seven years was a long time. The girl she'd been then bore little relation to the woman she had become. The Jack Stanton who had shown her around the building site was not the man who had asked her to marry him and then left without a word.

'Emma, what are you doing sitting alone? Has your father taken a turn for the worse?'

Emma hurriedly stuffed the letter under the blotting paper as Jack came into the room. He had changed from his work clothes, and his cream trousers once again showed the perfect crease. His cravat was immovably tied. The casual observer would think him a man of leisure, never suspecting that he had been clambering over stone and rock earlier.

'I was thinking.' Emma covered the letter with another sheet of paper. She would burn it later. There was little point in keeping it, or the dressmaking bills her mother had stuffed in the secret door.

'About anything in particular? There is a crease between your eyebrows. Have you found something else in the Goose Club list to perplex you?'

'Nothing important.' Emma smoothed her forehead. 'I had a bit of a pounding head earlier and took a tisane.'

'You look as if you have been crying.'

Emma scrubbed the back of her hand over her eyes. 'A trick of the light.'

She moved to go out of the room. Her nerves were too raw.

She wanted to blurt out what she had learnt, but it would only make matters worse. And how could she excuse her mother's behaviour? The inescapable fact remained that their courtship had been doomed from the start seven years ago.

'If there is anything I can do,' Jack said quietly. 'I am willing to help. Trust me.'

The words were tempting. Emma longed to lay her head against his chest and confess all—confess to the wasted years and the times when she had longed to be anywhere but here. Except it was not possible. She could not betray her past or her mother's machinations. Her mother had acted the way she had because she'd felt it right.

Jack raised an eyebrow, and Emma realised that silence had grown between them. Something needed to be said before she blurted out the sorry tale.

'The cook will shortly have supper ready.' Emma opted for a brave smile. 'I trust you will be joining my father and me?'

'I would like that very much.'

Still he did not move, but stood there. Emma remembered the way his hands had held her last night, and the way he had taken the time to describe his experiments this morning. She could feel the heat increase on her cheeks and hoped he would think it was because she was standing close to the fire.

'And, Mr Stanton…I am looking forward to the panto-mime.' She smiled and lifted her shoulders slightly. 'It strikes me that I may have sounded ungracious before.'

He was silent for a while. 'I have never thought you un-gracious.'

'You lie exceedingly charmingly. I was certainly ungra-cious when you appeared the other day.' Emma tucked a stray lock of hair behind her ear, fought against the warmth building inside her. 'I was preoccupied, not to mention annoyed at being caught in one of my oldest dresses.'

'It most certainly did not show off your charms as well as the ballgown you wore last night. Had I seen you in that first, I would never have believed you an acid-tongued spinster.'

'But now you do?'

'I know you for what you are.' Jack's gaze held her. She noticed how his eyes had taken on a slightly deeper, richer hue. They were the sort of eyes a person could drown in.

She forced her gaze onto the blotting paper, reminded herself of what lay underneath and why there were so many things between them—too many things. 'But you thought me a terribly interfering biddy when we first met at the bridge.'

Jack gave a short laugh. 'You were doing your best under difficult circumstances.'

'And you were right to step in. The building site positively rang with activity this morning.' The words seem to stick in her throat. Did he understand how much it cost her to say those words? 'I am grateful you are looking again at the line for the bridge. The bridge means so much to my father. Since my mother died, it is all that he has to occupy his attention.'

Jack's face betrayed nothing, but Emma thought she detected a slight softening of his eyes.

'The men reacted to your father's presence. They know who signs their pay cheques. He appears well recovered from his chill. One of these days he may consider remarrying.'

'My father?' Emma stared at Jack in astonishment. First Lucy at the ball, and now Jack. Surely they had to realise that her father had no intention of doing such a thing? But that fact would be impossible to explain without telling them about her father's illness and how Dr Milburn had said that there was very little hope. She regarded her hands. 'My father has no plans to remarry—none whatsoever.'

He paused and his eyes grew warm. 'Should you ever need a friendly ear, Emma…'

'I shall remember we are friends,' she said slowly, comprehension dawning. He thought she was upset because her father wanted to pay court to some woman and her own position in the house might be in jeopardy. It was ironic, but it saved her from having to explain the truth. She made sure her back was rigid. 'I value your friendship highly, Mr Stanton. I always did.'

'Yes, friends.' There was a bittersweetness to Jack's smile. 'I think you may say we are friends once again, Emma.'

'It is good to have a friend…Jack.' She felt very daring as she said his name, but it would go no further than that—light flirtation between friends, never anything beyond—as much as she might wish it. There was too much history between them, too many secrets. Even last night belonged to the past, and she had to keep her face to the future.

He paused with his hand on the doorframe, his dark eyes inscrutable. 'And, Emma, don't look back. Keep your face forward. The past is done and the future is yet to be.'

'Papa, are you sure you will be fine? Fackler has orders to send for me if anything should go amiss, or if you should start to feel under the weather.' Emma fastened a short cloak around her shoulders in preparation for her visit to the theatre. She was tingling with anticipation. The theatre—and most of all Jack.

Her father stood in the hallway, dressed in his silk dressing gown and carrying the latest news journals in his hand. Emma frowned. His face seemed pale, but it could be because he was wearing a burgundy silk dressing gown.

'Stop your fussing, Emma. I am as fit as I ever was. The cold was a blasted nuisance, but you shall see in the New Year…' Her father gestured towards the door with his paper. 'Go out and enjoy yourself. You know I dislike having several nights out in a week. I trust Lucy Charlton and that husband of hers will prove more than adequate chaperones.'

He gave a slight cough and pulled his dressing gown tighter around his body.

'Perhaps you should not have gone to the bridge two days ago.' Emma tilted her head. 'I could have reported back.'

'Perhaps you should pay attention to your own business. I wanted to see what Jack Stanton was up to. Satisfy my curiosity. See if he remained faithful to the ways I taught him.' Her father tapped the side of his nose. 'Besides, it would not have been proper for you to go on your own.'

'You let me go before.'

'I had no choice. And I had assumed you took Fackler or Annie. A woman's reputation reflects on her family, and in this case on the company. A man's private life shows the world how he conducts himself.' Her father held out his hands. 'Emma, I do want what is best for you.'

What *was* best for her? What she wanted, or what her father considered best? The clock struck eight, and Emma knew she did not have the time to argue.

'And do you approve of Jack Stanton's methods?' she asked, changing the subject away from her future. 'I thought the site looked clean and industrious.'

'There is not much one can do in the frost, but Stanton seems to have found work for everyone who wishes it.' Her father went over to the barometer, gave it a tap. 'If it gets much colder there will be snow, and skating on the pond. You used to enjoy such things. I can remember you and your sister coming back with rosy cheeks and pink noses.'

'That was a long time ago.' Emma's hand stilled, and she regarded her father in the looking glass.

'But I remember.' Her father put a hand on her shoulder. 'Here is Stanton. His tailor does right by him, don't you think?'

Emma turned her head and saw Jack coming down the stairs. No man had the right to look that good. It was not the clothes making the man, but the man making the clothes. The deep black of his evening suit fitted his colouring perfectly.

'Ah, Miss Emma, you are ready for your *educational* evening?'

'As ready as I will ever be.'

'You will find it amusing, I promise you.'

The pantomime *had* been amusing, and Emma had to admit that the company had been entertaining. She had not realised that Henry Charlton knew quite a bit about engineering as well as finance. His plan for a new engine was sound. He and Jack had spent a good deal of time discussing it, and possible modifications. Jack had agreed to look at the plans in greater detail if Henry supplied them.

'You look pensive,' Jack said now, as they waited in the Theatre Royal's portico for the carriage. A few of the Christmas broadsheet patterers could be heard singing out the verses of carols, hoping to entice the theatregoers to buy their wares. 'God Rest Ye Merry Gentlemen' vied with 'The First Nowell', a raucous but not discordant noise, somehow giving the usually austere portico a taste of the festive spirit. 'Or have you laughed too much? I know I heard a distinctly unladylike snort coming from your direction when Punch appeared.'

'There may have been.'

Emma's smile turned to a frown as she watched a ragged girl offer a sprig of holly to several of the theatregoers. Most were too busy adjusting their coats and bonnets to pay much attention.

'Something is troubling you.'

'How do you know?'

'Your brow has become furrowed and your expression intent.'

'It seems a shame that so many have so little.' Emma nodded towards the little flower girl.

'You cannot save the entire world.'

'I don't intend to, but it makes you think. Particularly at this time of year. I can see the first snowflakes falling.'

Jack gave the girl a coin, and then handed the sprig to Emma with a flourish. The little girl clutched the coin and ran off as fast as her little legs would carry her. 'There, now, does that make you feel better?'

'How much did you give her?'

'Enough to make her evening. She should be able to buy a hot meal or two.' His fingers touched her cheek, making a warmth grow inside her.

'I wish there was more I could do.'

'You are doing something. Or rather your father's company is. The railway bridge is vital to the future prosperity of this city. Without it you would see more children like that little girl. With it, and a proper station, the city prospers.'

'I suppose you are right.' Emma looked after the girl, but she had disappeared into the night.

'I know I am right. Progress will bring prosperity. It is the only way. Think about how far we have come in the last few years.'

'But we could be doing more.'

'At least you saw the girl. You did not pass her by, and you did not offer her charity.'

There was something in Jack's voice that made Emma pause.

'Is that really so important?'

'Yes, charity can destroy the soul. People want to feel valued. That they have given as well as received.' His fingers touched her elbow. 'Ah, here is the carriage.'

Emma kept her skirts carefully away from Jack, and chatted about inconsequential things as the carriage wound its way back to Jesmond, but her body hummed with anticipation. Would he attempt to take her in his arms? What should she do if he did?

In the dim light she could see his hands resting loosely on his cane, his eyes watching her face, watching her mouth. He had to kiss her. She wanted him to. Emma leant forward, her lips parting as the carriage swung into the drive. He put out an arm to stop her falling. Her body brushed his—but she pushed away as her attention became fastened on the light flooding the carriage.

'There's something wrong,' Emma said, and a shiver went down her spine. 'Something is dreadfully wrong.'

'How do you know?'

'Father would never have the lights blazing this brightly at night. He is very mindful of the cost of candles and gas.'

'I am sure it isn't anything.'

Emma leapt from the carriage without waiting for a hand and rushed in. Fackler was there, shaking his head and wringing his hands.

'Something is wrong!' Emma did not bother waiting for any pleasantry. 'What has happened here tonight? You should have sent the carriage for me.'

'We have had to send for Dr Milburn,' Fackler said. 'Your father took a turn for the worse soon after you left. He called for his tonic, drank it, then went rigid.'

'Emma, Emma—are you all right?' Jack's concerned voice broke through her misery. 'Give Miss Emma some space, Fackler. She needs air. Your news has been a shock, a great shock.'

He put his arm about her shoulder and led her into the parlour. The simple act calmed her, made her see that she had to take control of the situation. She could not give in to temptation and weep.

'My father has taken ill. The servants have summoned Dr Milburn.' Emma was amazed at how calm her voice sounded. But how faraway and distant. She shrugged his arm away, stepped from the warm circle of his embrace. 'I must go to him.'

She staggered a few steps, and was amazed at how light her head seemed. She should have eaten more at supper, but her nerves had been too great. The staircase appeared to grow with each step she took.

Then suddenly she was there, at her father's door. She peered in and heard the steady sound of her father's breathing, saw his form on the bed. At her footsteps, Annie looked up from where she sat and came hurrying over.

'How is he, Annie?'

'Sleeping, miss. Praise be to God, the worst appears to have passed.'

Sleeping. Emma dared breathe again. Her father was sleeping. The fit had passed. She had seen them so many times over the past few weeks. They were always the same. First the fit, and then the long sleep, as if life itself had exhausted him. But afterwards, when he had taken the pills Dr Milburn prescribed, he could remember little of it, and insisted that he was fit and well. 'Thank you, Annie.'

Annie's face creased. 'But, miss, he mustn't see you like this. You are as pale as a ghost. You know how it upsets him if he thinks you are perturbed, particularly after one of his turns.'

Emma put out a hand and held onto the doorframe. 'I am fine. Truly.'

'She is far from fine. She has had a shock and needs to sit down,' Jack said, and his strong arm went around her shoulder, led her out of the room. 'You may come down to the drawing room when you are certain he is settled, Annie, and tell Miss Emma all about it.'

Emma wanted to protest, but her knees were beginning to feel like jelly. She allowed Jack to take her down the stairs. When they reached the drawing room she paused and tried to pull herself together. 'It was the shock of it all. There is no need to fuss and fret.'

'You will do your father no good if you collapse as well. When you have recovered your breath you may go and sit with him for as long as you like.' Jack propelled her to an armchair. 'Fackler, get Miss Emma a brandy.'

'I never drink strong spirits.' Emma put a hand to her head.

'You need something to bring back the roses in your cheeks.'

Jack pressed a crystal balloon glass into her hand, and gave a stern nod. Emma was tempted to refuse, but she did need something. She took a small sip and felt a fiery trail go down the back of her throat. Her nose wrinkled. 'I can't say that I am over-enamoured of it. But I shall look on it as medicine.'

'It will do you good.'

'I suspect I might do better if I took some of Father's tonic.' Emma gripped onto the armchair, ready to stand.

'What exactly is wrong with your father?' Jack's eyes burned into her soul. 'And do not try to tell me that it is a simple chill. It is much more than that. Trust me with your secret, Emma.'

Chapter Eleven

Emma put her hand to her head and sank back down into the chair. The room gently swayed, merged, and then became clearly focused again. All the while the awful truth kept repeating in her head.

He knew!

Jack Stanton knew her father was ill. And he had known for some time. She had thought she was being clever and he had seen through her, toyed with her much as a cat played with a helpless mouse, waiting to see if she would confide in him.

Emma gulped air and tried to fill her lungs. She had to keep her wits and not give way to blind panic. Panic never served anyone. She had always known that she might have to face this one day, and that day had finally arrived. But all her explanations and half-truths vanished. Only the full truth would do.

'Yes, it is,' she said in a small voice. 'Much more than that.'

Her hands gripped the arms of the chair. She looked over his shoulder at the clock ticking. There was a muffled noise as the clock struck the hour, but beyond that silence grew. She tried to explain, but her voice refused to work. The prick of tears behind her eyelids grew stronger. Jack had to understand what she couldn't say. He had to see.

'I want to learn,' Jack said into the silence. 'I want to know, Emma. I want to know what I can do to help.'

Emma averted her head from his penetrating stare, focusing on one of the rivets that held the upholstery to the armchair. Help? Would he be so willing when he knew the full extent? Or would his predatory instinct come out? Her heart whispered that she could trust him. She had seen what he had done for Davy and the little holly-seller. He was a man with compassion in his soul. But her mind recoiled, remembering Dr Milburn's stories of how Jack had obtained his wealth.

A single tear rolled down her cheek. She brushed it away with impatient fingers.

'I am afraid. I have buried one parent in my twenties, and now it appears I shall have to bury my father,' she whispered, trying to keep her teeth from chattering. She looked up and saw compassion mingled with sorrow in his gaze. She swallowed hard and turned her face away, forced her voice to continue on. 'It has been awful living with the knowledge…keeping it from him, from you. I have felt dreadfully alone. There was no one I could turn to.'

'I waited for you to turn to me on your own, but you will have to trust me now.' Jack stood there, solid and real in his evening clothes. 'What ails your father precisely, Emma? Stop shielding him. You are doing him no favours.'

'He has turns.' Emma pressed her hand against her eyes and strove for control of her voice. 'Sometimes he goes rigid and his muscles shake. Afterwards he says that he remembers nothing, and chides me for being overly concerned.'

'When did these turns start? Is there any pattern to them?'

'Oh, God, I don't know.' Her hands curled around and held onto the arms of the chair as her body shook. Then the storm appeared to pass, and she regained control. She knew she could speak.

'Take your time, Emma.'

'They started just after my mother died.' Emma closed her eyes, remembering her terror at discovering her father slumped at his desk that afternoon. The papers, the pens and the empty tonic bottle strewn about the top as if some child had been playing. Her father was always precise in where everything went on his desk, always knew where everything was. He had been lying there, the man who had always been strong and who liked to boast that he had never been sick a day in his life. 'The first one came without warning. It was a bad one, and I called Dr Milburn.'

'And then what happened?' Emma could hear the tension in Jack's voice.

She forced her hands to relax. 'Back to his old self once he learnt that the bridge was a reality instead of a distant dream. He lives for that bridge. It occupies his mind, keeps him from dwelling on what could be.'

'And these fits—do they occur regularly now?' He leant forward. 'Think, Emma. Has he been doing anything in particular before they happen?'

'Most of the time he is fine, but occasionally he is vague, uncertain where he is. Dr Milburn keeps increasing the dose of the tonic and it seems to help for a little while.' She paused, and then continued in a trembling voice as she concentrated on the pearl button of her glove. She glanced quickly up into his eyes and then back at the button. She had to tell him. She had been a coward before. 'He makes mistakes, though.'

'Like the calculations for where the bridge should be. He was the one to make the errors, not you. You were covering for him.' He slammed his fists together, making her jump.

'You knew!' Emma's mouth dropped open as her mind

raced, grasping for bits of information, impressions. He had known, known and not said a word. When had she betrayed her father? She had been willing to take the blame. 'How did you? When did you?'

'I told you that you have a distinctive way of making your "e"s and equally your numbers. I told you I always recheck everything. I did so the night of the ball, when sleep evaded me.' His eyes darkened and his voice became hard and uncompromising. 'The figures in your handwriting were correct. Several in your father's hand were wrong, potentially dangerous.'

Emma put her head back against the chair as a great wave of tiredness washed over her. He knew, and he had never said a word.

'Why didn't you say?' She struggled to sit up. 'Have you told my father? It could kill him if you approached it in the wrong way. Things have to be put in a certain way, otherwise it agitates him. Dr Milburn explained this to me after the first fit.'

Jack made no move towards her, but continued to look at her with his deep black eyes. His hands were thrust into the pockets of his waistcoat. Uncompromising. 'Spare me Milburn's homilies.'

'He is a good doctor. He cares about his patients.'

'I had been waiting for you to explain,' he said quietly, 'but then I saw the relief in your eyes the other day, when we were at the bridge, and I knew there was more to it.'

'I only discovered the mistakes the day you arrived. I never thought my father would make errors like that.' A shiver went through her as she remembered her horror at the discovery. 'At first I did not want to believe it. I tried to tell you, but you thought it was my fear of the ball and Lottie Charlton. And then…then that day at the bridge I was too much of a coward. You were checking the calculations I had concerns about, and I had no wish to borrow trouble.'

'You thought I would blame you?'

'Never that.' Emma brought her head up. 'I was worried about what would happen to my father's business if the truth became known. I thought I could get the line of the bridge moved without….without explaining everything. I was willing to take the blame. That is the unvarnished truth.'

Her breath caught in her throat. He had to believe her. There was no sound in the room except the slight popping of the fire.

'Are you sure your calculations are correct?'

'I have gone over and over them. I don't understand where he got the information or how he did the calculations. It makes no sense.'

'Emma, I am checking all the experiments your father did. Your father taught me that—to check and recheck,' he said, breaking the silence. 'We shall see what went wrong. I blame no one at this point.'

'He was a great civil engineer.'

'You cannot change the past.' Jack made a chopping motion. 'But enough of this. The fact remains you were prepared to risk the fortunes, the lives of others, to preserve one man's vanity.'

'It wasn't like that at all. His turns have only just started to become more frequent. And I did discover the errors. I was trying to put everything right!'

'And if you hadn't done…'

A cold chill passed over Emma. She regarded her hands. It did not bear thinking about. All those lives, innocent lives. He was right. She had not properly considered the consequences. A life was more important than a reputation. It had to be. But the problem had been solved. Steps had been taken. She refused to dwell in the land of might-have-been.

'We are discussing what ifs and theory while my father lies immobile up in bed. I must go to him.' She rose, started forward. 'He will be devastated when he realises what he has done. The knowledge could kill him.'

'You should have tried harder to tell me.' His voice bounced off the walls.

'Me?' Emma stared at him in astonishment, anger growing inside her. 'I tried! It was you who encouraged my father to play that silly game of forcing me to go to the ball. I had to dance with you before you would even entertain any notion of speaking about the bridge.'

'And what of it?' A muscle jumped in his jaw, but he moderated his voice.

'You treated me like a brainless ninny. You made assumptions about me that were false.' She glared at him, daring him to say different.

'I have never thought you brainless.' A half-smile appeared on his face. 'Misguided, perhaps, but never brainless.'

'And that is supposed to placate me?'

'I hope so.' He held out his hands. 'What is done is done, Emma. The past is written in stone, unchanging. It is the future that is yet to be.'

'But you do believe me, believe that I tried?' Emma leant forward, staring into the abyss that was his eyes. He had to. He had to understand she had tried.

'God forgive me, but I do,' Jack replied after a long moment. 'You should know that I made an offer for Harrison and Lowe before I knew the full extent of your father's illness. I have every hope of him accepting it. You must make sure he accepts it.'

Emma stared at him as her stomach flipped over. He had made an offer. She should have guessed before. And now he would decrease the offer. She knew how these things worked. She knew what vultures businessmen could be. Friendship meant nothing in the world of finance. She doubted he would let friendship stand in the way of acquiring a company like Harrison and Lowe.

'I know what your business practices are like.' Emma looked at him with a level gaze. She knew what was coming next. He would lower the price. It was what she had feared. And the whole awful round of negotiation would begin, until they had nothing and he had everything. This night, which had started beautifully, was rapidly becoming a bad dream.

'You know nothing about my business practices!' Jack thundered, his fist hitting the table, making the Dresden shepherdess jump. He caught it before it tumbled off. 'How could you say such a thing? Think such a thing?'

'I have heard rumours…I have been interested in your career.' Emma pressed her hands together to stop them from trembling. She had to say it now. Before it ate into her soul. If she knew the truth, then it might serve to end her attraction. 'No one amasses that great a fortune without cutting a few corners.'

'Or without making a few enemies.' His eyes were hard lumps of black glass.

'Then how did you do it? How did you make it?' Emma pressed her hands against her stomach. She hated to ask the question. She wanted to believe Jack. But she had to know.

'I have been lucky. The right place at the right time with the right amount of grit and determination.'

'You make it sound like something anyone can do.' Emma gave a little laugh, more of a hiccup. 'No one amasses such a great fortune easily.'

'It was not easy. I gave my blood, sweat and tears.' Jack's face was grim, his lips white and his eyes shadowed. 'Do you think I would have lasted long if I had cheated men? Would men such as Stephenson have made me their partner?'

Emma shook her head slowly.

'I build my bridges and levees to last. I have done the same with my business. Its foundation is integrity, not deceit.'

Emma regarded her gloves. She had not really considered it in that light before, but she could understand what he was saying. She wanted to believe him. 'But your reputation in the press…'

'A man gets a certain reputation. I drive a hard bargain, yes, but it is always an honest one.'

Emma looked at him. Her heart whispered that she knew what sort of man he was. She needed no proof. 'What you say makes a certain amount of sense, but then I *am* an acid-tongued spinster.'

A ghost of a smile appeared on his lips. 'Thank you for that.'

'But this offer you have made my father—does it stand now that you have discovered the truth?'

'It is a fair offer. More than generous in the circumstances.'

Jack named the figure. Emma raised her eyebrows and her lungs filled with life-giving oxygen. Dr Milburn had been wrong. Jack was not about to cheat her father. 'And after what you have learnt tonight?'

'I want you to know that it stands whatever happens tonight. I put the offer in writing when I first arrived here. It won't be rescinded simply for me to make money in the short term. It is the long-term health of my businesses that I care about.'

Emma stared at him, allowing his words to sink in. He knew about her father's illness but did not intend to lower his price. Relief washed over her. Her shoulders eased. She hadn't realised they were tight. The burden she had been carrying for so long, ever since her father's first turn, had gone. Her head seemed positively giddy. Words failed her, and she stared at Jack.

'Thank you,' she whispered, reaching for his fingers and squeezing them as his eyes softened.

It seemed to be enough. Suddenly she knew she had the

strength to climb the stairs and face her father, face whatever ordeal lay before her.

'Miss Emma, Miss Emma.' Annie came hurrying into the room. Her cap was askew and her apron crumpled. Emma was hard pressed to remember when she had ever seen Annie anything but perfectly turned out. 'We have been so worried. But the master would have none of us calling for you. He wanted you to have fun, to enjoy the pantomime. You have little enough of that sort of thing, he said.'

'Tell me everything, Annie. Don't spare me.' Emma pushed her curls behind her ears. 'I should never have gone tonight.'

'It were a right to-do, like.' Annie's placid face creased, and tears threatened to spill from her eyes. Emma put her arm around the distressed maid. 'I never heard the like. It was right after he finished his bottle of Dr Milburn's tonic, or so Fackler says. Turned all purple and gasping for breath. I was certain he was a goner.'

'Miss Harrison needs to know his exact symptoms, Annie,' Jack said. 'Tell her in plain, simple language. We know that Mr Harrison is still alive and sleeping. We both saw him resting.'

'You are right, sir.' Annie bobbed a little curtsey. 'As I was saying…'

Emma listened intently while Annie related the evening's events. From the recounting, it appeared her father's fit had followed its usual terrifying course.

'I will sit with him for a while.' Emma started towards the stairs.

'He is sleeping like a lamb.' Annie held her nose and wafted the air with her hand. 'But his breath smells of garlic, like. And he ain't had any garlic. I checked with Cook. He barely touched his food today. His stomach was paining him that badly, and he said his mouth tasted like he ate steel. He finished his tonic tonight, no questions asked. Drained the bottle. It was then the attack happened.'

'That settles it,' Jack remarked decisively, his face suddenly wearing a very determined look.

'Settles what?' Emma asked in surprise. 'What are you talking about, Jack?'

'Do his turns always happen after he has finished a bottle of tonic?'

Emma tilted her head to one side, thinking back to the attacks. 'Yes, I think you are right. Does it signify anything?'

'It might do, but I need to know more.' Jack started to pace the room. 'Tell me everything you can remember about his most recent attacks.'

Emma explained, going back over the symptoms several times. When she had finished, she looked at him. His brow was furrowed. He had made several notes on a piece of paper and was reading them over. Did he really care about what happened to her father?

'What should we do? Can I go up and see my father?'

He jumped slightly, as if he had forgotten she was there.

'Do? You go up and see your father. Put your mind at ease. Leave Milburn to me.' He crossed his arms. 'I have some questions I want answered. Once they are answered, then the doctor can see his patient.'

'But…but…' Emma hesitated on the bottom stair.

'For once in your life, Emma, please do as I ask.' His hand enveloped hers. 'Trust me.'

Emma stared at him, met his intense gaze full-on, but hers was the first to falter. She had to trust him. She wanted to trust him. 'Send Dr Milburn up when he arrives.'

Emma gathered her skirts and raced up the stairs, taking them two at a time.

Jack watched her go, then rang for Fackler. He would do

what was necessary. Dr Milburn would only see Harrison once Jack was certain. 'Do you have the tonic bottle? The one Mr Harrison finished tonight.'

'It can be found, Mr Stanton.' The butler's face was perfectly schooled.

'With all speed and diligence, Fackler.'

'With all speed, sir.'

Jack smiled inwardly. Fackler thought him slightly unhinged, but it was important to follow his hunches, and the signs pointed to the tonic. Nothing happened without a reason. Everything obeyed the laws of nature. Everything.

The bell sounded—harsh, insistent. Jack stared at the solid door.

'I want to see Dr Milburn first.' Jack met the butler's stare. 'Miss Emma is not to be disturbed. She has had but a little time with her father.'

'Very good, sir.' Again the butler's face gave no indication that he thought the request odd or out of the ordinary. 'And if I might say so, sir, I don't put a huge store by medicine pedlars. A great big bunch of tomfoolery, if you don't mind me saying so.'

'Thank you, Fackler. I had thought that as well. Some tonics are good, and others—well, it doesn't bear thinking about.' Jack clenched his jaw. He was determined to give Dr Milburn a fair hearing, and as Harrison was now asleep, it would make no difference if he was examined in the morning or now.

'I have come from an important supper,' Dr Milburn pronounced when Fackler barred his way. 'And this man says that I am not required.'

'Please forgive the servants, Milburn, they overreacted.' Jack went to the door. The first few snowflakes drifted down, landing on Milburn's black coat. 'Harrison is resting comfortably after experiencing indigestion at supper.'

Dr Milburn carried his black leather bag in one hand and had a white silk scarf wrapped around his neck—the very picture of a successful doctor. His eyes slowly travelled up Jack's form. A tiny smile played on his thin lips.

'My patient is ill, Stanton.' He made an imperious gesture. 'Stand aside.'

Jack braced his feet and met Milburn's glassy gaze. With effort, he retained control of his temper.

'Your patient is resting. From what I know, sleep is often the best healer.'

'And what are you now? A doctor as well as an engineer?' The sneer on Milburn's face increased. 'For a charity boy, you express your opinion on a wide range of matters.'

'Out in the wild, you have to. Your men's lives depend on it,' Jack answered, allowing the charity remark to pass. He had proved his worth a thousand times over; no jumped-up doctor would take that away. Milburn wanted a reaction. 'I know what I am on about. Do you?'

'For the love of God, man, let me pass,' Milburn said, his voice thundering. 'I have work to do. A man's life depends on me and my skill.'

'I think not.' Jack lounged against the doorframe, giving the impression of great casualness, but in reality every muscle was ready to spring.

'What did you say? Are you threatening me? *Me*? A member of the Royal College of Physicians? How dare you?'

Milburn raised his bag, but Jack reached out and grabbed his wrist, holding him there.

'I dare all right.' Jack pushed the arm away. 'You forget yourself, Milburn, and you forget who you are dealing with.'

Neither man moved. The sound of his breathing, of Milburn's, echoed about him. Then Milburn blinked and lowered his bag, his shoulders slightly hunched.

'I have been summoned.' He tried again, his face flushing slightly. He spoke each word as if he were speaking to a backward child. 'Miss Harrison desires me to see her father.'

'You were summoned mistakenly. By the servants. Miss Harrison was with me this evening.'

'With you?' Milburn opened and closed his mouth several times.

'At a pantomime. The Charltons were in the party.'

'No one informed me of this,' Milburn muttered out of the corner of his mouth.

'I did not know either of the Harrisons were in the habit of telling you their social engagements,' Jack said through a clenched jaw.

Milburn blinked. A cold smile spread over his features. 'You are quite right, of course, Stanton. I have no claim over Miss Harrison…yet. But I do have hopes. Miss Harrison, despite her plain looks, would make an admirable helpmate for a doctor, don't you agree?'

Jack stared at Milburn. Emma? Plain? Infuriating. Maddening. Obstinate. But not plain. Her beauty might be unconventional, but he found it very pleasing to the eye. And her mind was first-rate. She had matured into an excitingly attractive woman. She deserved someone who appreciated her.

'If Harrison's condition has failed to improve by morning I will personally come for you. Until then, I suggest you go home.' Jack restrained his fist with difficulty.

'You are playing a dangerous game, Stanton.' The doctor's sneer resembled that of a snake. His eyes glittered. 'Harrison's condition is complex and complicated. I would hate to think anything untoward had happened to him because you refused me entry.'

'It is a risk I am prepared to take.' Jack moved solidly in

front of the door. He clung onto his temper, dared Milburn to make another move.

The sneer on Milburn's face increased, became more pronounced. 'It is on your head, Stanton, if Harrison dies since you play at doctoring. I will be quite happy to say as much to the authorities.'

'I welcome the responsibility.' Jack stared hard at the arrogant doctor. Emma as a dutiful helpmate to *him*! Impossible. Ridiculous. He refused to allow it.

'Until the morning, then. I pray to God that the patient lasts that long.' Dr Milburn stalked off to the waiting carriage.

'Old crow,' Fackler muttered under his breath as he banged the door shut. 'As you said, Mr Stanton, there weren't no need to call him out. I should never have listened to that Annie.'

'Miss Emma seems to set store by him.' Jack tried to keep his voice light. 'Their names have been bandied together.'

'Miss Emma?' Fackler shook his head. 'She don't like him. Not in that way. It were the late mistress, Mrs Harrison. She *did* set store by him. Called him her ministering angel. Wouldn't hear a word spoken against him. Not by nobody.'

Jack squared his shoulders and faced the butler. 'Mrs Harrison is dead. It is Mr Harrison and his daughter I am concerned with.'

Chapter Twelve

Her father lay in the centre of the double bed. His face pasty but peaceful against the white sheet. No rattling, no wheezing, just the steady breath of peaceful sleep. Annie was correct. His breathing was even and regular. There was no reason to disturb Dr Milburn. Emma offered up a prayer of thanksgiving.

Whatever her father had had, it had passed—just as it had done every other time. The fit had gone and he would be restored to the land of the living. But for how long? When should she tell him that he was dying? That Dr Milburn held out little hope? That she had confided everything in Jack? She would have to say something. Or Jack would.

She drew a sharp breath. Everything she had worked for these past few months gone. Her father had to survive—that was the main thing. Everything else could wait.

She was not ready to become an orphan.

'Papa, stay with me. Don't go to Mama.'

Emma stumbled forward and laid her head against the coverlet, her strong fingers curling around her father's limp ones.

'I have seen the good doctor,' Jack said, coming into the room.

Emma jumped up and made a show of securing the coverlet more tightly around her father. She brushed away the glint of tears and straightened her crumpled dress.

'Where is he?' Emma peered around Jack, trying to see the doctor's looming figure. 'Dr Milburn should be here by now. I distinctly heard the bell earlier. Why is he taking his time? Generally Fackler sends him straight up.'

Jack came closer. In the firelight, a pair of scissors gleamed in his hands. His face wore that same determined expression he'd had when he rescued Davy. 'I sent him away. His services were not required.'

'Sent him away?' Emma rolled her eyes heavenwards, choked back the anger. She had to remain calm. Shouting at Jack was going to make matters worse, but right now she wanted to throttle him. Of all the high-handed—! 'Why did you do that? How could you do that?'

'Your father is resting comfortably. After the shock he had, it is probably the best thing for him.' He paused and looked at her father's bedside table, where a variety of bottles and boxes stood along with a half-used candlestick. 'If needs be, Dr Milburn can call in the morning. I will personally fetch him. I think he is hoping to be able to say I told you so.'

'Will he?' Emma crossed her arms and narrowed her eyes. "My father is not a bone to be fought over by two men who have borne grudges since school. This is a man's life we are talking about. My father's life.'

'I doubt it. Your father is over the worst. He will live.' Jack nodded towards where her father lay. 'See, his breathing is easy. There is no sweat on his brow. You said that every fit he had, he had when he'd reached the end of a tonic bottle?'

'Did I? I don't remember.' Emma paced the room, clasping

and unclasping her hands. She found it difficult to think beyond the immediate room. 'Yes, I suppose that is correct.'

'Think. Take your time about it, but do you ever remember a fit that happened when he was in the middle of a bottle?'

Emma shook her head. 'It could be coincidence. Or perhaps my father tries to eke out the bottle. He has a great dislike of calling for the doctor.'

'I do not believe in coincidence. Nobody operates outside nature. A bridge falls down because of the forces exerted on it. People become ill for a reason.'

Emma swallowed hard, torn. Every instinct she had told her to trust him. It was a basic tenet of civil engineering—the forces of nature controlled everything. Every fit her father had had, had happened when he'd reached the end of a tonic bottle. She was sure of it now. She had never thought about it before. Jack was correct. Coincidence was highly unlikely. 'What do you intend on doing?'

'Following my hunch.' He gave a crooked smile. 'Check and recheck everything before coming to any definite conclusion. It is what I am good at. Details are important.'

'What sort of details?' Emma asked cautiously.

She glanced again at her father. He was sleeping comfortably. It would be a shame to wake him. She wrapped her arms about her waist and kept her mind away from what might happen.

'When he has the attacks, is there anything Dr Milburn gives him?' Jack paused and tapped the scissors against his thigh. 'What does Dr Milburn do? Does he bleed him?'

'No, not that. He has other methods.' She swallowed hard. 'I disapprove of bleeding. I think it made Mama weaker, despite what the doctors said. It is one of the reasons we changed to Dr Milburn. His methods are more modern. He believes in medicine-pills and tonics.'

'What methods? Think carefully, Emma. How does he control your father's attacks?'

'He has some special pills that my father is supposed to take if ever he is starting to feel dizzy. They seem to cure it, or at least make the fits less.' Emma rummaged through her father's top drawer and pulled out a glass bottle. She squinted at the spidery writing. 'Charcoal and sulphur. They are all gone. Is it significant?'

'Yes, I thought they might contain those two ingredients. It all fits.' Jack went to her father, snipped a lock of hair from his head, then captured it in a handkerchief before carefully transferring it to an envelope. He handed the envelope to Emma. 'Seal it.'

'I trust you,' she said.

'I would feel safer if you used your father's wax and ring to seal it. I want everything to be correct. You never know when it might have to be used in a court of law.'

Emma took the envelope and went over to her father's dressing table. She quickly sealed the envelope, pressing the ring into the warm red wax. Jack took it from her nerveless fingers. 'What will you do with it?'

'I will send this away, along with the empty bottle of tonic, to make sure my hypothesis is correct.' Jack ran his hand through his hair. She could see tiredness around his eyes. 'Milburn knows there is something in the tonic. Sulphur and charcoal are given for one specific reason. He knows what is causing these fits, even if he is not telling you.'

'Dr Milburn knows the cause?' Emma stared at where her father lay. Questions crowded in her brain. 'But he would dearly love to know. It would make his fortune, he says.'

'I suspect your father is suffering from arsenic poisoning. He has all the symptoms—confusion, garlic breath, metallic-tasting mouth and stomach cramps. Luckily Edward Harrison has a strong constitution.' Jack turned the empty pill bottle over. 'The cure for an accidental overdose is charcoal and sulphur. When your father feels up to eating he will need to have eggs and onions—foods that contain sulphur.'

'Poisoning?' Emma stared at Jack, incredulous. Her body became numb. Poison. Her father. Impossible. 'Who would do such a thing? How would he get arsenic?'

'Milburn's tonic most likely contains some,' Jack said quietly. 'A good many tonics do. In small doses it is supposed to be helpful in certain cases.'

'Dr Milburn is poisoning my father?' Emma looked at Jack. 'How could he do such a thing? Why would he do such a thing? If he knew, why would he have my father continue to take the tonic?'

She backed away from the tonic bottle as if it might bite her, trying to make sense of it. Dr Milburn was poisoning her father.

'I am sure it was not deliberate, Emma,' Jack said carefully. 'It is possible that the arsenic settled after being left too long. It needs investigating. We need to be certain before deciding what to do next.'

'You don't sound convinced.'

'I want to wait and weigh the options. I may not like the man, but I doubt Charles Milburn is a cold-blooded murderer. You say that he kept your mother alive. I have to trust your judgement.'

'Yes,' Emma breathed, and the word came out as a half-choked sob. Emma fumbled for a handkerchief but could find none. She gazed up at the ceiling. Why did she always get the temptation to cry when she was not in possession of a hand-kerchief? She blinked back tears and swallowed hard. Regained control of her emotions, then continued in a stronger voice. 'He saved Mama's life. I am convinced of it. We kept her going for as long as possible.'

Jack was standing right beside her. Emma turned slightly. His strong arms went around her, held her close in their gentle embrace. She laid her cheek against his starched white shirt-front and heard the reassuring thump of his heart in her ear. Nothing lover-like, a place of comfort. Safety. She swallowed hard. They were friends, and she had to be content with that.

'How long will it take until we know for certain?' she asked, fixing her gaze on his second shirt button down.

'I will have the answer before Christmas. Before I depart from Newcastle.' He spoke into her hair.

He loosened his arms and stepped away from her. The cold air rushed around her. She forced her lips into a brilliant smile. 'I imagine these things take time.'

'You won't have to wonder for long.'

All the while her mind kept echoing his words. Christmas. Christmas was when Jack would be leaving. He planned on going despite his new knowledge. Only a few days ago she hadn't been able to wait until he went, and now the thought of him going filled her with dread.

'What am I supposed to do in the meantime?' She struggled to keep her voice steady.

'Wait and watch. Hope.'

'And what of Dr Milburn?'

'I think it best if your father finds another doctor.'

'You may be correct.' Emma hugged her arms about her. She hated to think it had been she who had insisted her father take his tonic. She had thought that it was doing him some good, and instead she had been poisoning him. Her mind recoiled. She wanted to sink to her knees and weep. She forced her body to stay upright. 'Papa, you are not dying. We are going to get you well. You will live to see this bridge across the Tyne built. I promise you that.'

She heard the door click, and saw that Jack had quietly gone. 'Thank you,' she whispered to the emptiness he'd left behind.

'Fathers!' Emma closed the door to her father's room with a satisfying bang the following morning. 'One would think they enjoyed turning the entire household upside down and inside out.'

'You seem perturbed this morning, Miss Emma.' Jack lounged against the doorframe. 'Hopefully your father has not become worse in the night.'

'He agrees with you!' Emma put her hands on her hips and tried to forget that she looked a fright. Up most of the night, and with her hair hanging down her back in a loose plait, and more than likely dark circles under her eyes. Her only consolation was that he had seen her worse. But she wanted him to think her attractive. As excitingly attractive as the women in London or Paris.

'Agrees with me about what?' A faint dimple showed in the corner of his mouth.

'"There is no need to send for the quack."' Emma put her hands on her hips and mimicked her father's tone. '"Nor to take any more of that quack's medicine." Hooray! Hoorah! "Always knew it wasn't good for me," says he.'

'I thought we had decided not to send for Milburn anyway.' Jack reached out and grabbed her arm. 'We agreed to wait for the results.'

Emma stepped back and his hand released her. She held her elbows and did not meet his eyes. 'I thought maybe one of the other doctors, but Papa is refusing even that. He approves of your methods and is willing to wait for the results.'

Jack gave a satisfied nod. 'I would say that is a very positive sign.'

'Positive? It is infuriating!' Emma began to pace up and

down the hall. 'This is the first time in a long time that my father is not being sensible, and you are encouraging him in this foolish behaviour.'

Jack came forward, blocking her way. He reached out and gathered her hands in his. Emma found it difficult to breathe, her mind spun. She kept her gaze on his embroidered silk waistcoat.

'Emma,' he said, and his finger lifted her chin. 'Listen to me. Believe in me. Your father is recovering.'

'I am. I do. He must be.'

With the greatest of efforts she tore herself away from his hands. Took a deep breath. Her lips ached. In another moment her hand would have curled around his neck and pulled his mouth against hers.

There were too many servants about, and she hated to think about the scandal. And what it would do to her father. She had to be realistic. This was a flirtation for Jack. He had said when they first met that he was not interested in marriage. Nothing he had done since gave the slightest indication his mind had changed. Whatever chance they'd had, had been destroyed a long time ago, when her mother had not given her the letter. No. If she was honest, it had gone before then—when Jack had left without giving her a chance. His departure had nearly broken her heart. He would not have a second chance. And this time her heart was immune.

It had to be.

Jack made no effort to recapture her. He raked his hand through his hair.

'If your father was not feeling right within himself he would want to see the doctor. He'd welcome your suggestion.'

'He is talking about what will happen once he is in charge at the bridge.'

Jack's face betrayed no emotion. 'I would say that is a good sign.'

'He may change his mind about your proposal…I mean offer.'

Emma wanted the earth to open up when she realised which word had escaped.

'My proposal?' He lifted a brow. 'And which proposal would that be, exactly?'

Emma felt a tide of burning wash up her face. 'I was speaking about your offer for Harrison and Lowe. That is the only proposal I know about. Is there another one?'

'Not that I have heard of.' His eyes glittered slightly, and a half-smile appeared on his lips. 'I thought maybe you could enlighten me. Exactly what is your proposition, and will I enjoy it?'

Emma smiled back at him, feeling on firmer ground. Light-hearted remarks with no substance she had learnt to deal with years ago. 'I don't have time to stand here bantering with you. There is work to be done.'

'On a day like today? Have you had a look out of the window?'

Emma hurried over to the window on the landing. Snow-flakes were coming down in great piles, as if there was a gigantic pillow fight in the sky. The garden was rapidly filling up with huge white flakes. The muddy patches, the bare trees and bushes and the Greek goddess statue that had been her mother's pride, were all covered in a blanket of wet snow.

'You are right. There will be no work on the bridge.'

'It would be impossible,' Jack agreed. 'The men will work all the harder when the thaw comes and the ground is soft.'

'I pray when it comes the thaw will not be too rapid.' A shiver ran down Emma's spine as she thought of what the Tyne was capable of. Her father's previous project before this one had been strengthening the flood defences along the Tyne, and she prayed they would not be needed.

'You are too tender-hearted, Emma. The thaw needs to be rapid. We need to see what happens when the Tyne is in full spate. When I build a bridge it stands for all time, not just until the first one-hundred-year flood.'

'But think on the potential for devastation, the lives that would be ruined, the property.'

'If we can understand the pattern and the effects, we can save lives and ensure the bridge stands. The Tyne has washed bridges away before now. Every single bridge was lost last century due to a flood. It will not happen to my bridge.'

'Another of your it-can-be-done projects?'

'I am interested in taming the forces of nature, making them work for us rather than against us.' Jack paused. 'But you lead me from my purpose.'

'Your purpose?' Emma tilted her head.

Jack was dressed in his overcoat and top hat. Emma's brow wrinkled. Surely he could not be planning on going out in this weather? He had said that work was suspended on the bridge.

'To ascertain how your father fares.'

'I have told you that he is recovering—recovering all too quickly,' she said with a wry smile. 'He will be complaining about resting within a few days. You may go in and see him if you like.'

'It won't be necessary.' Jack waved his hand, but his face had turned serious. 'I must bid you adieu.'

'Adieu? You are leaving?' Emma looked at him in dismay, and her stomach dropped. The light appeared to go out of the day, and time stretched bleakly in front of her. 'But I thought you were staying until Christmas.'

'Urgent matters have arisen and I need to go to London. Stephenson needs to know about your father—about what we have decided.'

'Nothing is decided,' Emma said quickly.

'We agreed on the company, Miss Harrison.' Jack's face became stern. 'Stephenson and I have to discuss how best to proceed with the building of the bridge and its design. How to get the bridge built on time.'

'Until my father is well, I cannot say what he will do. I don't speak for my father.' Emma balled her fists. He had to understand. She had to give her father something to live for. 'He is alive. And he is going to recover fully. You said it was poisoning.'

'I hope and pray he does. In the meantime, someone needs to look after the bridge. It is too important a project to go unsupervised, and I do have other commitments, Miss Harrison. Places I need to be in the New Year. I accepted a contract in Italy. People are depending on me.'

Emma stared at Jack not quite taking in what he was saying. Other commitments. She had thought he would be staying. Another illusion. A great hollow place opened inside her. A huge Jack-shaped hole. She screwed her eyes shut, refused to think about that. She was overwrought about her father. That had to be it. It had no other cause.

'If it is arsenic poisoning, then my father will get well.' She forced the words from her throat.

'He should do, but it may take months.' He laid a hand on her shoulder briefly. 'You must face facts, Miss Emma. That bridge must have someone permanent in charge, whether your father retains ownership of his company or not. It needs a qualified and competent engineer.'

'The ground is frozen. Give my father time.' As she said the words she knew she was pleading for her own well-being.

Emma moved away from him. She had to think, to ignore the trembling that was developing in her stomach. Jack was making plans to go away—to go away and not come back.

'As you wish, but I need to speak with Stephenson in

person.' He gave a careless shrug. 'There is little good I can do here. The ground is frozen. But the trains are running.'

'And your experiments?'

'Davy Newcomb knows what to do. I have sent him a list of instructions. He is trustworthy.'

Emma forced her lips to turn upwards. 'You appear to have thought of everything.'

'I like to have the details correct.' His eyes darkened. 'They need me in London.'

Emma wanted to whisper that she needed him to stay here. But the words refused to come. What was between them was too new and fragile. Perhaps it was only her own longing and not his. He had been quite clear about things that first day.

She adjusted the shawl tighter around her shoulders. 'I shall wish you Godspeed on your journey, then.'

'I will return...before the thaw, Emma.' A half-smile touched his lips. He took a step closer. 'Wish me luck.'

'I thought I had already.' Her breath seemed to stick in her throat. She knew if she took one step closer her body would brush his.

'So cold, so formal,' he murmured.

He leant forward, and his fingertips delicately traced the outline of her eyebrows, the line of her nose and the curve of her jaw. Soft touches, as if he were memorising her face. Intimate touches, creating little ripples of warmth that flooded through her body. Her lips ached, and she wanted to taste his mouth again. What mattered was the feel of him against her.

Her hand reached up to drag his face down. But the clock chimed and he stepped away.

'Next time, remember to say goodbye properly without being asked.' He touched his hat.

And he was gone before her mind could think up a suitable

scathing retort. She heard his steady footsteps go down the stairs and the sound of the door closing.

She ran to the front of the house and rested her cheek against the windowpane, watching the black carriage disappear into the swirling white snow. She watched for a long time, until the tracks from the carriage became white and the world was covered with white down, refusing to think about trains becoming stuck or derailing.

The sound of the servants moving about the house roused her. She gave herself a shake. There was more to her life than mooning about like some schoolgirl. She had responsibilities, a life. But her mouth ached with the memory of what might have been.

Chapter Thirteen

'He will come back,' Lucy said, pressing her hand against Emma's as they sat in the little hut beside the frozen pond three days later. Her father had insisted she join the Charltons' skating party. He was tired of her fussing and fretting. 'There is no need to act the moon-calf about it either. He will be back before you know it.'

Emma froze. She thought she had been so careful. She had barely mentioned Jack Stanton. Only that he had gone just before the winter storm had set in. Newcastle and the rest of the North East slumbered under a blanket of snow and ice.

'What are you talking about, Lucy? Why this sudden penchant for riddles?' Emma bent her head and concentrated on fastening the strap of her ice skate.

'*Your* Mr Stanton.'

Emma pulled too hard and the leather strap broke.

'Now see what you made me do!' Emma held up the broken strap with a rueful smile. 'You should not tease me like that. I had not realised the leather was rotten.'

'Is that what caused it?' Lucy's eyes danced. 'And I thought you were remembering the way Mr Stanton could not take his eyes off you at the pantomime. I assure you the other ladies were quite jealous. Lottie fumed about it. Even Henry remarked on it to Dr Milburn. I am certain he will make an offer. I can see wedding bells in your future!'

'Must you always indulge in such fairytales?' A wave of burning stained her cheeks. Wedding bells? The idea was laughable. Jack Stanton had no intention of marrying anyone, least of all her. His sole concern and purpose was ensuring Harrison and Lowe became part of his empire. He had made that quite clear.

'You are being deliberately blind.'

'You are seeing romance where there is none. Jack Stanton is a family friend.' Emma held out her skate. 'Anyway, whatever the cause, it looks like I shan't be skating today.'

'I will get you another strap. I won't have you getting out of skating this easily, Emma Harrison.'

'How can I skate on one skate? Be reasonable, Lucy.' Emma gave a small laugh, and privately heaved a sigh of relief. The subject had veered away from Jack.

'Let me solve your problem.' Lucy signalled towards a footman, who brought another piece of leather. Emma waited while he threaded the strap through and then handed the skate back. 'You see—no excuse.'

'I do like to skate, Lucy.'

'It is good that your father has improved enough for you to leave him. I had worried you would not make Lottie's party.'

'My father was determined I would. Unlike Mama, he wants peace and quiet. He says I fuss.' Emma nodded to where Lottie stood, pretty and poised on the ice. 'She looks like a fairy child.'

'Ah, but she knows it, and that is the problem. She is rapidly turning into a flirt, and just think what that will do for her prospects.'

'Thus far she has been careful.'

'But she gets bolder and bolder. I am worried. One slip, one misjudgement, and her reputation could be beyond repair. But neither Henry nor Mother Charlton is interested.'

'Thankfully I listened to Mama about the pitfalls and avoided most of them.' A shiver ran down Emma's spine. She hated to think how close she had been to scandal with Jack. She did not regret it.

'Ah, Stanton, you have returned. In good time as well.'

'My meetings took less time than I anticipated. It is good to see you looking so hardy, Harrison.' Jack handed his top hat to Fackler. 'Where is Miss Emma? I thought she might like to try out my new sleigh.'

'She has gone to that Charlton chit's skating party. She was getting on my nerves, always fussing.'

Jack was dismayed at the wave of disappointment that coursed through his body. All the way up on the train he had pictured Emma's face, her eyes lighting up, her cupid's bow mouth softening when she saw the sleigh. And now she had gone out and the surprise would have to wait.

'I see. There will be other occasions, no doubt.'

Harrison tapped his fingers together. 'But this might prove fortuitous.'

'How so?'

'I have been thinking. I can not go on running the project much longer. I want to spend time doing other things.'

'My offer stands. Your recent illness makes no difference.'

'Ah, but I have my daughter to think of. She loves that bridge, and cares about the employees.' Harrison raised his eyebrows. 'I am going to give her the company as a dowry. It will be her problem then. I have enough from my various land investments. The railways have been driving the price of land,

and for a man with an eye on how the land lies there have been opportunities.'

Jack stared at him as cold seeped through his body. Harrison was giving the company to his daughter as a dowry. Exactly who was she marrying? What had happened while he had been gone?

'What are you saying?' He forced a laugh from between his teeth. 'Which man should I be congratulating?'

'Now, now, I am not blind and deaf, Stanton. I know a thing or two about these matters.' Harrison tapped his finger against his nose. 'I know which way the wind is blowing.'

'I made an offer to you in good faith.' Jack stared at Harrison, unable to believe his ears. Harrison was offering *him* the company as Emma's dowry. 'Does Emma know of this proposition?'

'No…I hadn't thought to say anything to her. I wanted to speak to you first. It was only right and proper.'

Jack resisted the urge to curse long and loud.

'If you know what is good for you, don't.'

A smile beamed across Harrison's face. 'I thought I could pick 'em. But Margaret had her heart set on her daughter being able to wear a coronet. She wouldn't settle for anything less than a title. It was a mistake, and Emma paid for it.'

'What was between Emma and I was over a long time ago.'

'I have eyes and ears, Stanton. You don't fool me.' Harrison cleared his throat. 'Anyway, I have taken the liberty of obtaining a licence—an ordinary one, to save money.'

'A licence?' Jack stared at Harrison. Had the fit caused him to become touched in the head? 'You have organised a marriage licence?'

'Between you and Emma. It took some doing, but I am not without friends.'

'Why?'

'As I said, I knew the way in which the wind was blowing,

and after my brush with death it came to me. Harrison and Lowe must be protected, and what better way to keep it all in the family, eh? And no point in shelling out for a Special Licence if one doesn't have to.'

'Harrison, I do my own courting.' Jack bit out the words. 'When I marry, and I have no plans to marry at present, I will marry for a far better reason than acquiring a company.'

Harrison's face fell. 'What are you saying?'

'I fear you have wasted your money. I have no plans to marry your daughter.' Jack crossed his arms and stared at Harrison. No man ran his life.

'No plans…but I thought—'

'You mistook my intentions. We are friends, Miss Harrison and I,' Jack said through gritted teeth. He had spent the better part of the time he had been gone trying to get her from his mind, and now he came back to this. It was not going to happen. Not in the manner Harrison prescribed.

'I can see I was a bit precipitous.' Harrison ran a finger around the rim of his collar. 'I had thought… Forget I said anything about it. Emma knows nothing about this.'

'You may call it what you like, but I never mix business with pleasure,' Jack said in a cold voice.

'Ah, but which is the business and which is the pleasure?' Harrison tapped his nose. 'It has been disputed before.'

'And if you are wise you will not say anything about it to Emma.' Jack clung onto the last vestiges of his control as anger surged through him. Harrison was prepared to sell his daughter in this way, to stoop to blatant manipulation. Emma deserved better than that. A marriage was more than a business arrangement. His parents' marriage had been. 'I bid you good day.'

'I do hope Emma is enjoying her skating expedition.' Harrison's voice trailed after him, causing Jack to pause in the doorway. 'I understand Dr Milburn is going. Her dear mama had high hopes for them once. In her final days she often used to speak of how well suited they were.'

Jack pulled on his gloves as he tried to refrain from shaking the man. Harrison's matchmaking attempts were pitiful. Emma had no interest in Milburn.

But… He paused, cold washing over him. What was Charles Milburn's interest? He could see the doctor's greedy eyes again, hear his voice proclaiming that he would soon marry Emma. An idle boast?

What if there was something more sinister afoot? The man had had no scruples as a boy. Jack clearly remembered the time Milburn had taken the opportunity to discover examination questions, and then blamed it on his hapless sidekick. Then there had been the time Milburn had lost the money from the charity box but had sported a new waistcoat. Nothing had ever been proved. It bothered Jack. Had Milburn really changed?

He quickly dismissed the notion as fanciful. But Emma could be in danger if she decided to quiz Milburn about the tonic. Jack's blood ran cold. Knowing Emma, she was quite capable of it. He cursed himself for being a thousand times a fool. Who knew what the doctor would do if he thought he was cornered?

Jack's heart skipped a beat. He had to make sure Emma was safe.

'You will forgive me, Harrison.'

'Where are you going?'

'To try out the sleigh.' Jack touched the rim of his hat. 'Good day to you, Harrison.'

'Give my regards to my daughter. You will find her on Gosforth Common. Her dowry remains the same, whichever man she chooses.'

Jack slammed the door to the echoing sound of Harrison's laughter.

* * *

All around Emma the shrieks of laughter rose. The Charltons' skating party was in full flow. The ice teemed with the Charltons, a number of Lottie's soldiers and a variety of friends. Mrs Charlton had set up a warming area, complete with a portable stove and a steaming bowl of her famous wassailing punch. Emma finished fastening her skates and stood. After years of not skating her ankles felt wobbly and threatened not to hold her. She looked longingly back at the warm hut.

'Are you coming out on the ice, Emma? I promise not to tease you any more.'

'Give me a moment.' Emma practised a few steps, felt her legs going and flailed her arms, but she didn't fall. She took a cautious step forward, and then another. The ice began to glide under her feet. 'I think my feet remember more than I give them credit for.'

'Do you need some assistance? I may not be Jack Stanton, but I reckon I can help hold you up.'

'Very amusing, Lucy.'

Lucy started to skate back towards Emma, stopped, and then gestured towards the centre, where Lottie stood surrounded by her admirers. She had a particularly mischievous look on her face. 'Oh, dear, Lottie has not given up the idea, despite Henry's warning. She is insistent on this pairing-off game.'

'Come and join us, Emma.' Lottie skated over. 'I am searching for another *single* lady, and I am sure one of the officers wouldn't mind being paired with you. It is quite harmless fun. Lieutenant Ludlow assures me that he is willing to be your gallant.'

'I shall pass. Not steady enough on my feet.'

'There is that. I shall just have to have two gallants, then.' Lottie gave a toss of her head and skated away.

'She skates very close to the edge, does my sister-in-law,' Lucy said with a pained expression, as Lottie laughingly grabbed onto the lieutenant's arm. 'She'll bring down scandal on us all if she continues in this manner. And then what will happen to her marriage prospects?'

'There are worse things than remaining single.'

'Sometimes, Emma Harrison,' Lucy said, shaking her head, 'I think you quite like playing at being the old spinster. And…'

'And what?'

'And at other times I am sure of it,' Lucy called as she skated away with firm strokes. Her blue eyes danced. 'Catch me if you dare.'

Emma laughed. Out here on the ice the years melted away. It was as if they were young girls again, with few responsibilities, instead of being in their mid-twenties.

'You will regret those words, Lucy Charlton!'

'Make me!' Lucy put her hands on her hips. 'You have not the stamina you once had, old maid Emma Harrison.'

'Neither your teasing nor Lottie's attempts to organise games will ruin the day for me.' Emma gestured out towards where the snow sparkled 'I plan to skate, skate, skate, until the sun goes behind the clouds or I become too cold. But on my own terms. It is how I live my life.'

'That's the Emma I know and love.' Lucy looked over her shoulder towards where a great deal of shrieking was coming from. 'I see one of my boys is getting into problems with his nurse. I did tell him no snowball fights. Sometimes I think he takes after his father, and at other times I am sure he does.'

'Go on. I will be here when you come back.' Emma waved Lucy away and watched her confidently skate over to where her little boy was looking mutinous. Emma watched for a little while, and then turned her attention to skating. She tentatively took a few more steps, found her rhythm and began to skate faster, her feet barely skimming the ice. The cold bit her cheeks as she remembered the soaring feeling. It had been far too many years. She circled around and decided to try to skate backwards, as she had been able to do once.

'Be careful, Miss Harrison.' Iron arms caught her and an imperious voice resounded in her ear. 'I would not want to be responsible for you receiving an injury.'

Emma froze, pulled firmly away from the restraining hands, and turned to face Dr Milburn. She fought to contain her revulsion at his arrogant expression.

Nothing had been proved. Jack's friend had not yet given his report. There was still a chance that Jack was mistaken and her father was truly ill.

'Dr Milburn, how pleasant it is to see you.' Emma forced her voice to be polite as she tried to peer over his shoulder to where Lucy ministered to her son.

'You are looking sprightly, if I might say so, Miss Harrison. And your father…is he here?'

'My father finds the cold difficult.' Emma took a deep breath. 'I was sorry that the servants over-reacted the other night. Thankfully, it proved a false alarm. My father is fully recovered now.'

'I am pleased to hear it. I feared the worst when Stanton barred my entry.' Dr Milburn's face assumed a sanctimonious expression. 'It does my heart good to know your father's health improves. In these sorts of cases there is no telling how long such patients will last. It is in God's hands.'

'He has recovered.' Emma swallowed. She had to fight against being too cynical. Nothing had been proved. It could all be coincidence. She had to believe that somehow this had been a mistake. She gave a light laugh. 'But I am surprised to see you here in this party.'

'Do you think me too old and staid for such doings?' His smile did not reach his dead eyes. 'I am but a few years older than Jack Stanton. We knew each other as young men. Did he ever say?'

Emma fought to keep her face pleasant. 'Not too old. I had merely wondered about your patients. I thought they would have first call on your time.'

'Thankfully they, like your father, are being healthy at the moment. I must take my pleasures while I can, Miss Harrison. My bag is in my carriage in case I am required.' He touched his hand to his hat. 'I do like to think ahead. When I was a boy, I used to skate on the rivers all day. It appears such a perfect day for this type of innocent pleasure.'

'Yes, I agree.' Emma bit her lip. She had no wish to spend any more time than absolutely necessary in this man's company.

'Perhaps you will do me the honour of skating with me for a short while?'

Emma saw with relief that Lucy had finished with her son. 'I am sorry, but I promised Mrs Charlton…'

'Maybe later, then?'

'If it does not turn too cold.'

His eyes narrowed, and Emma's breath caught in her throat. A cold wind blew around her. She willed him to go.

'I hear your overseer has left Newcastle, Miss Harrison.' He cleared his throat. 'Do you know when he plans to return?'

'Mr Stanton did not tell me. Was there any particular reason?' She tilted her head to one side.

'There was a business opportunity I wanted to discuss with him, that is all. Henry Charlton was saying that he might be amenable.'

'I will be sure to tell him you were enquiring after him.'

'You do that. And, Miss Harrison, pray do be careful. I have no wish to see any harm come to you.'

'I always am.' Emma skated away with forceful strokes, trying to ignore the sudden chill that went down her spine.

* * *

'Once more around the pond and I am finished,' Emma remarked. 'My legs are positively shattered.'

'You have kept going far longer than I thought,' Lucy replied. 'It is pleasant to have a skating companion who is older than five. Henry used to skate when we were courting, but these days he is far too busy.'

'My nose is getting very cold, and I lost feeling in the tips of my toes aeons ago.'

'Come and have a cup of Mother Charlton's lamb's wool punch. She reckons it is more potent than the insipid drink they served at the St Nicholas ball.'

Emma began to move forward, towards where the Charltons had set up their punch bowl.

'Watch out! Watch your back! Man out of control!'

Emma felt a bump from behind, and then she fell onto the cold ice. Lay there with a heavy weight on her back. She struggled to breathe, to move.

'Terribly sorry. I didn't see the good doctor, and I appear to have careened off in the wrong direction. High spirits and all that,' Lieutenant Ludlow said, holding out his hand. 'No harm done, what?'

'Nothing worse than a bruised elbow.' Emma started to lever herself off the ice and sat back down again. 'My ankle is slightly twisted. The new strap did not give as much as I thought it would.'

'You are as pale as a ghost.' Ludlow's face creased. 'I will get the sawbones for you. Put you to rights. I can't have a pretty thing like you blaming me for a sprain.'

'No, no, I am fine.' Emma attempted to smile but knew it was probably more of a wince. 'It is my injured pride, nothing more.'

'I must insist, Miss Harrison.' The Lieutenant helped her to stand. 'Dr Milburn! Dr Milburn! I need your assistance and some of your marvellous tonic for this woman. In avoiding you I ended up colliding with this good lady instead. She is rather shaken.'

'Not the tonic,' Emma protested, scrambling to her feet. 'I have no need of the tonic.'

'Shouldn't we let the doctor be the judge of that?' Lieutenant Ludlow replied. 'He's the one qualified in medicine.'

'Yes, Emma, you must be cautious,' Lucy said. 'Here is Dr Milburn.'

Emma bit her lip and forced her head up. She would refuse to take the tonic, but what if Jack was wrong? She did not want to be responsible for ruining Dr Milburn's reputation.

'What appears to be the trouble?'

'Miss Harrison and I were involved in a collision. I believe she needs some of your excellent tonic. She looks a bit piqued.'

'Not the tonic,' Emma said hastily, and then stopped, glancing from Dr Milburn to the Lieutenant and back again. 'I don't want to…I am not ill.'

'She does indeed look pale.' Dr Milburn's eyes glittered like a snake's. Emma wondered if he had noticed her hesitation. 'But I don't think she requires my tonic…yet.'

'What does she need?' Ludlow asked. 'I certainly did not intend any harm. It felt as if I was pushed from behind just after I passed you, Doctor. What can I do to make amends?'

'Besides skating with more care?' Milburn said. 'You nearly knocked me down as well.'

'But what does she require?' Ludlow persisted.

'She needs a cup of Mrs Charlton's excellent hot punch. It is guaranteed to put the roses back in her cheeks.'

Emma released her breath, felt her lungs fill with cold air. Silently she offered up a prayer. Punch, and not tonic. 'A cup of punch would be lovely.'

'I will get it for you, Miss Harrison.' Dr Milburn gave a low bow and skated off.

Emma allowed Lucy and Lieutenant Ludlow to help her over to the side. She sat on a long bench and shivered slightly.

'Are you positive that you suffered no injury, Miss Harrison?' Lieutenant Ludlow asked again. He hovered over her in a possessive manner. A lock of fair hair fell over his forehead, making him look barely out of his teens. 'I do not know what came over me. High spirits.'

'I think it is merely because I have stopped skating.' She shivered as a bitter wind swept across the pond. 'After I have had my cup of punch no doubt I will feel better.'

'I have arrived just in time.' Dr Milburn pressed a steaming cup into Emma's hand. 'As requested, my dear Miss Harrison, your punch. I trust it will be as the doctor ordered.'

His laughter sounded hollow to Emma's ears, and did nothing to dispel her unease, but the soldier appeared amused by the quip. She was seeing shadows where there were none. Had to be. She had known Dr Milburn for years, and he had been most attentive to her mama in her last days.

She lifted the cup and took a tentative sip, choked, and resisted the temptation to spit it out.

'Thank you, Doctor. You have been most kind,' Lucy said. 'Now, drink it all up, Emma.'

'It will do you good, Miss Harrison.'

'I will in a little while. Just sitting is quite pleasant. I had not realised quite how tired I was.' Emma eyed the cup. She planned on pouring away the liquid once everyone had left her alone. It tasted foul. She had no idea what Mrs Charlton used in the celebrated punch, but she seriously wondered about people's tastebuds.

'I must insist, Miss Harrison. You need warming up. Drink it. I shall stand here watching until you do.' He gave a laugh, but she noticed his eyes had an intent look about them, much like a cat watching a mouse hole.

'It is a little warm for my tongue. I shall leave it to cool—' she began.

'Emma, do be sensible and do as Dr Milburn says,' Lucy implored. 'I want my partner back on the ice. You are wasting the daylight. I have never known you to be missish.'

Emma gritted her teeth. She wanted to be rid of the doctor and his stare. She made a face and forced the liquid down her throat, nearly gagging as she did so. She wiped her hand across her mouth. 'There—are you both satisfied?'

'Hugely satisfied,' Dr Milburn replied. His face assumed a very smug expression.

'I shall just take a turn around the ice,' Emma said. She wanted to get away from the doctor, and the prickly feeling that she had at the back of her neck. Something was not right. But it was probably an over-active imagination.

She set out with fast strokes, feeling the wind against her cheeks. It had turned much colder during the time she had been in the hut. Fewer skaters were on the ice. Emma started to go faster, turned a corner, and a wave of dizziness hit her. She shook her head to clear it.

In the distance, a broad-shouldered figure appeared, watching the skaters. His hands were behind his back, and his face shadowed, but Emma's blood gave a sudden leap. Jack! She started towards him. He wavered slightly. But she dug in, head held high. Every stroke of the blade seemed harder. Emma swallowed and redoubled her efforts, but when she got there he had vanished.

'Miss Harrison.' Dr Milburn's voice echoed in her brain. Emma squinted, managed to see straight. She put a hand to her face. As suddenly as the strange sensation had started, it ended, leaving her clear-headed, if a bit giddy. 'Are you sure you are all right?'

'I thought… That is…' Emma tried to explain the strange sensation that had filled her, filled her and then vanished. She readjusted her hood. 'It was nothing.'

'Perhaps the fall you took was greater than you imagined.' Dr Milburn gave a small bow. 'Allow me to escort you home.'

Every nerve screamed a warning. Dr Milburn's features swam in front of her, fading in and out. Emma attempted to concentrate. 'I don't think I want that. I really don't want that.'

She knew she sounded like a petulant child, but it made no difference.

'Nonsense,' Dr Milburn said. 'You need to return home before anything else happens to you. Look at you. You hardly know what you are saying. I must insist.'

Emma shook her head and refused to give in to the urge to sit down on the ice. She forced her back to remain straight, looked Dr Milburn in his fish eyes. 'I will find my own way home. I came with Mrs Charlton. There is room in her carriage.'

'You don't know what you are saying. The fall has addled your wits.'

'I don't think so.' Emma stood straight and stared determinedly straight ahead.

'You will be coming with me,' Dr Milburn said.

His fingers closed around her wrist like a vice. Emma tried twisting, first one way and then the other, but his fingers held firm.

'Unhand me. Now,' she said, in a low furious voice. 'Unhand me and we will say no more of this ungentlemanly behaviour.'

'I am afraid that would be impossible, Miss Harrison. I have your health to think of.'

Chapter Fourteen

'I believe the lady has spoken, Milburn.' Jack's voice resounded across the icy pond. Clear. Crisp. Firm.

Emma turned her head to see if she was simply hearing things. Relief flooded through her as she spied the tall man on the edge of the pond, muffled against the cold, but his outline clearly discernible. Jack had returned. *Returned!*

Suddenly, as if it were nothing, she could think again. She was not going anywhere with Dr Milburn—not if she could help it.

Dr Milburn turned his head slightly. Taking advantage of his distraction, Emma brought her arm down sharply, and Dr Milburn let go. Taking a step backwards, she caught her aching wrist with her other hand and tried to rub some warmth back into it.

'It is very kind of you to offer, Dr Milburn, but Mr Stanton will see me home.' She nodded towards where Jack was striding towards them. 'No doubt he has come from my father.'

'No doubt.'

Dr Milburn's eyes narrowed. Emma caught a look of intense hatred that was masked so quickly she wondered if she had imagined it. She pressed her hand against her forehead and tried to get her head to clear. The cold revived her a little, and focus returned to her world.

'I will see the lady home.' Jack's gloved hand caught her elbow. A very different sort of grasp from Dr Milburn's. His shoulder touched hers. Emma looked at him through her eyelashes, trying to see if he had changed in the few short days that he had been gone. If anything, his features seemed finer than before. She had not realised quite how much she had missed him until he was standing there. Solid and real. 'I positively insist.'

'I leave it for the lady to decide,' Dr Milburn said, his face taking on a plump, sleek look.

Emma took a deep breath, forced air into her lungs. She no longer knew if her head was spinning because she was cold and tired or if it was due to Jack's nearness. 'Mr Stanton is here, and as he is lodging with my father and me it is not out of his way. I would hate to think I have deprived any of your patients of your attention.'

'If that is your choice, Miss Harrison, I must abide by it.' Dr Milburn made a stiff bow and stalked off.

Emma was relieved to see Lucy skating towards them.

'I shall leave you in Mr Stanton's capable hands,' she said with a beatific smile. 'My children are anxious to be off home. Look after her well, Mr Stanton. She is very precious to me.'

'I intend to.'

Before Emma could protest at such blatant matchmaking, Lucy had skated away, leaving her standing facing Jack. He lifted one eyebrow. Her heart sank. He knew what Lucy was doing.

'She worries…about her children,' Emma said, to explain away Lucy's behaviour. He had to believe her.

'Did I say anything?' Jack regarded Emma. The tip of her nose was bright pink and matched the colour in her cheeks.

Her woollen hood emphasised the oval of her face. Her eyes sparkled. The dull ache inside his being vanished.

He had missed her. It had not occurred to him until he saw her exactly how much he had missed her. And what did he do about it? Harrison had made life more complicated, not less.

'No, it is just that…well, I thought you might wonder.' She wrapped the ribbon of her hood about her hand.

'Mrs Charlton appears to be an admirable mother. Her devotion to her children's welfare is to be commended.'

'She lives for her children. Until she married I don't think she ever thought much about being a mother. I am not sure if she even knew which end was up. But now she does. She is a very good mother.'

'Is that something you aspire to?' Jack watched for her reaction. How much did she know of her father's plan? Had she been party to it? He wondered if he should broach the subject and explain that he never mixed business with his private life, that he would never marry for the sake of a dowry.

'I have told you that I am on the shelf.' She gave an uneasy laugh.

'I had forgotten.' Jack touched his hand to his hat, satisfied. Emma had no notion of her father's plans, and he intended to keep it that way.

'Pray don't forget again.' She raised her chin and met his gaze full-on. 'I value my independence highly. It has allowed me to develop my mind, to realise there are things beyond balls, routs and dances.'

'But they do have their place.' Jack watched her mouth, remembered the feel of it against his, and her soft sigh. 'Waltzing can be a pleasurable pastime. Don't you agree?'

Waltzing with him? Emma forgot to breathe. The dizziness in her head increased. All too clearly she remembered what had happened when they'd waltzed—the pressure of his hand against her back. She gulped a mouthful of air, tried to focus somewhere other than his hands, his shoulders, his face, his mouth.

'How did you know where I was?' Emma asked, striving for a normal voice. She forced her body to ignore the dizzy feeling. If she didn't think about it, it would go away. Had to.

'I arrived back from London and your father sent me to fetch you.' His eyes were shadowed.

'He did?' Emma tried to control the sudden lurch in her stomach. The fizz in her veins had disappeared as though it had never been, leaving her empty and flat.

Jack had not come looking for her. He was here at her father's request. Here probably because he wanted to buy the company, and humouring her father was the best way to go about it. And her father was playing at matchmaker. He had to be. Everyone appeared to be. She pressed her hands together and strove for a normal tone.

'How is he? I mean, he was in good spirits when I left with Lucy earlier. Has he taken a sudden turn?'

'He is fine, but he feared you might be overdoing it. We decided it was for the best if I came out here and offered to take you back in my sleigh.'

The lines around his eyes crinkled, and Emma's heart turned over. It was as if she wanted to capture each moment and remember it for ever. She was certain his hair had grown slightly in the time he had been away, and the cut of his coat was different.

'My father worries too much. I was fine until one of Lottie's admirers collided with me.'

'Are you hurt?' Jack's hands reached out, stopped. 'How did you fall? Have you hurt your head?'

'Nothing but my pride.' Emma gave a small shiver. There was no point in telling Jack about her trepidations. Dr Milburn's sinister behaviour had melted away like snow in the sun now that Jack was here. 'I told Dr Milburn that. He appeared to believe me.'

'What Milburn believes is of little interest to me.'

'He gave me a cup of Mrs Charlton's punch. I assume that is safe.'

'I have no reason to doubt it. Is it any good?'

'It is a secret recipe for lamb's wool, perfected over the years.' Emma thought it best not to mention the awful taste of the punch. It seemed improbable that it had caused her problems. Other people, including Lucy, had drunk cups of it, and they seemed to be behaving perfectly normally. 'Lottie's young lieutenant thought some of Dr Milburn's famous tonic would set me right, but Dr Milburn said that I didn't need that.'

'Intriguing. Did you say anything about the tonic?'

'I am no fool, Mr Stanton.'

'I never said you were, Miss Harrison. And I make no judgement until the results come back.'

'But you distrust Dr Milburn.'

'Milburn and I have never been friends. I see no reason to start now.'

Emma examined her hands. This was not going the way she had planned over the last few days. She had thought of many things to say to Jack, and how she would say them. And now, when she did meet him again, she was entirely at a disadvantage.

'Which shall it be? Home, or a longer sleigh ride?'

Emma realised with a start that Jack had lifted an eyebrow and was staring at her with a quizzical expression. He had obviously been saying something. She had been paying attention to the way his mouth formed the words, rather than to what he was saying. 'You choose.'

'Then we shall try out my new sleigh and see how the

blades grip the snow. The Town Moor should provide a good clear run. I only thought about it on the way out here.'

A sort of reckless happiness infused her. He wanted her opinion, her help. He had not been simply doing his duty towards her father. She swallowed hard, and tried to banish the wooziness from her brain. He had come back to Newcastle to do a job, not to see her. She had to keep that in the forefront of her mind.

'Is there something special about the sleigh?'

'I have modified the runners. It is based on a Russian troika that I saw when I had business there last winter. Mine is pulled by two horses, not three. This is the first opportunity that I have had to conduct experiments with it. See if my theories actually work.'

'And I presume they do?' Emma hoped her words were enough.

He smiled and his face was transformed. 'I can see from the way your eyes shine that you do want to go.'

The past suddenly no longer mattered. Jack was right. It was only the here and now. She clasped her hands together. The slightly woolly feeling her brain had would vanish once she sat down. She was certain of that. 'Yes—yes, I would like that very much.'

Emma noticed how smoothly the modified troika ran over the snow. It was black, with red leather seats that matched the lap robe, and the grey horses wore a double set of sleighbells. She would not have thought the snow quite deep enough, yet it glided. Most of the others had used carriages to arrive at the pond.

The crisp air was filled with sounds—each separate and distinct—the falling of snow from the bare trees, the swish of the runners and the peal of the sleighbells as the pair of greys stretched out their necks. A piece of ice plopped onto the red plaid blanket. Emma leant forward, tilted it out, and replaced the blanket more firmly about her legs.

'Cold?' He reached into his pocket and withdrew a silver flask. 'Here—this will help keep you warm. Only a little as the brandy is quite potent.'

'Happy,' Emma replied, after she had taken a small sip and felt the fiery liquid trickle down her throat. Somehow it seemed very daring to be drinking from Jack's hip flask. She carefully wiped the top, replaced the stopper and handed it back to him. He returned it to his coat pocket. The pain at the back of her head had ceased, and a wild exhilaration had replaced it—as if she had been reborn and lived now only for this. 'This must be what flying feels like.'

'Some day man will fly. I don't mean simply float in the sky in a gigantic balloon, but actually soar like a bird.'

'You sound confident.' Emma glanced at his profile. His eyelashes were spiked with little crystals of ice. Each individually picked out. She wanted to think of a word to describe it, but her head felt heavy, didn't want to work properly. She would think of the exact word—the word to describe how his lashes looked—later.

'As I told you, we live in an age when someone says I wish to do something and it is done.'

'I will not quarrel with you today. I will agree with you instead. Some day men will fly, but how or why I have no idea.'

'Nor will I quarrel with you. It is far too lovely a day.'

She concentrated on the way his hands held the lines. Strong hands encased in kid gloves, holding the leather lines with ease and confidence. It was hard to believe that when they'd first met Jack had never ridden a horse, let alone driven a spirited team like this pair obviously were.

'Do you want to drive?' he asked.

'Me?' Emma asked in surprise.

'I seem to recall you used to be quite handy with the whip and lines. And you are looking at the lines with such an intent expression.'

Emma inclined her head. 'Again, it is something I have left behind me. There isn't time to drive out any more. And a lady never drives in town.'

'Is there anything you didn't leave behind?'

Devotion to my parents and to duty. An attachment to a young civil engineer I thought had left without a word. A lump rose in Emma's throat. She should say something about the letter she'd found. But not now. Not when they were getting on so well. Perhaps he was correct, and the past no longer counted for anything. It was the future that was important.

She gave a brief laugh. 'Many things. I have no wish to tell you all my vices.'

'Vices? I didn't know spinsters were allowed vices.'

'They are allowed more than young ladies who are active in the marriage market. Spinsters are positively encouraged to be eccentric.'

'If they have money.' Jack's face sobered. 'I have seen many who become pale shadowy companions to even older ladies, living a sort of half-life, dependent on the good nature of their relations.'

'It will never happen to me.' Emma put her hand on the bar. On a day like today she refused to consider a bleak future. Her mind did not want to consider much of anything. It was a strange but not unwelcome sensation—rather like when she had had too many cups of punch, only this time the blood in her veins appeared to be moving more quickly. 'Can these horses go faster?'

'They can, but they need a steady hand.'

Jack clicked his tongue. The larger grey pricked up his ears and gave a low whinny. The pair then surged forward. The wind caught Emma's hood, sending it backwards. She reached up and set it more firmly on her head as the sleigh skimmed over the white snow. The horses shook their heads, seemingly simply for the pleasure of hearing the double set of sleighbells ring.

'They are wonderful animals…' She paused, carefully considering the lines, and the sleigh. She had never driven a sleigh before. The last thing she had driven was the governess cart this summer, but she knew her hands remembered. She watched as the lines stretched and pulled. Did she dare take a risk? 'Yes—yes, I would like to have a try at driving.'

'That's my Emma.'

His Emma. A warmth grew inside her, reached down to her toes. More fiery than the sip of brandy or even the hot punch. She had no desire to analyse the words and read more into them yet. They were carelessly spoken and meant nothing. Later, she knew she would turn them over and over in her mind, trying to remember the exact nuance of his words. Right now she was content with the slight thrill.

He pulled back on the lines and the horses instantly slowed their gait, first to a steady trot and then to a sedate walk. The bells slowed and then quietened. The whole world became wrapped in a hush, as if it were waiting for something to happen, something wonderful.

Emma drew in a deep breath, and focused on a point beyond the horses' ear tips. The dizziness that had threatened a moment before faded and the world became beautifully clear. She could do this. She took the leather lines, flicked them, felt the horses surge forward.

'It is almost as if the lines are alive. Are they strong enough? It would be dreadful to become stranded out here. No one is around to help.'

'They will hold. I had the leather waxed and the joints reinforced. I did not want anything to happen.' He touched his hat. 'Attention to detail saves time in the long term.'

'Are the horses liable to run away, then?' Emma swallowed hard, and tried to keep the horses at a steady gait.

'They are from Tattersall's, and are well trained but lively. I like to drive horses with a bit of spirit.'

And how do you like your women? Emma bit back the words and wondered where the thought had come from. Something inside her insisted on being reckless, grabbing life with both hands.

'You like to live dangerously, then?' she said carefully.

'Dangerously? No, I like to take calculated risks.'

Emma glanced at him out of the corner of her eye. A calculated risk? Was that what she was taking? She turned her attention firmly to the horses, and watched the power of their stride as they moved over the unbroken snow of the Town Moor.

She pulled back slightly, and the horses responded much more sharply than she'd thought they would. The sleigh turned, rising slightly on one runner. She slid into Jack, her thigh touching his through their clothes. She forgot her lungs needed air.

'Everything will be fine. Keep calm.' Jack's voice rumbled in her ear. He put his hands over hers. 'Like this. Steady, with a firm but gentle touch.'

She gave a brief nod. 'They respond quickly.'

'As I said—they are lively. A bit dangerous.'

Like their master. Emma held back the words, only allowing herself to nod. She screwed up her eyes, feeling a dizzy excitement rise within her. Emma did not know which unnerved her more—the horses' abrupt turn or the pressure of Jack's thigh against hers and the warmth of his hands. She had to remain in control. Keeping her attention focused on driving this team would help her do that.

'I believe I can handle them.'

'As you wish.'

Jack withdrew and settled himself against the backboard. He laid an arm across it, not exactly hugging her, but it was there, tempting her to lean back. Emma forced her back upright, reached forward, and gave the lines a flick.

The horses responded, and this time she was able to complete a turn without rocking the sleigh.

'It is amazing how things come back to you. Things you never forget.'

'Your confidence is returning.'

'Something like that.'

Jack glanced over and saw the brightness of her cheeks had increased. They were unnaturally pink, almost as if she had drunk far too much. There was something unusual about her, but he could not put his finger on it. A missing detail.

'Your horses are wonderful.' Her laugh rang out, tinkling like the sleighbells, and Jack decided to concentrate on that instead.

'I am pleased that my sleigh meets with your approval.'

'More than my approval. My admiration. It is very impressive. It is like something from a storybook—a dream.' His warm laughter resounded in the frosty air, warming her insides as surely as the lamb's wool punch had warmed her before, but somehow more potent—much more potent. The world appeared to spin slightly, as it had just after Dr Milburn had given her the drink. She glanced at Jack from under her eyelashes. 'Are you sure I am not dreaming? In many ways I think I must be.'

'If you are, we are experiencing the same dream. And that is an impossibility.'

She pulled the lines, slightly more jerkily this time, and the sleigh slid once more. Her body hit his, her soft breast meeting his chest. Her hands slackened, and the lines fell between them. The sleigh rocked violently.

Jack took the reins from her slack grasp, concentrating on regaining control of the horses, of his body.

'Be careful. You nearly turned us over.'

'I am trying my best,' Emma whispered. How could she explain about her increased dizziness? He would insist on returning to her father's, and she did not want the sleigh ride ever to end. She wanted to be out here, with him. The chance might never come again. Tomorrow she would return to reality, and he would go away again. The thought sobered her. 'I lost concentration, that is all.'

'Losing concentration is when accidents happen.'

'I know.' Emma looked at her hands. 'It won't happen again. Let's stay out a bit longer…please.'

Jack pulled the lines and brought the horses to a stop under the shelter of some trees at the edge of the common.

'Do you want to explain what happened?' he asked. 'It was more than a momentary lapse. You are an expert driver. How badly did you hit your head?'

'It has been a long time since I have driven. That is all. Nothing more. My head feels perfectly fine.'

Jack noticed the red ripeness of her mouth—a ripeness that demanded tasting. Her mouth was inches from his. And there was no sound but the soft plop of snow as it fell from the trees. It was as if they were cocooned in their own little world.

He lifted a hand and touched her cheek. 'I share some of the blame, Emma. These horses are high-spirited, and the sleigh responds instantly.'

'That is kind of you.' Her voice was small, her eyes big.

Jack fought to keep from taking her in his arms. Once he began kissing her he knew that he'd be unable to stop.

Things were too complicated. Business before pleasure. Once ownership of the company was settled, then he could

pursue Emma Harrison properly. She had to know that she
meant more to him than a means to an end. This sleigh ride
showed he had been mistaken. He wanted her in his life. But
on his terms, not Harrison's.

'We will go back.'

Go back? The fizzy bubbles in Emma's veins burst. She
slumped against the backboard and braced her feet. She had
been sure Jack was going to kiss her. Her whole body ached
for the touch of his mouth against hers. Nobody was around.
They were safe. No one would ever know.

Suddenly she knew she had to know how he felt about her.
Once again the strange reckless feeling filled her. Acting on
pure instinct, she leant towards him, lifted her mouth.

'Kiss me.' She caught his face between her fingers. 'Kiss
me like you mean it, Jack.'

He swore, and pulled her into his arms, their bodies colliding once again.

Then his mouth descended on hers, devoured, feasted, and
she knew she had never been kissed before. Everything that
had gone before was tame. This was the essence of danger.

His tongue traced the edge of her lips, demanding entrance.
She parted them, and plunged into a whole other world. Dark.
Dangerous. Carnal. Her tongue touched his, retreated then
advanced. A sigh was torn from her throat.

Her body arched forward and his arms tightened around
her, holding her tight against his chest. The reckless feeling
changed to something warmer, and her breasts began to ache,
new feelings flooded through her. Everything in the world had
stopped, had come down to one thing—him, his touch, his
scent, his everything.

His lips moved from her mouth to her eyelids and face. Hot
against the cold, creating a heat that was burning inside her.

A tiny voice in the back of her mind warned her to stop,

to protest. But her body seemed to have a will of its own. A hot fire was coursing through her body.

She reached up, sank her hands into Jack's hair and pulled his face closer, recapturing his mouth. This time their tongues touched, played, entwined. A wild dark thrill that somehow did not lessen her desire but increased it.

She wanted more than this. A deep burning sensation was growing within her. His body seemed impossibly hard against hers and yet she wanted to feel that hardness, feel his skin touching hers. She wanted… Her hands went to his shoulders.

'We must go back,' he growled in her ear as his tongue licked her earlobe. The briefest of touches, but it sent pulses of warmth through her body.

'Back? Why?'

He lifted a hand and brushed the hair off her face. His lips skimmed her forehead. 'Because.'

His eyes were dark pools fringed by even darker lashes. She wanted to stay here, in this little world they had created. She wanted this fiery ache to continue and grow.

She pressed her lips against his ear. Her breath fanned his hair just above the earlobe. 'That is no answer. You enjoyed the kiss as much as I did.'

He gave a groan and slid his arms around her. Iron bands holding her fast to him. His hand slipped downward, cupping her bottom, pulling her more fully on top of him. Emma allowed herself to fall, encountered the full hardness of his body. She allowed her mouth to echo his, to trail down his throat. Her hands pulled at his stock, releasing a small patch of skin—skin that begged to be touched, to be tasted, feasted on.

'What is going on? Why is this sleigh here?' The voice was sharp, insistent, and horribly familiar in its piercing tone, penetrating her mind.

Emma froze, looked at Jack in horror. They were discovered. Her hair was about her shoulders in waves. His stock was mussed. He put his finger to his lips and gave a slight shake of his head. She nodded her understanding. The people might move on. If she remained quiet there was a whisper of a chance.

'Has there been a crash?' another female voice asked. 'Why has it stopped here under the trees?'

'The horses seem perfectly content. The sleigh is upright.'

'We should leave them,' a masculine voice said. 'It would be folly to pry.'

'Nonsense. They might be hurt. I am going to see. It will be fun. A mystery to be solved.'

'I really shouldn't do that if I were you…'

Emma's eyes widened. They were about to be discovered. Jack's hands released her, pushed her away. Emma hastily sat up, trying to straighten her clothes. She offered up a prayer that no one had noticed, and that she had been mistaken in the voices. They could be from anywhere. The Town Moor was popular with all sorts of people. It could be anyone. Total strangers. She had to be mistaken.

The golden light of a lantern blinded her. She raised a hand and saw several black silhouettes.

'Oh, my, oh, my, oh, my—Miss Emma Harrison. Who would ever have guessed?' Emma winced at Lottie Charlton's smug lip-smacking tones. 'I thought you were far too proper to indulge in such games, but obviously I was wrong.'

'You may lower the lantern, Miss Charlton,' Jack said, and his tone held ice.

'Mr Stanton—such an unexpected pleasure,' Lottie purred.

'We had some difficulties with the horses, but they are now solved.'

Emma's heart pounded in her ears. She knew what was happening. Her head began to spin as the enormity of what she had done hit her. She should protest, or at least make a pretence of being overwhelmed. Something to save her reputation. She should feel ashamed of what she had done. But huge great waves of tiredness hit her. Where there had been giddy excitement now there was only numbness and weary recognition. She was ruined. She was ruined, and furthermore she didn't care.

Shock, horror and general revulsion should be her emotion, she knew, but all she felt was regret and disappointment that the kisses had stopped.

Her eyelids felt heavy. Darkness pressed against her eyeballs. And the cotton wool feeling in her brain returned with a vengeance, swooped down and claimed her. She closed her eyes, intending to rest for a moment before she explained. There had to be a rational explanation for what she had done, what she longed to do again. Something she could say.

Perhaps it was all a dream? Perhaps she had hit her head in the collision with Lieutenant Ludlow and everything since drinking the punch was a dream? If she rested a moment, then she'd wake and discover what was real and what was fantasy.

'Jack,' she breathed, before the darkness claimed her.

Jack swore under his breath. He should have expected this. It had been far too easy. The woman far too willing. And now she had decided to faint. A soft snore came from her lips. No, not to faint, but to fall asleep. Almost as if she was drunk.

He gazed up at the treetops and tried to control his temper. What had she had to drink? Milburn had given her something to drink. There had been something in the way she'd said that. And why hadn't he realised the difference in her behaviour? He gritted his teeth. The truth was that he hadn't wanted to. He had taken because he'd wanted to.

'You saw nothing,' he said, looking at the redness of a major's coat. 'We stopped for a moment when the lines became entangled. We were in the process of untangling the lines.'

'That is not what I saw!' Lottie Charlton's voice held a tone of amused outrage. 'You and Miss Harrison were in an embrace—an intimate embrace.'

'It would be wise to keep your views to yourself, Miss Charlton. You are out here without a chaperon.' Jack glared at her.

'I know what I saw.' Lottie made a little moue with her mouth. 'It is quite shocking. And you the confirmed spinster, Miss Harrison. Tsk, tsk, tsk.'

Jack gritted his teeth. He should have erred on the side of caution. Emma's head lolled against his shoulder.

He tried another approach. 'Miss Harrison is unwell. She needs to get home to her bed.'

'She appeared well when she left the skating,' Lottie answered. 'Otherwise my sister-in-law would not have let her go, and Dr Milburn would have insisted on looking after her. He fetched her some lamb's wool punch. I heard him ask most particularly for it. He wouldn't let my mother take it to her either.'

'Are you sure?' Jack looked at the blonde woman. Could it be possible? Jack frowned and dismissed the thought. He had to stop thinking the worst about Milburn. He might be obnoxious, but it would be an incredible risk to take. The doctor did not even know about his tests for arsenic.

'I think she is shamming.' Lottie Charlton reached into the sleigh. 'Emma—Emma, say something.'

Emma gave a quiet sigh, and snuggled closer to Jack. Her full lips parted as if she had fallen asleep. Asleep, or something worse? Jack frowned. She had avoided saying how badly she had hit her head. Or was she feigning, hoping that everyone and everything would go away? And yet Milburn had been less than pleased to see him. He had had Emma by the wrist. What had he intended? Jack felt a deep anger grow through him.

'I do hope you intend to do the decent thing, sir,' the other female voice said. 'There is only one honourable way to rectify this situation.'

'Yes—you have ruined Miss Harrison.' Lottie Charlton smacked her lips. 'Think of the scandal. Poor, poor Emma. My heart positively bleeds for her. What will Mama say when she hears? And Lucy won't be able to look down her nose at me quite so much now that Emma has behaved like this.'

Jack ignored the pair of harpies. He stared hard at the Major, who was shuffling his feet. 'What was your purpose in coming here, and who sent you?'

'I saw the sleigh skimming across the moor,' the Major answered. 'Lottie thought it would be good fun if we could catch it. We lost sight of it, but Lottie's sharp eyes spied it here in the trees and we decided to investigate.'

'You saw nothing untoward.' He looked hard at the Major, who gave a slight nod.

'Are you going to deny your responsibility?' Lottie gave a faint gasp of horror. 'I know they have always said that you are not quite a gentleman…'

Jack stared at the group in astonishment. He curled his lip. 'I am in the process of taking Miss Harrison home. The sooner she gets there the better, for all concerned. Gossip and idle chit-chat will not reflect well on anyone.'

'But…but…' There came a little squeak of protest from Lottie Charlton, and Jack knew that gossip would spread and grow. The silly woman would be unable to resist.

'I would think a modicum of tact might be worthwhile.' Jack regarded the man. 'I would take it amiss if gossip was spread about her. I would take it as a very great personal favour if it was not.'

'I can see no reason for any of us to say anything, provided the decent thing is done,' the Major pronounced. 'Miss Harrison enjoys a sterling reputation.'

'I always do the decent thing.'

Jack gritted his teeth. He was trapped. Emma was trapped. This was to have been a very different sort of sleigh ride, building their friendship. But he had been unable to resist.

He glanced at her oval face, now quiet in sleep. What would she say when she woke? Who would she blame? Neither of them had a choice.

'But he *is* going to make it right?' the silly blonde asked. 'Poor, poor Emma. Ruined. It would be the gentlemanly thing to do.'

'You do not know very much about me, Miss Charlton, if you call me a gentleman. That is a title I have never claimed.'

'Of all the nerve!'

He heard the shocked gasps with satisfaction as Emma snuggled down against his chest, warm and delightful.

The Emma he knew would never have behaved in such a manner. But did he really know her? She had kissed him with an expert passion.

He clicked his tongue and the sleigh began to move.

'Where are we going, Jack?' she asked in a slurred voice, heavy with sleep. 'I have had the strangest dream. You kissed me, full on the lips. It was lovely.'

Jack gave the lines a tremendous shake, gave the horses their heads, and braced his feet against the dashboard.

'Off home. We go home, Emma,' he said, forcing the words out one at a time. 'And then we see about making this right.'

Chapter Fifteen

'Do you wake, or do I carry you into the house?'

Rough hands shook Emma's shoulder. Her body protested at the sudden rush of air, and sought warmth again, but nothing was there. Her neck ached from being in the wrong position, and her nose was numb from the cold.

She sat up and tried to figure out where she was. The shape of her house loomed above her. She frowned and rubbed her hand against the back of her neck. How had she got here? The last thing she remembered was the sleigh ride and the lines slipping.

'I must have fallen asleep. I had the strangest dream.'

'You are back home. Do you feel capable of walking?' Jack's voice was hard and uncompromising.

The inside of her mouth felt woolly and her lips bruised. She ran her tongue along them and tried to rid herself of a sense of impending disaster.

'What is happening?'

'I am going to see your father.'

'Why?' Emma clambered down from the sleigh and put one foot in front of the other, slipping slightly. Instantly Jack's hand was there, catching her. There was nothing lover-like in his hard fingers.

'We were seen. Your reputation is in tatters. That Charlton chit's mouth flows as freely as the Tyne.' Jack's face was hard and intent—nothing of the lover, everything of the irate businessman.

'But nothing happened.' Emma drew herself up with dignity and tried to remember the lovely dream she had had, with Jack kissing her. His lips had been soft and his voice caressing, bearing little resemblance to this. 'It was just a dream, and dreams don't count.'

'The devil you say.' The words were low and furious.

Emma rubbed a hand over her eyes, saw two doors. If she closed her eyes again all this would go away. It had to.

Emma stretched, pointing her toes and lifting her arms above her head. The linen sheets felt cool against her cheek. She regarded the bright light that shone through a crack in the bed curtains.

She tried to sit up, and rapidly put her head down on the feather pillows again. Pain shot through the front of her head. All her limbs were weak, and the ceiling showed distinct signs of moving. She closed her eyes, opened them again, and tried to focus.

'Annie,' she called. 'What time is it? I have had the strangest dreams. Dreams so vivid and real I could swear they happened, but they were sheer fantastical nonsense.'

'At last you are awake, miss.' Annie twitched back the curtains and daylight flooded into the bed.

Emma put up a hand to shield her eyes and squinted towards the mantelpiece clock. She scrubbed her eyes, focused, and then gaped. Her first glance had not lied. She doubted if she had ever slept so late in her life—not even when she was ill.

'You appear worried, Annie.'

'Your father wishes to see you directly. He has asked several times over the past few hours.'

'Why didn't you wake me?' Emma swung her legs over the end of the bed. 'I feel as weak as a newborn kitten today. Mrs Charlton's hot punch is notorious, but I only had the one cup. Is my father well?'

'Your father has been up since daybreak, miss, bustling about, sending letters here and there, barking orders.' Annie twisted her apron between her hands. 'And I would have woken you, but Mr Jack insisted I was to let you sleep.'

Emma grabbed onto the bedpost and sank back down on the bed. So Jack Stanton *had* arrived. She had thought it a dream. She wrinkled her nose. No, most of it had to be a dream. It had a dreamlike quality to it. More than likely she had hit her head, come home with Lucy and simply then heard Jack's voice as she lay dreaming. She closed her eyes with relief. That was what had to have happened. The alternative was too terrible to contemplate.

'Since when do you obey Mr Stanton?' she asked, keeping her voice calm.

'Since he became your fiancé, miss.' The maid gave a swift curtsey. 'I thought it best. He does appear concerned about you.'

All notion of sleep and beautiful dreams vanished, to be replaced by the ice-cold feeling of dread. Emma put a hand to her head and tried to think. Exactly how much had been a dream?

The sleigh with its bells and runners gliding over the snow? The feel of Jack's leg against hers? His warm lips seeking hers as his hands pulled her close? All of it? None of it?

Her lips ached faintly in remembrance. Had she acted in that brazen manner? Pressing her body against his? She could not imagine doing such a thing. Her entire being became numb. She blinked twice, going back over the events. It had to have been a dream. Was she dreaming still?

She pinched her wrist and discovered that she was definitely awake, and Annie was looking at her with an increasingly puzzled expression on her face.

'I don't believe I am anyone's fiancée, let alone Mr Stanton's.'

'Mr Stanton did say that you had bumped your head, miss. Are you sure you are fit?'

'My head hurts.' Emma explored the base of her scalp and found an egg-sized lump. 'But not in the manner I would expect. I think Mrs Charlton's punch must have been stronger than I first thought.'

'Bound to have been, miss,' said Annie, bustling about the room. 'It is an old wassailing recipe I had from Jeannine, Mrs Charlton's lady's maid. But you are definitely Mr Stanton's fiancée. There can be no doubt about that.'

Emma pressed her lips into a firm line. An old wassailing recipe? But that begged as many questions as it answered. No one else appeared to have suffered the difficulties that she had.

'Exactly when am I to be married? My memory is a bit vague on the precise details.'

'As soon as possible, or so the servants say.' Annie put her hands on her hips. 'And it is hardly surprising your memory ain't good. You were bundled up to bed the moment your foot touched the hall. On Mr Jack's orders. Right angry he was about everything, too.'

'Christmas is only three days away, and there are still preparations for the Goose Feast to settle. It will have to be in the New Year.' Emma tapped her finger against her mouth.

'It would not be for me to say.' Annie stood with her eyes downcast. 'But there was talk of a Special Licence. Servants' gossip only, mind. Rose the under-housemaid had it from Fackler, who heard it from Mr Stanton's valet.'

'Servants' gossip?' Emma gave her maid a stern look. 'You should know better than to go repeating tales.'

'Very good, miss, but I know what I heard.'

Emma pressed her fingers into the bridge of her nose. There was a slim chance that this was simply gossip—misheard rumours and innuendo. She had not agreed to marry anyone! She would know if she had. It was not something one easily forgot. 'It has to be just rumours, Annie. I would remember if Jack Stanton had asked me to marry him. I know I would.'

'I thought you would like to know, miss, just in case.' Annie bobbed a curtsey. 'I must say the thought of a Special Licence sent a little tremor through me.'

Emma drew in a breath, the woolliness vanishing as sweet relief flooded in. She *knew* she had not agreed to anything. She would not forget a detail like that.

A Special Licence…

Despite everything, a small thrill went through Emma as well. When her hair had been in plaits and she had dreamt of dancing all night, and of tall, broad-shouldered dukes who would sweep her off her feet, she'd also had a wish to be married by Special Licence. It had a certain ring to it, and was certainly more attractive than eloping to Gretna Green. Her mother had been furious when Claire had married simply by ordinary licence.

She forced her mind away from girlish thoughts. What sort of licence did not matter. What mattered was that everyone was under the impression that she was going to marry Jack Stanton. And he had never even asked her!

'I am certain you have heard wrong, in any case.' Emma started to dress, tying the tapes of her petticoats with practised fingers. 'When I go down I shall prove what nonsense this conversation has been.'

'As you wish, miss, but what shall I do about your trousseau?'

'My trousseau?'

'I can't have my lady being married without a proper one.
I know your under-things are serviceable, but a married lady
requires more. And there simply is not time to send a Marriage
and Outfitting order out to the linen warehouse at Bainbridges.
Even with the best will in the world it will take a few weeks.
Christmas is nearly upon us.'

'I can always acquire the things later, if it is necessary.'
Emma gave a smile and wished the pain in her head would
cease. She would clear up the mystery and life would go on
as before. This talk of trousseaux was premature. Things were
rapidly spinning out of control—like a trickle of water that
had become a stream and then a torrent, carrying all before
it. She drew a deep breath and refused to panic. 'I am positive
we shall have time. Bainbridges are very efficient.'

'But, miss, your wedding dress… You should send to
London for that. I wouldn't trust any in Newcastle for such a
thing as that.'

'My wedding dress will be dealt with when the time
comes,' Emma said firmly.

She regarded her dresses. The one thing she absolutely
refused to think about was a wedding dress. But Annie was
correct. None of them would do. She raised a hand and stroked
the rose silk. Jack's eyes had shone when he saw her in this.
And when they had danced in the drawing room— She drew
her hand back as if the dress had bitten her.

Enough of this foolishness.

She refused even to allow herself to build castles in clouds.
Her life had to be real and solid. Her future was not married
bliss with Jack Stanton, despite the longings of her heart. She
had to be sensible. She had spent seven years being sensible
and mature. Now was not the time to revert back to the girl
she had been. Dreams were for other people.

'I think my grey poplin would be best for today. It is serviceable, and I have much to do about the feast today. After I have spoken with my father and laid this bit of gossip to rest I have the twelfth cakes to inspect. Can you imagine how Mrs Mudge will click her tongue if the royal icing is not just so?'

Annie did not give an answering laugh. Her brown eyes sobered and she tucked her hands under her starched white apron.

'It is your choice, miss, but I think the blue brings out your eyes more. And grey always robs the colour from your face, if you don't mind me saying. Mr Stanton's face lights up when he sees you in the blue dress.'

Emma gritted her teeth as a pulsating warmth flooded through her. 'You are becoming very bold, Annie.'

'Someone has to take you in hand, miss. Don't you want Mr Stanton's eyes to light up?'

She wanted that, and more. Her treacherous body wanted the feel of his hands and his lips again. She wanted to taste his mouth. Emma put her hand to her head, tried to clear it of the image of Jack's expression just before his lips touched hers, of his hands entangled in her hair, the tiny beat of his pulse at the base of his throat.

'You are being ridiculous, Annie! Please get me a tisane for my head, and kindly refrain from comments about Jack Stanton.'

'Sometimes I think there are those that don't know what is good for them, like.'

'I do know. And concentrating on the upcoming Goose Feast is what I need to do. It means a great deal to the employees and their families.'

'Very good, miss.'

The worst part was that a large chunk of her hoped the servants' gossip was true—all of it.

She did want to marry Jack Stanton. She wanted his eyes

to light up each and every time they saw her. She wanted to feel his mouth against hers again. But more than that she wanted to be with him. To spend hours discussing bridges and other engineering projects. To travel to unknown places and see the sights he had described. Just to be with him. But she wanted him to marry her because he wanted to. Not because he had to, because society dictated it.

It did not matter if the whole of her dream was true—including the nasty bit with Lottie at the end. Emma caught her lip between her teeth, considering the implications if the worst should happen.

Lottie would make much of it. She'd be unable to help herself from giggling and gossiping. The story would fly from lip to lip, become embroidered. Some women might even pull their skirts away from her as she walked in Grainger Town near the Theatre Royal, or refuse to return her calls. The penalties for such scandals were severe, and strictly enforced for some time. But she would recover from the scandal… eventually. Such talk would die down and disappear over Christmas. Scandals were always nine-day wonders.

She was on the shelf. It was not as if she anticipated a brilliant alliance such as her mama had dreamt about. She'd rise above it. Hold her head high. Show it did not matter. What more could they do to her?

And Jack Stanton was not the marrying kind. He had made that quite clear that first day at the bridge. And after what had happened between them, would he risk humiliation by asking her?

No, she could not be engaged to Jack.

Emma forced down the tisane. The infusion of herbs and barley helped restore a measure of confidence. She was not stupid. She would know if that were the case. However much her heart whispered that she wanted it to be true.

* * *

Emma discovered both Jack and her father in the study. They were sitting in front of a blazing fire with cups of coffee at their sides, discussing bridges. Jack's legs, encased in tight-fitting cream trousers, were stretched out in front of him, and Emma glimpsed the tops of his black leather shoes.

Emma listened, half hidden by the door. Jack's voice flowed over her, making her heart pound. It had been just a dream last night. It had to have been. She forced her breath to come naturally.

Jack's long-fingered hand held his cup, and Emma was forcibly reminded of how his fingers had intertwined in her hair. How they had felt skimming her jawline. A warm fluttering sensation grew in her belly as she felt her jaw. It had to have been more than a dream. Surely she could not remember such a thing so vividly if it had never occurred? And yet she could not imagine what had caused her to so forget all notions of propriety.

She was glad that she had listened to Annie and chosen the blue wool in the end, rather than the much more practical grey.

The two men paused in their conversation when she rapped on the door. Only Jack rose, and as Annie had predicted his eyes did light for an instant, before becoming veiled.

Her father lifted a lazy hand but remained seated. 'You took your time, daughter.'

'My eyes have just opened. I have come down with a pounding head and little memory of yesterday afternoon.' Emma gave a smile, but there was no answering one on either man's face. 'Events appear to be a little hazy. The only thing I know for certain is that I left this house to go skating and Mr Stanton arrived to take me home in his sleigh. My eyes must have closed the moment I sat down.'

The explanation would have to suffice. To reveal her dream was unthinkable.

'Hazy?' Her father's face turned the colour of the Turkey pattern carpet. 'How much punch did you have to drink yesterday, daughter?'

'I had the one cup of lamb's wool that Dr Milburn brought me, and a sip of brandy from Mr Stanton's flask.' Emma kept her head high, but two spots of heat formed on her cheeks. 'I had thought my mind was clear, but it appears not.'

'Shamming serves no useful purpose.' Her father's voice was deceptively quiet. Emma shifted in her slippers. She could have dealt with him if he'd shouted, but when he was quiet like this she knew worse was to come. 'This is a scandal of immense proportions.'

She looked from his face to Jack's, found comfort in neither.

'I went for a sleigh ride. Nothing happened.' Emma wrapped her arms about her waist. 'Anyone who tries to say differently is mischief-making.'

Her father harrumphed. 'It all depends on what you call nothing. I never thought you a flirt, my girl. I thought your mother and I had brought you up better than that.'

'My head is so woolly this morning, Father, please try to understand.' Emma bit her lip. The last faint hope she'd had faded. Everything that she'd been certain had been a dream had in fact happened—her insistence on a kiss, and then the aftermath. Her cheeks flamed. She had behaved in such a brazen fashion, pressing her body against Jack's, demanding more. Her father was quite right. She was ruined. Her future lay at her feet, broken and shattered.

'I believe we have already discussed this, Harrison.' Jack moved between her father and herself. 'We have already determined the fault was mine.'

'You have behaved admirably without question, Stanton.' Her father harrumphed again.

Jack held up a hand, silencing him. Her father covered his

mouth and nodded. 'We have reached an acceptable arrangement, with good will on both sides.'

'Your fault? An arrangement?' she whispered. Jack made it sound like a formal business deal. Good will on both sides, indeed.

'In light of what has happened I have offered to do the decent thing.' His eyes became hard black lumps of granite, his mouth uncompromising. 'We will marry with all speed.'

'And I have no choice in the matter?' Emma hated the way her voice squeaked.

'Neither of us has any choice.' Jack's voice was cold, his stare hard.

'There is always a choice.' Emma raised her head and glared back at Jack. 'No one has asked me to marry.'

'The asking was unnecessary,' her father blustered. 'It is all settled. You will marry and marry quickly, daughter.'

'Is it necessary for us to marry quickly?' Emma stared at Jack. His words from that first day clearly reverberated in her head. He had no wish to marry her. It was only the circumstances. How could she marry a man like that?

'I consider it a necessity,' her father said.

'Would we not be better to wait until the scandal has died down? See what happens then? This whole sorry episode will be forgotten by New Year.'

'No.' Jack's dark eyes pierced her and his lips became a thin white line. 'We marry tomorrow.'

Emma's heart pounded in her ears. She stared uncomprehending at Jack, hoping for the slightest sign of softening. There was none.

'Tomorrow? But that will create a bigger scandal.' Emma stared him. Tomorrow was tomorrow. Even for Jack Stanton and his money it was surely an impossibility. There were conventions to be followed. Rules. Regulations. She had to concentrate. There had to be a way. She refused to be married in such a fashion.

'I don't think so.' His mouth took on a cynical twist. 'We shall explain that you and I were close seven years ago, but parted. Now that we have become reacquainted we have discovered our hearts remained true. In light of your father's recent illness we wish to marry quietly but quickly, so that your father can see you as a blushing bride.'

Emma walked over to the fireplace and looked at the embers. *Our hearts remained true.* She rejected the idea. It had not happened. On either part. A cynical tale served up for public consumption. She spun round on her heels.

'But the banns will have to be posted. Those take three weeks.'

His lip curled upwards. 'Not with a Special Licence. You know that as well as I do.'

'A Special—?'

'No need for such a thing. A common licence has already been obtained,' her father said.

This was going altogether too fast. Emma clasped her hands to her head. 'Stop—stop.'

'Is there something wrong, Emma?' Jack asked, in an infuriatingly calm voice. He raised an eyebrow and his fingers beat a slow tattoo against his thigh.

Emma struggled to contain her temper. 'I have not said yes. I have not agreed to marry Jack Stanton or any man.'

She heard the sharp intake of breath, saw Jack's eyes glitter, and she took a step backwards.

Her father pounded his fist against the table. 'You will cease this nonsense and do as I say.'

'Are you ordering me?' Emma put her hands on her hips. 'I am a grown woman, Father. I should have the right to decide my own life.'

'This discussion has little merit.' Jack's words cut through the room. 'Your father and I have reached an agreement.'

'I shall leave you, Jack, to explain the situation to my daughter. Perhaps you can make her see sense where I cannot. You are a man who can make things happen. Here and at the bridge.' Her father turned on his heel and stalked out of the room.

Make things happen. Here and at the bridge. A slight chill went down the back of Emma's spine. Jack and her father had intended on this happening. No one could get a common licence that speedily. It was a physical impossibility.

This marriage had already been decided. Signed and sealed. She had fallen into the trap. Jack's offer to buy the company at a decent price had been a ruse. All the while he had intended to acquire it in a different fashion.

The room started to spin slowly, and Emma sank down into the chair that her father had vacated. She put her head in her hands, willed it to stop.

The deal must have been done the night of the St Nicholas Ball. It must be why her father had allowed her so much freedom. She had been naïve. She had tumbled headlong into a manipulation—a merger between companies. She had been used as a pawn. What exactly *was* the agreement between her father and Jack? She did not doubt Jack had used it to his advantage. Her father must have bought her respectability with his company. It had to be her dowry. There could be no other.

Jack had cynically kissed her. Pretended to be her friend. Damning thought piled on damning thought. And all the while her mind was crying no, somehow she was mistaken, over-reacting. He was interested in her. It was not all pretence.

'You appear less than pleased, Emma,' Jack said. 'I would have thought avoiding a scandal would be something you'd desire. You always set such great store by what society thought.'

Emma raised her face from her hands and looked directly

into his uncompromising face. She refused to let him twist things. This wedding was happening because it suited Jack's purposes—his business purposes.

'You are marrying me for my father's company. It is the price you have exacted for marrying me. You made my father promise it as my dowry.'

A muscle jumped in his cheek but he stayed stubbornly silent.

'I need to know,' she begged. Her insides were jelly. She wanted him to say that it did not matter, that he was marrying her because he could not imagine a future without her.

His eyes raked her up and down. Emma's heart beat so loudly she thought he must hear it. He had to say something. Her throat closed and she struggled for breath.

'I am a businessman,' he said, breaking the stretching silence. 'I have made no secret of wishing to acquire your father's company. That is the truth.'

'I see.' She kept her head high, ignored the sudden prickle of tears behind her eyelids. Whatever happened she refused to cry. She gazed up at the ceiling, blinked rapidly, regained control. Then she looked him directly in the eye and smiled. 'It makes perfect sense now. Thank you for being honest.'

'But perhaps you want soft meaningless words?' His mouth twisted into a hard smile. 'Should I say that I am suffering from an undiminished passion for you? That I have carried a torch for you these past seven years? That not a day has gone I did not think of you and wonder how you fared? What words do you wish me to say? Tell me, and I will say them.'

Emma held up a hand. 'Stop, please. Such cynical sentiments do not become you. You must not think that because I am a woman I spend my day reading Minerva Press novels where the hero declares undying passion for the innocent maiden. Such things do not happen in real life.'

However much we might like them to, she added silently.

'Very well.' Jack gave a slight shrug. 'I won't say it.'

'It is not good to pretend things that one doesn't feel.' Emma strove for a normal voice, but it sounded high and strained to her ears. The knots in her stomach ached and her feet were rooted to the spot. She longed for him to draw her into his arms and whisper that he wanted to marry her, and only her. She wanted to believe his kisses had been real, that he hadn't simply been pursuing her for the sake of acquiring another company.

'Honesty is always best.' He checked his pocket watch, the gold gleaming in the sunlight, and closed it with a snap.

Emma wanted to scream. To do something to end this terrible formality. He had to see that marriage between them would be disaster. 'You caused this situation.'

He raised an eyebrow and a half-smile crossed his lips. 'Me? Miss Harrison, your recollections about yesterday's events may be hazy, but mine are crystal-clear.'

'What do you mean by that?' Emma put her hand to her throat and attempted to look anywhere but at his mouth. Yet every time she attempted to look away something dragged her gaze back, fastened it to that spot, the fullest part of the curve.

'It was you who asked me to kiss you. Begged me.' Jack's gaze never wavered. 'How could I refuse such a request when it was so prettily offered?'

'You should have known the impropriety.' Emma swallowed hard. She was being unfair. She knew it. But this situation was not of her making.

His eyes hardened. 'Perhaps it is I who should be complaining of manipulation?'

'How do you mean?' Emma's jaw dropped, and then she closed her mouth with a snap. She had not trapped him into anything. She hadn't... She stopped as the memory of her voice echoed in her brain. She had asked him to kiss her, begged him.

She wanted to die. Emma fought against the tide of heat that was washing over her. 'What are you accusing me of?'

'Not accusing, merely pointing out the details.' He settled himself on the chair-arm, his right foot swinging slightly. 'It is vital to get the details correct. It makes for a firm foundation.'

'In what way?' Emma crossed her arms and glared at him and his maddening complacency. 'What are you accusing me of doing? I am the injured party here.'

'It was *your* friends who discovered us,' he said, ticking the points off on his fingers. 'And it was *you* who initiated the kiss. You demanded it. Let us be clear on that.'

His dark eyes flared with something, and Emma took a step backwards. Surely he could not think that she would be so underhanded as to try to get a husband in such a fashion?

'It was a series of unfortunate coincidences,' Emma said through gritted teeth. Lottie was not her friend. Never had been. Never would be. How that witch must be enjoying this, crowing to any who'd listen. 'That is all.'

'Tell me, Miss Harrison, do you often behave like that with men?' he asked softly 'Not being raised a gentleman, I sometimes lack the finer details.'

'You should know that it is unlike me,' she said to the fire. 'I have never said that sort of thing to a man before. I have never kissed a man like that before.'

'I am relieved to hear it. I should dislike it intensely if my wife behaved in such a manner with any other man.' He paused and his voice dropped an octave, his eyes flaring with sudden intensity. 'I should welcome it if she decided to act that way with me.'

A tide of heat washed up Emma's face, and she hoped that he would think it was from the fire rather than from the memory of their impassioned kiss. Her hand plucked at her skirt, twisting it, and she tried not to see entangled bodies in the flames.

'Ah, you *do* remember more than you pretended earlier.' There was a definite note of derisive laughter in his voice now. 'I find it best, when one has taken too much alcohol, not to feign ignorance. You were a willing partner last night.'

'I have never denied it. My recollections of the actual event are hazy.'

'And how should I make you remember?' He tapped a finger against his mouth. 'Do you have any suggestions? A repeat performance?'

'You are teasing me now.' Emma's mouth twitched upwards. She knew she was on firm ground. The sinking sensation had vanished. He had not really meant it. He would not kiss her in her father's study. She looked again at his intent expression. Would he? Her pulse jumped slightly.

'What else would I be doing?' He gave a small shrug and strode over to where the silver coffee pot stood. 'The offer and the warning are both there. I expect my wife to cleave only to me.'

Emma wrapped her hands about her waist. This conversation was all wrong. She wanted Jack, she desired his kisses, but not like this, with this hard, mocking expression on his face.

'You said that you had a licence—a common licence. You were expecting this.'

'Expecting you to demand my kisses? No, that was an added bonus.' His eyes blazed and then became cold. 'I like to be prepared for all eventualities, Miss Harrison. I spoke to your father. My time is limited here. There are other projects that clamour for my attention. We must make the best of the situation.'

'And when did you know of my dowry?' She forced her voice to sound calm and not to break. 'When did it become certain that to get your hands on my father's company you would have to marry me?'

'Your father has ensured that you are adequately taken care of.' He examined his cuffs.

Emma gritted her teeth. The worst thing was that a man like Jack Stanton did not need a dowry. He could afford to marry whom he pleased. Why had he done it? She peered at him, but his face offered no clues.

'You are not going to tell me.'

'It is a matter between your father and me. He should tell you, not I.' His eyes burnt with a sudden intensity. 'You will not want for anything.'

Emma's jaw hurt. She wanted to reach out and shake some of the complacency out of him. 'It would have been better if you had spoken to me before getting the licence.'

'I prefer things to be done correctly as well.' His eyes were hooded.

'Then it would have been better if you had asked me to marry you rather than simply announcing it.' Emma crossed her legs and tapped her foot. 'It is insupportable. It makes me seem as if I am a puppet, a doll without any mind.'

'After what happened in the sleigh there was no choice for either of us, Miss Harrison, much as we might wish otherwise.'

'We do have a choice. There has to be another way.' Emma heard the desperation in her voice. Didn't he understand? She wanted him, but not like this.

'I will not risk my business and all the employees who depend on me by being outside of society. Are you prepared to risk your father's?'

A lump rose in Emma's throat. She wanted to go to him and lay her head against his chest. She wanted to feel his hands on her back. Wanted the reassurance that she meant more to him than simply keeping society at bay. That she meant more to him than a means of securing the company. A company that would have been nothing without her interven-

tion earlier this year. She had worked tirelessly to save it…for
what? For him. Her heart bled at the thought of the employees and their families. What would it be like for them with a
new master?

If she did not marry him, would they lose their jobs as the
work ebbed away? She knew the power of whispers, how they
could ruin a man.

'But—'

'No buts, Emma. A quiet yes will do.'

Emma attempted to hang onto some sort of reason. There
had to be a way out.

'As neither of us desires this marriage, I expect it to be in
name only.' She tilted her chin and gazed directly into his eyes,
and was unprepared for the sudden blaze of fire.

'You are in no position to dictate terms.' He stepped closer.
'Shall I demonstrate?'

He reached and grabbed her shoulders, pulling her towards
him, making her body collide with his. His mouth swooped
down and took her breath. Plundered until her legs became
jelly. Her hands lifted and clung to his shoulders. A soft sigh
was drawn from her throat.

He let her go and she stumbled back.

'Point proved. Next time try telling the truth.'

Emma put her hand to her mouth. Tender, bruised, and
aching for more. 'That proves nothing. You have not asked
me to marry you.'

He looked at her. A half-smile curled on his lips. He made
an oh-so-correct bow. 'Very well. Miss Harrison, will you do
me the honour of becoming my wife?'

'I have not considered the matter fully.' Emma kept her
eyes downcast. There had to be a way. She could not marry
Jack like this. There had to be another way.

'You have one hour to decide. There will be no repeat of

the offer.' His smile became crueller, more mocking. 'Remember that more than just your own personal happiness rests on your answer.'

Chapter Sixteen

Emma sat watching the clock tick past the quarter hour on the mantel. She'd give Jack fifty-five more minutes and then she'd give her decision. He deserved to sweat for his high-handed attitude, but he was correct. She could not think of a way out of the situation. They had to marry—or else be outside society.

She might be able to exist—just—but what about her father's business? She knew how many times her mother had said that a man's reputation stood or fell on his wife's. How she and her sister had to behave properly or their father might not win contracts. What if contracts were withdrawn? And the employees—why should they suffer simply because she'd been foolish enough to be compromised? And yet how could she marry simply for business reasons? How could she have a marriage with Jack on that footing…when she wanted more?

Emma willed the clock to stop, but the minute hand slowly headed for twelve.

'My dear Miss Harrison,' Dr Milburn said, barging into the room. 'Your butler said that you were in seclusion, but I insisted. I may have a solution.'

'A solution?' Emma stared at the doctor. What was he going to offer her—more tonic?

'To the dreadful thing you are going through right now.' His smile was a little broad, a little too many teeth.

'How can I help you, Dr Milburn?' Emma forced herself to remain seated, to stay calm. She folded her hands in her lap and kept her back straight.

'My dear child, I cannot help but feel responsible for your current predicament.'

'I doubt you have anything to do with it.'

The doctor started to pace the small room, his coat-tails billowing out behind him. Emma sneaked another look at the clock, willed him to hurry.

'I have thought and thought and I am almost positive I made you drink the punch from Mrs Charlton's special cup.'

'What was in her cup?' Emma's hand trembled. Had this whole thing been a dreadful mistake? If she had been less worried about the tonic would she have drunk the punch? She should have said something.

'I do not wish to betray confidences, Miss Harrison.' He assumed a pious look. 'I have my professional oath to think of.'

'I cannot see how you will be able to remain silent, Dr Milburn. You must tell me all.' Emma leant forward. 'What was in that particular cup? Why should my drinking from it have any bearing on my situation?'

'The senior Mrs Charlton is overly fond of laudanum.' Dr Milburn raked his hand through his hair, but did not meet her eyes. 'I fear she poured a portion into her cup and I took it by mistake. I have turned it over and over in my mind. I am now certain of it.'

Emma stared at the doctor. Her stomach dropped. She had told Jack and her father that something was amiss, but they had not believed her. And now Dr Milburn was admitting to giving her the wrong cup of punch. It made no sense. Was this the miracle she had been praying for? And, if so, why did she feel so curiously deflated? 'What are you saying?'

'I have heard about the terrible scandal this morning, and want you to know that I do not hold you to blame.' He puffed out his chest. 'You did not know what you were doing.'

'It is kind of you, sir.' Emma pressed her fingertips together. 'But I do not believe there will be much of a scandal, or that it will be very long-lasting.'

'You are sadly mistaken there.'

Dr Milburn shook his head and his eyes grew troubled. The 'concerned doctor' look if ever she had seen one. Emma tried to control a sudden stab of anger. If what he was saying were true, then he was to blame…for everything.

'It is only a minor scandal. Nothing happened.' Emma aimed for an unconcerned laugh.

'This is not a minor scandal that will be forgotten by New Year.'

'Why not?'

'They are saying dreadful things—truly dreadful things about you and Mr Stanton. I have heard from three of my old ladies already. By nightfall all of Newcastle will know, and after that all of England.'

Emma forced herself not to flinch. 'Exactly what are they saying?'

'That you were caught in the embrace of that man Stanton, behaving as if you were the worst flirt imaginable.' His face took on a pious expression. 'I know you are not like that, Miss Harrison. I have never known you to behave without decorum. I want to do what I can to help.'

Dr Milburn stood upright, his feet slightly apart, certain that his words must be of great comfort.

'Thank you, sir, for supporting me.' Emma inclined her

head and blinked back sudden tears. It seemed impossible that the odious Dr Milburn should be the only person to think well of her. Everyone, even her own father, was so quick to condemn. 'I am glad you think the best of me.'

'And to silence the whispers I wish to offer you my hand.'

'Your hand?' Emma stared at the pallid fingers, then back up at Dr Milburn's bulging eyes. 'My mind appears to be working slowly this morning. Why would you wish to do that?'

'I wish to marry you and save you and your father from this dreadful scandal. It will circle round and round you.' Dr Milburn placed his palm on his chest. 'I am sensible that Mr Stanton is no gentleman, and cannot realise the harm this little escapade will do to your reputation.'

Emma nearly opened her mouth to inform him that Mr Stanton was indeed determined to put matters right, but closed it. Obviously Dr Milburn had not heard the latest rumour. Nor did she quite believe his story about Mrs Charlton and laudanum. It was far too easy. He had some other motive— one that she could not discern.

'Pray enlighten me.' She leant forward. 'Why did you take the wrong cup?'

Dr Milburn blinked and shifted from foot to foot.

'I was in a hurry. Mrs Charlton had placed it down. I picked it up, and then I forced you to drink. I should have seen by your face that you found it distasteful.'

Emma stilled, remembering. He had known what was in that cup. He had made her drink it. He had wanted her like that. A cold shiver ran down her back. No, that was impossible. This was Dr Milburn, the man who had devotedly tended her mother in her last days. She had to give him the benefit of the doubt…for her mother's sake. 'Dr Milburn, neither of us can change the past.'

'I have thought it over, and it is the only thing to do. You must allow me to repair the damage to your reputation. You must marry me.' His mouth pursed, as if the very idea was distasteful. He captured her hand and held it between his clammy ones. 'You would do me the greatest honour.'

Emma drew on her inner resources and kept her face blank. 'You need not fear, Dr Milburn. I have already taken steps, and I regret that I must decline your offer.'

'Decline my offer?' Dr Milburn opened and closed his mouth several times. 'Are you mad?'

'I know what I am doing.' Emma withdrew her hand. 'I have accepted a prior offer.'

'Whose?'

'Mr Stanton's.'

'It is good to know that you have finally seen sense, Miss Harrison,' came Jack's cold voice from the doorway.

Emma turned and saw him lounging against the doorframe. 'How long have you been there?'

'Long enough.'

'It is not the done thing to listen at doorways.' Emma silently cursed her wayward tongue.

'That is one of the reasons I am very glad not to be well bred, Miss Harrison.' He inclined his head. 'And now I believe I must ask you to depart, Milburn.'

Dr Milburn's face turned red, and then white. 'I was only doing my duty as I saw it.'

'As you can see, there is no need.'

'Ah, yes…well, that is to say…' Dr Milburn placed his hat on his head. 'Should you change your mind, Miss Harrison—'

'She won't.'

Emma heard the door close with a decisive click, but did not turn from where she faced the fire.

'I thought you were going to give me an hour.'

'Shall I call Dr Milburn back?' His voice, silken-smooth, slid over her. 'But then I forget—you have already given him your answer. You are engaged to me.'

'I wanted him to leave with the minimum of fuss.' Emma closed her eyes. Trapped, and she had no one to blame but herself. She slowly opened her eyes and discovered Jack regarding her with an amused expression. 'I thought you were going to give me an hour. You weren't meant to hear.'

'One can learn such interesting things, and your voices were raised.'

'It is a bad habit.'

'Forgive me, Miss Harrison, but circumstances dictated.' Jack held out a piece of paper. 'This arrived by messenger. I thought it best to inform you at once.'

'What is it?'

'The results from the laboratory. My friend was most thorough.'

'What does it say? You mustn't keep me in suspense.' Emma looked over the spidery writing, and the notations. She could follow most of it, but some of it made little sense.

'It is as I suspected. Your father has been ingesting arsenic. You are lucky that he has a strong constitution. The amount in his body would have killed a lesser man.'

'It does explain why he was getting ill. But was it the tonic?' Emma started towards the door. 'Why did you not confront Dr Milburn?'

'I am having them check other bottles of tonic.' Jack hooked his thumbs in his waistcoat. 'I need to be certain if I am to go to the authorities.'

'But my father has high levels of arsenic in his body?'

'Yes.' His expression offered her no comfort.

'That means someone was trying to poison him. Who would do such a thing?' Emma clasped her hand over her mouth. 'I cannot think of anyone in the house. They are loyal servants. And I would never, ever hurt my father.'

'I never suspected you.'

'Thank you.' Emma closed her eyes briefly. Someone had tried to poison her father. His fits had definitely been caused by someone rather than something. He was not dying. She put her hand to her mouth and looked towards the door. 'You don't think it was Dr Milburn?'

'I may not like the man, but he is well respected in the community. He has a following, a reputation.' Jack shook his head. 'I cannot fathom a reason why he should want to poison your father.'

'Or why he might give me the wrong cup of punch,' Emma said quietly.

'I am sorry? I don't follow your line of thought.' Jack looked at her intently, his eyes suddenly flaring with emotion. 'The wrong cup of punch? How could that have bearing on anything?'

'That is why Dr Milburn offered me his hand, as distasteful as it was to him.' Emma bit her lip. 'He believes that he took Mrs Charlton's cup by mistake and says Mrs Charlton is a secret laudanum user. Therefore his sense of duty compelled him to offer for my hand as I am now a fallen woman.'

'Have you heard this of Mrs Charlton before?'

Emma paused. Her brow wrinkled. 'I have heard Mrs Charlton called many things. She and my mother were great rivals once. But never that. She is highly respectable, a pillar of the church. Though the punch did taste foul…'

'And…?'

Emma thought back to her encounter with Dr Milburn. The cold, inexplicable fear washed over her again. 'What if Dr Milburn had planned on kidnapping me?'

'For what purpose?' Jack crossed his arms and his mouth

turned down in a frown. 'Why would Dr Milburn wish to kidnap you? Did you tell him of your suspicions about the tonic?'

'No, I never did.' She put her hand to her head. 'It makes no sense. Nothing makes much sense. Why would he offer me his hand in marriage?'

'People need motivation to act, not some melodramatic reason.' He gave a sudden heart-stopping smile. 'And if his purpose was to marry you, I believe the situation has been remedied.'

'How so?'

'You have agreed to marry me…tomorrow…and there is very little Dr Milburn can do about it.'

'But what will we do about the tonic? Someone has tried to poison my father.'

'There is very little we can do without proof. I will find that proof. Then act. Never fear.' Jack's fingers caught her elbow. 'Dr Milburn will have no escape if he is to blame.'

The expression on Jack's face made her shiver. He was not marrying her for love, but out of duty. And now it was duty that compelled him to protect her. To protect her, or the company? She longed to know which.

Grey light filtered through stained glass, providing the only light in the church. Staff from the house occupied a few of the pews but the rest remained empty. Even Emma's sister had been unable to attend. The journey from Carlisle was too long for her and her children at this time of year.

Emma risked a look at Jack, perfectly correct, with not a hair out of place, the very image of the successful gentleman. His expression bore no signs of welcome, but was black and furious, leaving her little doubt that he was not pleased with the state of affairs. Any doubts she'd had about her father's hand in the matter were dispelled by the radiance of his smile as he gave her to Jack and the vicar began speaking.

Emma concentrated on looking at the altar and the vicar. She recited her vows in a mechanical voice and barely heard Jack's deep ones. She kept feeling that this was somehow not right. They were marrying for the wrong reasons. And yet she was not unhappy to be married to Jack.

'And now I pronounce you man and wife.'

The vicar's words resounded in the nearly empty church. To Emma, it seemed like the closing of a door. It had happened. She was married. There was no going back. She could only face the future and hope.

'You may kiss the bride,' the vicar intoned.

Emma could not control the slight surge in her pulse. Would he kiss her like yesterday? Or the day before? Something to demonstrate his power over her?

His cool lips brushed hers. A quick, impersonal kiss. Emma bit her lip.

'Shall we go, Mrs Stanton?' He held out his arm.

'We have no cause to linger. We are married. The wedding is over.' Emma kept her voice brisk. This was not what her wedding was supposed to be like. She had always envisaged white silk and roses, but there hadn't been time. Instead it was her best blue dress and a nosegay of white narcissi and green ivy. Emma forced her head to be held high as they exited from the cold dark church, blinking into the sunlight. A loud cheer rang out.

Emma's feet skittered into each other and she looked about her in amazement. The churchyard was full of people. She recognised a number from the company. She glanced up at Jack, who shrugged but did not appear displeased. Had he known?

'Best foot forward, Emma,' he said in a low undertone. 'They have come to see the blushing bride.'

'What is going on here?' she asked. 'Who told them?'

'That is not for me to say.'

'We wanted to wish you and the gaffer well, like,' Davy Newcomb said, plucking at her sleeve.

'You mustn't greet the bride yet, lad,' Davy's mother said, pulling him back. 'I am begging your pardon, miss…I mean Mrs Stanton, ma'am. It wouldn't be right and proper until the sweep has been.'

A very blackened and sooty man came up and grabbed Emma's hand, shaking it heartily. 'May much good luck come to you and your marriage.'

A ragged cheer rose from the crowd. 'Three cheers for the gaffer and his missus.'

'Exactly what is going on here?' Emma asked again.

'Harrison and Lowe belongs to me now. The employees and their families have come to wish us well.' He touched his hat. 'As I plan to marry only once, it seemed like the right thing to do. I do not plan to have our marriage spoken of as a hole-and-corner affair. Appearances matter.'

'Me mam went and suggested it to him once she heard, like,' Davy remarked.

Jack laughed. 'Yes, I am afraid young Davy here has been my partner in crime. Are you upset by the attention?'

'Upset?' Emma shook her head. 'More surprised.'

'And we shall celebrate well at the Goose Feast tomorrow. Eh, Davy?'

Jack ruffled Davy's hair.

'Yes, Mr Stanton. That there pine tree has been delivered to the hall, just as you asked. It's huge, like!'

'Good lad.'

'The feast is going on as planned?'

'I told you before, Emma, I keep Christmas as well as any man. A change in ownership means nothing.' He glanced up at the heavy skies. 'I hope for a thaw soon.'

Emma nodded. She knew what he meant. He would keep the employees on as long as possible, but if the present weather continued he would have to start letting them go. At least he was waiting until after Christmas, she thought.

'Emma—Emma, you bad, miserable excuse for a friend.' Lucy came hurrying up. Her little girl held out a sprig of holly for Emma. 'You might have confided in me. This has apparently been planned for ages.'

'We wished to keep the ceremony quiet as my father has not been well.'

'And to think how you must have laughed when I told your Mr Stanton to take care of you on your sleigh ride.' Lucy pressed her hand against Emma's. 'I nearly died of shame for you when I first heard Lottie's lurid account.'

'I am sure Lottie spared no details.' Emma cringed when she thought of Lottie's superior tone.

'Henry was furious with her when he heard. I thought he was going to shake her. He told her to stop spreading lies and rumours. He fairly thundered it, slapping his fist on the table. Mother Charlton was very taken aback as well. I was proud of him.' Lucy lowered her voice. 'Lottie has been sent to live with Mother Charlton's sister in Haydon Bridge in strict seclusion until Henry decides what to do with his sister. She won't be able to spread the tale any further. Her tricks have finally caught up with her.'

Emma reached over and squeezed Lucy's hand. 'Henry did not have to do that.'

'Henry cares about you, and about what happens to you. He was most distressed.' Lucy gave a smile. 'But sometimes he is forgetful. He told me that he'd thought Dr Milburn would marry you. That he would make it all right. But I knew Jack Stanton would prove his worth.'

'Dr Milburn?' The back of Emma's neck pricked. Henry

had made a pairing of her and Dr Milburn? How curious, as she had never said anything to Lucy about Dr Milburn. 'I have never wanted to marry him.'

'And I know it is a real love-match, despite what everyone is saying.' Lucy pressed her gloved hand to Emma's cheek. 'You may try to hide it from everyone else, Emma, but I saw the way you two looked at each other by the pond.'

Emma shifted uneasily. She glanced to where Jack stood, speaking to a few of the employees. The black material of his jacket was pulled tight across his broad shoulders. And she saw the spot where his hair curled as it met his neck. A lump grew in her throat. A love-match. Lucy was correct. It *was* a love-match. A one-sided love-match. She wrapped her fingers tighter around her bouquet. She had done the unthinkable.

She had fallen in love with Jack Stanton.

She watched Jack move down the line, chatting and laughing. Jack would never know. She refused to give him that sort of power over her. He was only interested in the company, in business. He was marrying her for the company and for social respectability.

It was impossible to discern a time or a place, but it had just happened, and now she knew. The full evidence of the emotion hit her between the eyes. She had fallen hopelessly in love with him, despite everything that he'd done.

'Are you all right, daughter?' her father asked. 'You are frowning. All is well that ends well.'

'Perfectly well, Father.' Emma leant forward and gave his cheek a quick peck.

'I thought just then you looked unhappy. I am doing what is best for you. It seemed the most sensible solution to the problem.' He gave her hand a squeeze. 'After my illness I knew I wouldn't live for ever. The company needs to be in safe hands. I needed to know that you would be looked after properly, just as I saw your sister looked after properly. I have a duty towards you. You are ideally matched, if I do say so myself—you share the same interest in civil engineering. I wish your dear mama had.'

Emma nodded. When the time came she would have to let Jack go. She remembered his words from the first day—he had too many projects, a wife and children would tie him down. 'I am sure it will be fine, Papa.'

'Emma, there are a few people here who would like to meet you,' Jack called.

Emma hurried forward and was swept into congratulations from the crowd. Jack and her father had been right, she thought. No one was questioning the suddenness of their marriage. As far as scandals went, it would be forgotten easily.

'You have married Stanton,' Dr Milburn said, coming up to her when Jack had turned to greet some well-wishers. 'Do you know what your dowry was? What your father had to pay?'

'I do not believe it is any of your business, Dr Milburn.' Emma's smile became more fixed. Now was not the time or place for accusations.

'What are you doing here, Milburn?'

'I came to wish you and your bride Godspeed, Stanton. You cannot object to that.' He raised Emma's hand to his mouth. Her flesh crawled, and it was all she could do to endure his touch.

Why had Dr Milburn wanted to marry her? And why had Henry Charlton considered the match already made? The only person who could have told him that was Dr Milburn himself. But why?

'You are wearing a pensive face,' Jack said. His warm fingers guided her through the crowd and he settled her in the carriage, solicitously tucking the robe about her. But Emma knew it had to be for show, to dispel the rumours. 'Are you preparing yourself?'

'Preparing for what?' She pushed away all thoughts of Dr Milburn. She was safe. She had to concentrate on the man beside her—her new husband. 'What should I be ready for?'

'For the wedding breakfast your father has kindly laid on.'

'And after that?' Emma asked, finding breathing difficult.

'We stay here for a few days. I have things to do in Newcastle.'

Emma played with the button of her glove. She knew she should not feel disappointed, but somehow she did. Once when she had thought of her wedding she had thought of white lace and wedding trips to Europe, not a quick trip to the local church and then continuing on as if nothing had happened.

'Of course. I want to stay here in case my father has a relapse.' She kept her head high and stared out of the carriage window.

Jack's hand turned her head to face him. 'We shall stay the night in a hotel. I do not want my wedding night interrupted for any reason.'

Her cheeks prickled with sudden heat. To hide the telltale flush, she bent her head and pretended to smooth the folds of her gown. 'I had not really thought.'

'Has anyone told you what to expect?'

'I know the theory,' Emma said, with what she hoped was dignity. 'Lucy Charlton told me years ago, just after her mother spoke to her.'

'There is a world of difference between theory and practice.'

A warm tingle of anticipation rippled down Emma's spine. 'I doubt it,' she said.

He reached and enveloped her hand in his.

'It is all right, Emma Stanton, you are safe with me.'

Safe? Emma felt anything but safe as she waited in the hotel suite. The room was beautifully appointed and a fire burnt cheerily in the fireplace.

Emma paced the room. She should have found a solid reason to stay at her father's house. Then she would not have had to wonder what tonight would entail. She would have had an excuse to be elsewhere.

There were no flutters of anticipation. Nothing but a numbness. Everything had happened so fast. The only thing she felt was a great lump of fear. She wished she had taken more time, asked more questions of Lucy today. What if what she remembered was wrong? What if she did something wrong? The doubts crowded around her head like crows.

Emma fingered her white lawn nightdress as she looked at the large double bed, piled high with quilts and white pillows. She should get in the bed—or would that seem too forward? So many things she knew she ought to know but was in ignorance of.

It was probably her one chance to bind him to her.

'Shall we begin where we left off?'

Emma jumped at the sound of Jack's rich voice, a voice that flowed over her and teased her senses, promising much but revealing little.

She turned, and her breath caught in her throat. Jack had discarded his coat, waistcoat and stock. His fine white linen shirt was open at the neck. Pure male.

A shiver went down Emma's back. She drew a deep breath and attempted to remain calm, outwardly cool, when her insides appeared to have become molten.

'Whatever you want.'

He came to her. His hand caught hers, held it lightly in his grasp. 'Exactly how much do you know about what is going to happen here…tonight?'

'Enough.'

Emma gave a little shrug of her shoulders to show she was unconcerned. How could she admit that she knew next to

nothing, just quick whispered gossip and the memory of
Jack's lips against hers? No doubt he'd expected her to be in
bed already. A mistake? She moved her hand and his fingers
let her go.

'Women do talk,' she said brightly, and the double bed
appeared to grow larger with each breath she took. 'Shall I get
into bed first?'

'If you wish…'

Emma took a step towards the bed. If she lay there without
moving a muscle it might be over quickly, and then she could
get on with the rest of her life. Jack had married her for the
company, not for her companionship.

'No, wait. I have a better idea.'

Emma paused and half turned round. He held out his
hands, his eyes twinkling. 'May I have the pleasure of this
dance, Mrs Stanton?'

'Dance?' Emma hesitated. All too clearly she remembered
their waltz in front of the fire. Then things had ended in a
heart-stopping kiss. Where would they end this time? But
anything to delay that inevitable moment when he discovered
she knew next to nothing. She tucked a strand of hair behind
her ear. 'What sort of dance do you want? A polka may be a
bit lively for here.'

'A waltz will suit my purpose.'

His hand caught hers, lifted it to his lips. She had expected
a soft brush, but his tongue made a lazy circle on the inside
of her wrist. He repeated the movement on her other wrist and
a deep molten warmth rose within her.

'I believe I can manage a waltz.' She tried for a smile, tried
to forget the warmth building inside her. She had to concentrate. 'Who will hum? Dancing is impossible without music.'

'Allow me.'

He put his hands on her shoulder and waist, and drew her

in close. Their bodies touched. Emma realised with a start that, rather than being constrained in a ball gown and lots of petticoats, it was only fine lawn between them.

The warmth of his body radiated through and enveloped her. She could feel the strength of his thigh muscles, the hardness of his chest. She looked up and was submerged in his inexorable gaze. She should move, but had lost all power to do so.

'My feet are like blocks of lead,' she whispered. 'I am not sure if I can do this.'

'You will get the idea,' he murmured against her hair. 'Trust in me. Follow my lead.'

He started to hum a waltz—a Strauss waltz—in her ear. They moved about the room, but with each turn their bodies moved closer together, until it was as if they were one being.

She half stumbled and his hands came to catch her, pulling her firmly against his body. She glanced up and saw his dark gaze, tumbled into it and could not look away.

A sudden trembling filled her body. A sort of nervousness combined with something else.

His lips touched hers, drew back. A butterfly's kiss, but one that sent ripples of aching tension throughout her body.

She ran her tongue over her lips, tasting them. They seemed to have become fuller in an instant.

'There is no mistletoe here,' she said, with a smile and an attempt at a laugh. Her voice sounded husky and unnatural to her ears.

'How remiss of me.'

His hands cupped her face so she was looking up at him, and she could see every lash, and the fact that his eyes were not black at all, but filled with a myriad of dark colours, eyes to lose herself in.

His mouth swooped down and claimed hers. This time they were firm and lingered long. A heady warmth washed over her and she forgot to be nervous, forgot everything but the feel of his lips against hers.

She gave a sigh and curled her arms about his neck. She wanted, needed more.

He deepened the kiss, demanding entrance to her mouth. Her body responded with an aching need. He moved his legs so her body was positioned between them, the hardness of muscle pressed in on her.

Her lips parted and allowed him entrance. For a long time they stood there, mouth against mouth, tongues exploring, sampling, feasting. Everything had come down to this sensation.

A dark, raging sensation.

The fire grew within, and with each passing breath seemed to grow until it threatened to engulf her whole being.

'We take this slow…very slow,' he murmured against her mouth. His hands undid the ribbons that held her nightcap, let it fall to the ground, and then he ran his hands through her hair. 'I have dreamed of doing this. Pure silk.'

Emma shivered.

Her hands reached and entangled themselves in his hair, pulling his mouth closer. Then she felt herself falling as her knees gave way. Jack scooped her up and carried her to the bed.

He set her down and she sank into the soft cushions. In the firelight, she watched him divest himself of his shirt, and his chest was broader than she'd thought possible. She reached out a hand and touched the warm sculpted flesh while his fingers worked on the tiny buttons that fastened around her neck.

He trailed kisses down her neck, and she knew what she had felt that night in the sleigh was nothing compared to this burning ache inside her.

She started to speak, but he put a finger to her lips.

'Hush, we have all the time in the world. It is time to show you how imagination and creativity can add to the experience.'

He bent his head, and Emma knew everything before had been pure theory.

Chapter Seventeen

Jack propped himself up on one elbow and looked at his wife. Her dark hair was spread out like a carpet on the pillow. Her limbs were entwined with his and her skin still bore a rosy hue from their lovemaking.

She belonged to him now, and it was up to him to keep her safe.

Jack's lips thinned. He did not believe Milburn's story, nor did he think Emma melodramatic. Something had happened to her at the pond. Something had happened, she had not been herself, and he had taken advantage of it. He gave a wry smile. And would continue to take advantage of it for the rest of their lives.

He lifted a strand of hair from her cheek, let it slide between his fingers. Would she have married him otherwise?

Now it was his duty to make sure she was safe. And, until he had confronted Milburn with solid evidence, that meant keeping her away from things.

She gave a murmur that might have been his name and snuggled closer.

He had no wish to worry her. He would deal with the feast,

and then take her away for a protracted wedding trip. Edward Harrison could take care of the bridge for a while, and the rest of his investments were running smoothly. It would give them a chance to get to know each other better, to build on their foundation. But first he had to keep her safe.

'One more day, that's all and then we leave,' he whispered, and then stood up. If he stayed, he'd take her in his arms again and, as delightful as that would be, he would be no further forward. 'Sleep well. Dream of me…please.'

She moved into the warm spot he had vacated.

His heart clenched. Until he knew for certain, he did not want to worry her.

Emma woke to sunlight streaming into the room. She blinked her eyes, intending to call for Annie, and then stopped. The memories of last night came flooding back.

Her body ached in places she had never dreamt possible. She reached out a hand and encountered empty space.

She propped herself up and looked. There was an indentation in the pillow, but the bed was cold. Jack had left. He had gone without saying a word.

She flopped back down on the pillows and stared up at the ceiling. Without a word! She had meant that little to him.

No doubt he was out working…somewhere.

She sat up. But she had work to do as well. The Goose Feast would not run itself. She had planned it all, but there were always last-minute problems. A thousand things could go wrong, and then good will would be lost for ever.

She had to be there.

She wanted to be there.

Emma did not bother ringing for the maid, but started to dress, quickly and with practised fingers.

Within moments she was ready. She gave one more glance

in the pier glass. Serviceable. Her eyes were perhaps a little larger and her mouth fuller, but outwardly nothing had changed. Nothing inwardly as well.

Emma placed her hand over her stomach. She had no reason to think that last night would bring forth a baby, but her arms longed to hold one. A child of her own to love and take care of. Unlike her mother, she would not try to relive her life through the baby. If she ever had a child, she vowed, that child would grow up to do what he or she wanted to do.

She put her hands on her face. *If* was a big word. One she was not going to think about. Later, her attraction to Jack might fade, become something manageable instead of this great aching need. She was pleased that she had not given in to temptation, had not whispered her love.

How he would have laughed and felt pity for her. The one thing she did not want. She could abide many things, but not pity.

She grabbed her cloak and bonnet, opened the door and gave a small cry. Davy jumped backwards, banging his crutch against the wall.

'Davy, you startled me. I wasn't expecting you. I wasn't expecting anyone.'

'Begging your pardon, miss…Mrs Stanton ma'am, but I was told to be here, like. It's my duty, see.' He took off his cap and twisted it.

'Why are you here?' Emma glanced up and down the corridor, but there was no one else. Jack had really gone, left without saying a word.

'The gaffer told me that I was to make sure no one went into your room. And I have been doing that, like. Right boring it is too.'

'No one has gone into my room.' Emma gave a smile and started forward. She would go to the hall and see how the preparations were progressing. It would keep her mind from Jack and wondering why he had left.

Davy nodded, but did not move from where he stood, blocking her path.

'Are you going to let me pass?'

'Begging your pardon again, like. The gaffer did not mean for you to come out. Not now anyhow.'

'Where is Mr Stanton?'

'The gaffer? He has gone to help out. It's the Goose Feast today, like.'

Emma pressed her lips together. She could readily imagine it. Jack wanted to use the Goose Feast as an occasion to consolidate his power, to show to the employees of Harrison and Lowe that he now owned the company. She crossed her arms. He had forgotten one small detail.

'I believe you are mistaken, Davy.'

'You reckon?' The boy tilted his head to one side. 'Where exactly do you think I have gone wrong?'

'Did he actually say that I was to be held here? A prisoner?'

The boy's eyes widened, and his brow furrowed. Then he shook his head. Emma resisted laughing in triumph. She had no doubt that Jack wanted her to stay put, but she had other plans.

'You say that Jack—Mr Stanton—has gone to see about the preparations?'

Emma drew in a deep breath. She had guessed right. He was going to use the occasion to consolidate his power, but he had forgotten one thing—this company was her dowry, and she still retained some vestige of control over it. She was not about to become some milksop miss. She wiped her hands against the skirt of her gown. 'Can you take me to him? We can ask him then.'

'That wouldn't be wise, ma'am.' Davy readjusted the angle of his crutch. 'Really, you are better off staying here, like, until

Mr Jack comes back. If you want to go back in quiet, like, it will be the best for the both of us.'

Emma knelt down so her face was level with Davy's. 'Would you like to see the German Christmas tree? I understand there is going to be a gigantic one—one that reaches up to the ceiling. There are going to be candles, white candy canes and presents. Old Christmas is going to come and give each person at the feast a present. Won't that be splendid?"

Davy slowly nodded his head. 'I never seen one 'fore. Decorated, you see. I have seen lots of pine trees before. It's a monster tree, like. Do you think they will have a present for me?'

'I am sure they will. Mr Stanton and I think you have been a very good lad…all year.' Emma resisted the temptation to pat Davy on the head. She would go and see what was happening. She would not be stuck here in this lifeless room with nothing to do but sit and watch the clock, going quietly mad. 'Mr Stanton is there now, getting things ready.'

'That's right, ma'am. He wants to make sure every detail is correct. I don't know if we ought to. He's in a right fearful temper.'

Emma pressed her lips together. *He* was! What about her? No word of goodbye or anything. He had to learn that he was not going to have everything his own way. There was no way she was going to sit around placing pins into cushions to make sweet mottos. She had had a taste of life and she intended to keep it.

'And once we have found Jack Stanton we shall ask him if I can come out of my room or not.'

'If you say so, ma'am.' Davy gave a shrug and adjusted the crutch under his left arm. 'But seeing how's you are going to anyway, what is the point, like?'

The hall bustled with activity. Everything appeared to be happening at once. Wreaths of holly and garlands of ivy hung from the bare walls, transforming the hall into a Christmas wonderland. The scent of pine and spices filled the air. Along one beam the geese and one large turkey hung, each with a number brightly displayed. The twelfth cakes and mince pies were piled underneath along with brown nuts, winter pears, and all sorts of apples, all hues and sizes, from the brown russet to the rose-cheeked pippin. Bunches of purple hothouse grapes vied with red pomegranates.

Christmas bounty waiting for the employees to arrive. Everything ready, everything going on without her.

A lump formed in her throat. She had worked hard to get this feast organised, had thought herself vital. She'd believed the deception. The reality was far harsher—she was not indispensable, not missed, not needed. Was this the way it was going to be in the future? She wanted to be needed, to make a difference.

'Will you look at that?' Davy gave a low whistle. 'You were right, ma'am, to say I should come. That tree is a monster— a real monster. Can you see what is hanging from it?'

'Yes, it is.' Emma regarded the tree. Pen-wipes, needle cases and smelling bottles vied with less practical items, such as humming tops and little china dolls. White candle tapers stood on the ends of branches, waiting to be lit. It would in time be transformed into a magical paradise for children. She had to admit Jack's idea of a large German Christmas tree with presents was inspired. She could easily imagine the tree being talked over and marvelled at again and again throughout the coming year.

Emma scanned the room and discovered her husband—up a ladder, putting the final touches to a holly wreath. He clambered back down and gave Mudge a slap on his back. The sound of laughter echoed in the hall. Emma's throat closed. She was not required. She had no place here.

'Are you all right, ma'am?'

'Yes, of course,' Emma said quickly. She gave Davy a small push against his shoulder. 'Why don't you go and see the tree? See if any present has your name on it?'

She watched Davy go over to the tree. Jack stopped him, asked him a question. Davy pointed back towards her. His eyes searched the hall and came to rest on her. Emma shifted as they grew dark. She had thought that maybe they would light up, but if anything the light died.

She squared her shoulders and started forward. Her stomach appeared to be in knots, and the distance from the back of the hall to where Jack stood seemed to grow with each step she took.

Then suddenly he had crossed the distance and his fingers closed about her arm. 'Emma, you should be at the hotel, resting.'

'I am here now.' She kept her chin held high and met his gaze directly. 'I did not know where you had gone.'

'I planned on returning in time to bring you here for the start of the feast.' A flash of a smile showed on his face. 'I wanted you well rested. You did not have much sleep last night.'

Emma's heart began to melt. Her body clearly remembered what it was like to be held against him, to have him murmur soft words in her ear. It would be very easy to forgive him. To forgive and forget. But that way led down a slippery slope. She had every right to be here.

'You did not leave a note.' She gave a small shrug and played with the ribbons of her bonnet. 'How was I expected to know?'

He raked his hand through his hair. 'Shall we speak of this somewhere more private?'

'If you wish.' Dimly Emma was aware that everyone in the hall was staring at them. Emma allowed him to lead her away from the others. She kept her head held high. She was in the right.

'Why shouldn't I be here?' she asked when they were alone in the corridor.

'There's no need for you to be here. Everything is in hand.'

'I have worked long and hard for this feast. I have as much right to be here as you. More, even. Now, let go of me.'

His hand fell away from her arm as if it had burnt him.

'Everything is under control. You should be resting, or whatever it is that ladies do on the morning after their marriage. I thought you would sleep longer.'

Emma cast her eyes heavenwards. His reaction was not the one she had expected. She was not so naïve that she'd thought he would scoop her in his arms, but she had expected some sort of civility.

'I *am* doing what ladies do. I have come to supervise the decorating of the hall, to make sure everything is done properly. I have duties and responsibilities, regardless of our marriage. The feast must be right. The memory of my mother demands it.'

'It is all under control.'

'Are you asking me to leave?'

'Yes.' The single word fell from his lips and hung between them, as uncompromising in its tone as his face.

'I see.' She spoke around the huge lump in her throat. 'You have what you want. You have made sure the marriage cannot be annulled, and therefore I am to fade away.'

'You are putting words into my mouth!'

'It is what you think,' Emma countered.

'I am not going to have a silly argument with you, Emma.'

He turned to go. The gentle lover of last night had vanished as if he had never been. Here was only the hard businessman. Emma swallowed hard. All the doubts and fears of yesterday came crowding back in. 'Tell me this—why did you marry me? Was it to get your hands on my father's company?'

His eyes widened. 'Who has been talking to you?'

'I want to know. I deserve to know.' Emma crossed her arms

and stared at him. Her life was about to become devoid of everything—with only a husband who did not love her and no place for her in the company. She had become meaningless, redundant. And he was about to dismiss it all as if it were nerves or an attack of the vapours. 'Was your price—the company?'

'You will have to ask your father.' His eyes burned with rage.

Emma took another step backwards, stumbled. His hand went out but she brushed it away. She straightened her spine. 'I intend to.'

She turned on her heel and marched out of the corridor, forcing her eyes to stay focused ahead and not glance behind her. She had thought he would come running after her. She reached the door, stumbled through it. Outside a fine mist was beginning to fall, making the grey snow become pock-marked.

Hot tears went down her cheeks. She scrubbed them away with the back of her hand. Her marriage was over before it had ever began.

'Emma, why have you returned home?' Her father put down his copy of *Punch* and stood up. Emma was struck by how much brighter his eye was. He was improving. He would get well.

She pressed her hands against her skirt, straightening the folds. She had to ask. Now, before her nerve failed.

'Papa, did you offer Harrison and Lowe as my dowry?'

Her father bit his lip and turned his face away. The pit in Emma's stomach grew bigger. She wanted to bury her hands and cry.

'Papa, tell me. Is that why he married me?'

'It is not something a man likes to speak of.' He held out a hand. 'You are married now, and all your wants will be taken care of. Jack Stanton assured me. Why all this talk about your dowry?'

'I want to know.' Emma clasped her hands under her chin,

forced her tone to be measured. 'I believe I deserve to know. I am not a child to be kept in ignorance about such matters.'

Her father shifted from one foot to the other. 'Some things are better left unsaid. Your dear mama was not interested in such things at all.'

'How can you say such things? I want to know. I *am* interested in the company, and its future. You cannot have sacrificed all the employees for my sake. They have worked for us for a long time.'

'What did Jack tell you?' Her father's gaze pierced her and his voice became stern. 'You have had a fight with him, haven't you? That is why you are spouting this nonsense about wrecking people's lives. I have done no such thing, and neither will Jack Stanton. You are attempting to find excuses, daughter.'

'Papa!'

'You love him very much.'

Emma put her hand to her face and started to pace the room. Was her face that transparent? How had everyone guessed when she had only fully known yesterday?

'My feelings don't come into it,' she said with dignity. 'It is what society demanded. I simply want to know the price you paid for my folly.'

'Oh, but your feelings do come into it. They have to. I told that to your dear mama when she wanted to marry you off to some jumped-up title-holder with no chin. We have to do what Emma wants, and never mind the social consequences.'

'Papa, what are you saying?'

'Daughter, do you love Jack Stanton? Would you have married him if this mess had not come about?'

Emma straightened her shoulders and looked her father in his eye. She knew she could not lie. 'Yes, I would have married him. But I wanted to marry him because of who I am now, and not because of my dowry.'

'I think I may have done more harm than good.' Her father dropped his head to his chest. 'I acted out of the best of motives. But, daughter, your quarrel is with Jack Stanton. You need to go back. You cannot stay here, hiding from the world.'

'I don't want to hide from the world. I want to be there, experiencing life.'

'But you have been. You gave up so many things to look after your mother, and then to look after me.'

'I thought that was what you wanted.'

'True love comes but once in a lifetime. Your mama thought she was doing what was best. She told me that if you and Jack Stanton were meant to be together, somehow you would be.'

'She did what she thought was right.' Emma gave a tiny shrug. 'And she did it out of love. I know that. But she should have given me the choice.'

Her father walked over to his desk. 'I took this letter from her. It explains everything. She would have wanted you to have it. Perhaps it will explain why I offered Jack the company. Why I felt the need to atone.'

Emma looked at the bold writing and knew it was Jack's. The letter he had sent years ago. Her father had it, had kept it. She shook her head. 'That letter is many years too late.'

'Are you sure, daughter?'

The pieces of paper were tantalisingly close. She scanned the first few lines. The words described another person—an angel lighting the darkness, a brilliant dancer, a paragon of virtue. Someone she never had been, could never hope to be. Was this who Jack thought he'd married? She could never be that person. Surely he had to understand that she had changed? She quickly read through to the end. His undying devotion. This proved nothing. He had changed in the past seven years, just as she had.

But what if he wanted the girl from the past? Had thought

he was marrying that girl? A person she could never be? She wanted to know. She needed to know.

Emma folded the yellowing pages up small, stuffed them into her reticule. 'I have to go back. I have to go to the feast. There is little point in living the past, Father.'

The hall that had been empty before now teemed with people. Emma filled her lungs with air. She would go in now and brave them, brave Jack. It would have been easy to stay where she was, but she was determined to fight. Emma felt her father's hand on her shoulder. 'You will be fine, daughter.'

'I have every expectation of being so.' Emma kept her head up. She was pleased that she had decided to wear the rose silk. Her beaded reticule went well with it.

'Emma, I see you have returned.' Jack came up, perfection in his evening clothes. His eyes glittered dangerously.

'As I said before, I planned this feast. I could hardly let the people down.' She tightened her grip on the reticule's handle.

He raked his hand through his hair. 'Emma, we need to speak. But not here, not now. There are too many people.'

'I agree.' Her voice was tight. Emma concentrated on a point over his left shoulder. 'My father and I will be having Christmas lunch. Perhaps you will consider joining us? Unless your business takes you elsewhere.'

There was no change to Jack's face. If anything it became colder. A wall of ice. Emma knew in that instant she had lost him—if she had ever had him.

'I regret that I will be leaving tomorrow. The train leaves for London quite early.'

Emma smiled, but inside her she knew a large piece of her was bleeding. He was leaving. Without her. 'How good of you to inform me of your movements. I shall look forward to your return.'

'Emma, I have said this badly.' He held out his hands. 'There has been no time to talk. I didn't think about your Christmas dinner.'

'It is fine.' Emma ignored the tightness in her throat. Her father was wrong. Jack didn't care for her. He was going to leave. 'If you will excuse me, there are people I need to greet. It would not do to let the company down.'

'We need to speak, Emma, but here is not the time or place.'

'Later, Jack. When you can fit me into your schedule. I understand completely about the demands of business.' Emma turned her shoulder and concentrated on greeting the employees and accepting their good wishes, keeping her head high and her smile bright, drawing on all her social skills. When she glanced back, Jack's eyes had become stone. He moved away from her, leaving a wide, cold chasm between them.

She scanned the crowd and stopped.

'Why is Dr Milburn here?' she asked her father, who had come to stand beside her.

'Dr Milburn?' Her father looked towards where she was pointing. 'He is the company doctor. He always gets an invitation.'

'But I thought...'

'You thought what?'

Emma shook her head. 'It is not important.'

Her father obviously did not know about Dr Milburn's treachery. As Jack still had the piece of paper, there was little she could do. She had to concentrate on what was happening.

'If you say so, Emma.' Her father gave a bemused smile. 'I have lost months with being sick. There are people I need to see—get everything set up for when work begins again in the New Year.'

'The New Year? But I thought Jack ran the company now.'

'He has other things he wants to do. Places he needs to be.'

Emma gave an unhappy nod. He was leaving. He simply had not found a way to tell her yet. It was what she had feared. They had married, and now she was going to be abandoned. Hadn't he said that he moved around too much for a wife?

'Be happy, daughter. Tonight is Christmas Eve.' Her father laid a hand on her shoulder. 'Come, your quarrel will be soon forgotten. Join in with the carolling and the feasting.'

Emma tried to smile. The carols all sounded hollow to her ears. There was no merriment here for her. She could see Jack up by the tree, surrounded by people.

'You had better get ready. The children are expecting Old Christmas to give them their presents.'

'I had forgotten that. Where are the robes?'

'They are out in the back room, I believe. Shall I fetch them for you?' Anything to get away from Jack. She couldn't bear another scene. Not now.

'Very well daughter, if you insist.' Her father held out his cup. 'Wassail, daughter, wassail.'

'Ah, Miss Emma.' Mrs Mudge came up, blocking her path. 'I wanted to say how pleased Mudge is with his bonus. Your father has been generous—very generous indeed this Christmastime.'

'It will be my husband who has been,' Emma said with a polite smile as her insides twisted. 'He owns the company now.'

'That's right.' A frown appeared in Mrs Mudge's face. 'He bought it from your father—cash. That is why your father has given all the employees a bonus. A pretty penny he paid for it too, I heard. Your father stays on to oversee the project along with Mudge, as Mr Stanton is required elsewhere, and once it is done there are many more projects for Mudge to work on—branch lines to be built, stations. All the jobs are safe. Better than anyone could hope for. Mudge tells me everything, he does.'

'But I thought… I thought…' Emma looked up at where Jack stood, surrounded by men. He had done far more for the employees' security than she could ever have hoped for. And he had allowed her father his dignity. She swallowed. Hard. But he was going away…without her. Where to this time? Back to Brazil? Or somewhere else exotic? She didn't know. All she knew was that he had no desire to take her with him.

'If you will forgive me, I see Mrs Newcomb,' said Mrs Mudge. 'Yoo-hoo, Mary! You will never guess what has just happened.'

Cash. Money. Jack had purchased the company. Harrison and Lowe was not her dowry. All the things she had said, all her accusations. All false. A thousand questions sprang to her mind. Jack's broad back was towards her and he appeared in deep conversation with some of the men. She would not give in to impulse and demand an answer. She would have to wait. Patience.

Later she would find out the truth. She'd use the time it took to get the Old Christmas green robes and crown to regain control of her emotions.

All the way to the small room her heart pounded. She had been wrong, but she could do something about it. She could apologise, work to put things right. Ask to begin again.

The corridor was empty, and Emma's shoes sounded loudly against the tiled floor. She opened the door to the small room and her heart sank. The robes and the holly crown had obviously been moved from the wardrobe. A single holly leaf remained in the bottom. Her journey had been in vain. She needed to get back to the others. It was too quiet here, too remote. She wanted to find Jack and apologise. She had to do that.

'Well, well, well, who do I find here? Mrs Stanton, you should not be on your own. You never know what sort of folk might be about, particularly on Christmas Eve.'

Dr Milburn's cold voice made shivers run down her spine.

'I was looking for the Old Christmas robes for my father.' Emma resisted the urge to barge past the doctor and run. She was safe now. She had married Jack. She forced herself to gaze at the pale eyes and smile brightly. 'Do you know where they have gone?'

'Me? Why should I know where such things are?' The doctor gave an elaborate shrug.

'Well, then, I had best be going. I dare say someone has moved them.' Her laugh sounded brittle to her ears, and she tried to ignore the growing pit of nerves in her stomach. She willed the doctor to move.

'I dare say.' Dr Milburn remained where he stood, blocking her path.

Emma clung onto her temper. She had no desire to fight with Dr Milburn, no desire for a scene. 'Please let me pass. I am expected.'

'I am sorry, I can't let you do that.' Dr Milburn advanced towards her and put a cloth over her face. 'One way and another, Miss Harrison, you have been a terrible burden to me.'

Emma struggled against the sickly sweet smell that invaded her senses, but the doctor's grip was too strong and she found the world going black. She tore at his jacket and her fingers closed around a button, ripping it off. She dropped it and her reticule, sent them flying under the wardrobe.

The last sound she heard was a great cheer as Old Christmas appeared.

Chapter Eighteen

'Where is Emma?' Jack asked Edward Harrison.

Harrison took another sip of punch. 'She was around here a few moments ago. I saw her before I started to give out the gifts. She was supposed to find my robes, but in the end, Mrs Newcomb found them for me. I have no idea what she is up to. Emma used to be so reliable.'

A cold fist closed around Jack's insides. Something had happened to her, despite all his precautions. He turned to his young employee. 'Davy, have you seen Mrs Stanton lately? Have you noticed anything amiss?'

'Not since before you sent me to check the experiments, sir,' came the answer. Davy fingered his pile of books. 'The thaw's progressing right fine. There was a light bobbing about in the keep, but that was all.'

'Did you investigate?'

'No, I was too busy thinking about the monster German Christmas tree.' Davy hung his head.

'But that was earlier,' Harrison said. 'The light will have nothing to do with Emma.'

'I am sure you are right.' Jack felt the small box in his

breast pocket. He had wanted to give it to Emma when the others were around, so there could be no refusal. And now Emma had disappeared.

The crowd merged and parted, laughing and happy, showing off the various geese, twelfth cakes and presents they had received. A merry, pleasant scene—but something was wrong. His instinct told him just as surely as he had known the design for the bridge was off. Emma would never have left on her own.

'Where is Milburn?' Jack asked, looking around at the thinning crowd. 'I saw his oily face before.'

'Dr Milburn was called out on an urgent call ages ago. He gave his regrets to me,' Harrison said. 'He always enjoys the Goose Feast, you know.'

'Before or after Emma went for the robes?'

'Before, I think. That's right. He left just before, because Emma remarked on how strange it was for him to be here. Is it important?'

'It might be.'

'I trust Dr Milburn implicitly.' Harrison rose up on the balls of his feet. 'He has never done anything to harm me.'

Jack pressed his lips together. He should have denounced Milburn when he'd had the chance, but he had wanted to give the doctor an opportunity to reveal himself. He had wanted the doctor to explain why.

'Where were those robes kept?' he asked, focusing on the details. If he got the details right, where Emma was would become clear. He should have done things differently. He should never have let this quarrel go on.

'Mrs Newcomb can show you,' Harrison said, gesturing to the overly plump woman. 'She was the one who found them for me. She knows where they were stored.'

'Take me there now.'

* * *

Emma's eyelids were like lead. She forced them open. The ground against her cheek was hard, cold stone. Her mouth tasted as if it had been stuffed with cotton rags. She moaned slightly and moved her head, trying to get a better idea of where she was.

'Ah, good, you are awake,' Dr Milburn said, holding up a single lantern. 'I had worried that I might have given you too much.'

'Too much?' Emma struggled to sit up. Her hands were securely fastened behind her back.

'Too much chloroform. I doubted if you would come with me willingly. But sometimes, if the patient has had too much, the patient does not recover, and I rather thought that would be regrettable with you.'

Emma squinted in the light. Dr Milburn's features swam in front of her, barely discernible in the faint light. She wondered that she had ever thought him a kindly man. He looked pinched, and his face bore the certain sign of madness.

'Where am I?' she asked.

'That would be telling. But you are in no danger, Miss Emma.' The doctor rocked back and forth.

'Are you planning on killing me?' She forced the words from her mouth.

'Killing you? You mistake me, my dear.' The doctor leant in, so close that she could see the beads of sweat forming on his brow. 'You are still useful to my plans. You have a while to live yet.'

Emma turned her face away, unable to suppress a shudder. A while longer to live. There were so many things she needed to do, things she needed to explain.

'Where am I?'

'That is for me to know and for those searching for you to

discover.' Dr Milburn put his fingertips together. 'And there is no use struggling, my dear. I made sure the knots were good and tight. You'd need a knife to cut them. And, alas for you, this room is bare.'

'You are insane!' Emma stared at him in astonishment. His lips were drawn back, baring his teeth.

'No. Determined. I am going to get what is rightfully mine.'

The distant pealing of bells sounded. St Nicholas's. It was at least eleven o'clock at night. She cocked her head. If she concentrated, she could hear the river. The walls of her prison were grey stone. She had to be in the keep, near the building site, but she doubted anyone would look for her here.

'There's no sign of her,' Mudge reported back, shaking his head. 'We have searched and searched, but Miss Harrison… Mrs Stanton…has vanished completely.'

Jack paced the small room. She had to be somewhere. People did not just go. And Emma would not have left without a word. She was far too responsible.

'Search again.'

'Begging your pardon, but where? It is getting late, like.'

'I've found something.' Mrs Mudge knelt down and pulled out a beaded reticule and a brass button. 'The button looks like one from the doctor's jacket. I remarked on them brass buttons to Mudge, I did.'

'Emma was definitely here, in this room. That's my daughter's reticule.' Harrison put his face in his hands and wept. 'She would never voluntarily leave it anywhere.'

Jack opened the clasp with a click. Several sheets of yellowed letter paper greeted him. He instantly recognised his own youthful writing. When had these come into her possession? He took them out and put them into his breast pocket. She always seemed to want to preserve the past—first the

castle, and now these letters. His hand stilled. He picked up
the brass button, sent it spinning into the air. Dr Milburn had
to have seen her drop these. He wanted to be found. Why? If
he had harmed one hair on her head, Jack would not be held
responsible.

'Where can Mrs Stanton be?' Mrs Newcomb's face
creased. 'It is so unlike her.'

'Your Davy said he saw a light earlier in the keep,' Mrs
Mudge said.

A surge of excitement went through Jack. He had him.
'Has anyone checked there?'

'No, it's haunted, like,' Mudge answered. 'No one goes
there. Unsafe, like.'

'That's where he will have taken her. He wants us to find her.'

'Who?'

'Milburn. Milburn has kidnapped Emma for some reason,'
Jack said through clenched teeth. 'She will be alive.'

'I am confused,' Harrison said. 'Dr Milburn is a trusted
member of this community. He has been my doctor for years.'

'There is no time to explain.' Jack ran his hand through his
hair. Everything could wait until he had found Emma. Without
her, life was meaningless. 'You need to go and rouse the authorities. Milburn must be brought to justice.'

'What are you going to do?'

'Save my wife.'

'What exactly do you intend doing with me?' Emma
brought her knees up to her chest as she tried to ease the pain
in her wrists. 'Exactly how long do I have left to live?'

'My dear Emma, you do like a touch of the melodrama,
don't you?' Dr Milburn's smile did not reassure her. He
reached out a hand and lifted her hair away from her shoulder.
'I have no intention of harming you. I have every intention of

marrying you. I told you that several days ago. Unfortunately you chose to ignore me.'

'I am already married,' Emma said carefully. She eyed the distance between where she was and the door. There was an outside possibility that she could run. The rose silk with its many petticoats would hamper her, but she might make it. Anything was better than being here, locked away with a madman. 'Married in a church before witnesses. There is no possibility of the marriage being set aside.'

'You were.' He reached over and lit his pipe from the lantern, pausing to take a long draw. 'It is such a shame that your first marriage was short and you will now have to wear widow's weeds.'

Short? Widow's weeds? Emma's mouth went dry. She fought against the ropes binding her wrists, twisting first one way and then the other. 'What have you done to Jack?'

'Such devotion is touching.' Dr Milburn's face became stern. 'I thought your marriage would be the end to my plans, but now I see it was divinely inspired. I am meant to have more—more of everything.'

Emma swallowed hard. She had to keep him talking. She had to find out.

'What plans?'

'It came to me after your dear mother died. I needed finance for my projects. Henry Charlton had refused me more money and threatened to pull out. Your father was ill and not getting any better. I heard about the plans for the bridge and purchased the land near the castle. Once the bridge's line was chosen it would become valuable, as they would need the station there. No one thought that they would tear down the keep, but I made sure your father saw otherwise.'

'How?' The cold seemed to creep into the very fibre of

Emma's being. Dr Milburn had planned this. He had somehow changed the calculations.

'You father is very suggestible after he has had a fit. It was a simple matter. I knew no one would ever discover the errors. But the money from the sale of the land was not enough. Costs had gone up. The tonic was not selling as well as I had anticipated. I needed more money.'

'And…?' Emma breathed the word. The full horror was starting to creep over her.

'I came upon a way to truly finance my needs. You. You would marry me after your father met his end. I explained the delicate situation to Henry, and he was content to wait and see if I managed to find someone wealthier. He knew there was no other suitor for your hand.'

'I had no plans to marry you.'

'You would have done. That or faced imprisonment for your father's murder.' Dr Milburn shook his head in mock sorrow. 'Nasty, nasty business when one finds poison in medicine. Particularly when it is more than in the other bottles.'

Emma gasped for air. She could see the future Milburn had mapped out

'You knew he had arsenic in his tonic. You were deliberately feeding him poison. First to control him and then to finish him off.' Emma bit her lip. 'But his bouts of recovery came when you were chasing that wealthy widow from Harrogate. Then she married a peer, and your attention once again fell on me.'

'Very clever of you to guess.' The light in Milburn's eyes burnt. He wiped his hand across his mouth. 'Who told you it was arsenic?'

'Jack had the bottle checked after my father's last fit.' Emma raised her chin and stared defiantly at Milburn. 'It had too much arsenic in it. He will ensure the truth comes out.'

'Stanton pays attention to too many details. It will be the death of him.'

'My father is going to get well again. His mind will be as clear as ever.'

'Your father is going to have an unfortunate relapse.' Dr Milburn's face became solemn. 'I shall weep.'

Emma stilled. Her ears strained. She was certain she had heard a noise. Whatever happened she had to keep Milburn talking, distracted. There was a slight chance that he hadn't heard.

'You are insane.'

'I assure you that I am quite sane, my dear.' He smiled. 'Once Stanton reappeared, I had to make sure my investment was safe. Otherwise Henry Charlton would have called in his loan. As it is, I don't have much time. I have thought through my plan long and hard. It suits my needs.'

'But it doesn't suit mine.'

'Your needs are of no concern to me.' He put his hand under her chin. 'Yes, you will serve me well, until I don't need you or your money any longer. Just think—the very wealthy young widow, grief stricken at the loss of her husband and father, consoled by her doctor.'

She wrenched her face away. 'That is something I would never do.'

'But you will.' His leer increased. 'My knowledge of drugs is extensive—a pastime, you might say. That is how I was able to spirit you away from the party. There is a lovely new compound called chloroform, and what people will do after they have tried opium—well, you really don't want to know.'

Emma heard the thump of something falling. She swallowed and tried not to let her emotions run away with her. Was it someone trying to rescue her? How would they know she was here unless…unless Milburn meant her to be found. At

a time of his choosing, with the way prepared for Jack. Sh
closed her eyes and prayed it was not the case.

'How…how are you going to get rid of my husband?'

'You insisted on marrying him. If anything, his demise wil
be at your hands, not mine.' He gave a laugh that echoe
eerily off the stone walls. 'He is just a jumped-up charity boy
A person of no importance.'

'You are wrong. Wrong, I tell you. He has done more fo
this country than anyone. And I for one am proud of him.'

'Such devotion is touching, but misguided. He cares for n
one but his business.'

Emma closed her eyes and acknowledged the truth.

'You are wasting your time,' she said at last, watchin
Milburn move about the room. 'He won't come after me
Jack Stanton only married me for Harrison and Lowe. He i
sure to stay away from here!'

'You underestimate the man's attraction to your charms.
the doctor said with a sneer. 'Such as they are.'

The door crashed inward with a splintering sound. Milbur
was up, pulling her away from the door. His arm encircled he
neck, squeezed, and then released her. She gasped for breath

'That is one of her worst faults.' Jack's voice resounded i
the room. 'Believe you me, Milburn, you would not enjo
being married to Emma. She is far too independent. Neve
stays where you think she will. Always follows her own path.'

Emma's heart gave a leap. Jack was here! He had come afte
her. But he had to realise that it was he who was in danger.

'Ah, Stanton.' Milburn lit a cigar from the lantern. 'You ar
a bit early. I was not expecting you until tomorrow.'

'Sorry to disappoint, but I happen to want to spend tim
with my wife at Christmas.' Jack shrugged. 'A little quirk o
mine, shall we say? Paying attention to little details, particu
larly where my *wife* is concerned.'

'Jack, be careful. He's dangerous,' Emma called. She felt her body fly backwards as Milburn shoved her against the wall.

'You are right,' he sneered. 'The witch does speak too much.'

'You ought not to have done that, Milburn.' Jack's eyes were cold black lumps of stone. 'Nobody touches my wife like that and lives.'

'Jack, this is no joking matter.' Emma tasted the trickle of blood that was running down her mouth.

'Did I give the impression that it was?' Jack lifted an eyebrow. 'How very remiss of me.'

'Jack, he means to kill you,' Emma said urgently as she watched Milburn move about the room.

'I am certain that he means to try,' Jack remarked in a calm voice. 'Whether he succeeds or not is a moot point. Don't you agree, Milburn?'

'Exactly what do you intend, Stanton?'

'I intend to take my wife away from here unharmed, and to celebrate Christmas with her properly.' Jack permitted a smile to cross his face. Later he would think about punishing Milburn, but right now Emma had to be rescued. Milburn would not escape this time. Jack struggled to hang onto his temper. This was not like the time before, when they'd fought. Milburn then had held the advantage. This time, *he* did. He was certain of it.

'I am afraid I can't allow that.' Milburn tossed the cigar onto the floor and ground it in with his foot.

'Then I shall have to fight for her. It will give me great pleasure to tear you limb from limb.'

'I had rather thought you would say that.' Milburn gave a yawn. 'In many ways, Stanton, you are predictable. Breeding will out. You will lose, as you have always done. Who was it that won the house cup? And the school prize? Not you, but me. There is a certain order to this country. Tradition. It will give me great pleasure to re-administer the lesson.'

Jack crouched, tensed his muscles and charged. His shoulder connected with Milburn's stomach. 'Fighting is what charity boys do well.'

Milburn reacted, landed a punch to Jack's jaw and sent him flying backwards.

'I forgot to warn you, Milburn,' Jack said, fingering his jaw. 'I don't intend to fight like a gentleman.'

He threw a knife over to Emma. The knife landed inches from her feet. Emma scooped it up, understanding what Jack meant. She was to cut herself loose and leave.

She worked feverishly and felt the rope begin to give, but her feet were rooted to the ground as the men sparred with each other, neither one gaining the advantage. How could she leave when Jack was in trouble? She had to stay. She rubbed her wrists, and tried to look for an opening.

'Emma! Be sensible!' he cried as she hesitated. 'Go now. Get help. Get to safety.'

She shook her head. 'Not without you. We go together.'

'How touching.' Milburn drew out a handkerchief and a tiny glass vial from his pocket. 'But you need to be ruthless to survive, Stanton, and you have gone soft.'

'Jack, be careful. He has chloroform.'

'Chloro—what?' Jack yelled over his shoulder as he side-stepped Milburn's charge.

'It made me go to sleep.' Emma watched as Jack and Milburn lined up again. Each circling the other. The sickly sweet smell filled the room. 'Be on your guard.'

Jack beckoned Milburn closer. Milburn advanced with the handkerchief, a broad grin on his face. Jack reached out and put Milburn's head into a lock.

'Get the handkerchief,' he said as Milburn tried unsuccessfully to put it in front of Jack's face.

Emma darted forward, snatched the handkerchief, and held

it firmly in front of Milburn's face. He tried to move his head, but Jack increased the pressure. Emma watched as Milburn's eyes rolled back and he ceased to struggle.

'You can drop him now,' she said. 'He has gone to sleep.'

'Powerful stuff that,' Jack remarked.

'Aren't you going to tie him up? I have no idea how long it lasts.'

'It will last a while yet, but what you say makes sense.' Jack used the remains of the rope that had bound Emma to tie Milburn up. 'He won't be bothering anyone for a very long time.'

'I only wish I had seen through him earlier. Did you know that he convinced my father to change his calculations? He had bought the land around the keep and thought to sell it at a high price. Later he hit on the idea of marrying me.'

'It explains much.'

Jack reached and held up the lantern, signalling out of the narrow window.

'Why are you doing that?'

'Mudge had instructions to storm the keep if I hadn't emerged by midnight. I'm telling him to come up now.'

'How did you guess where I was?'

'Davy saw a light earlier. I decided that it was worth a shot.' Jack's face became grim. 'Luckily I was in time.'

'It was you he wanted to destroy.' Emma started to shake.

Jack reached out and gathered her into his arms. 'You are safe now, my love. Your poor wrists. I can never forgive myself.'

His love? Emma wanted to sigh and rest her head against his shoulder, but there was still too much between them. Did he want her, or the girl she had been? How could she ask? The room was suddenly full of men, shouting. Mudge arrived with a rope and took charge.

'We are not wanted here, Emma,' Jack said. 'Mudge is

highly capable once he is given the right sort of direction. I want to get you away from here.'

They left the keep. The cloud had lifted and the starlight cast a soft glow over the snow-clad world. The bells of St Nicholas's Church began to toll, and a quiet hush filled the air.

'It's Christmas,' Emma whispered as Jack drew her into his arms again.

'So it is,' Jack said, against her hair. 'If you reach into my pocket, I have a gift for you.'

'Why can't you?'

'Because I am holding you, and I never intend letting you go again.'

Emma reached in and fished out a small box. She squinted. The box was emblazoned with the name of one of the best jewellers in London. With trembling fingers, she opened it. Inside was a diamond surrounded by two pearls. On the gold band two hands were clasped.

'Let me put it on.' Jack slipped the ring onto her third finger, over her wedding band. 'I bought it in London.'

'But…but…' Emma looked down at the ring.

'I intended asking you to marry me at the Goose Feast, but events overtook me.'

'You let me think that you had married me for the company.' Emma looked up into his face.

'I never mix business with pleasure. How many times do I have to tell you that? I wanted my business concluded with your father before I asked for your hand.'

Emma stared at him in wonderment. He had intended asking her to marry him. The proof was on her finger. It had nothing to do with Harrison and Lowe and everything to do with her. She paused. What if he expected her to be the same as she had been seven years ago? She took the ring off her finger and held it in her palm.

'My mother hid the letter you sent seven years ago,' Emma said. 'My father gave it to me today. It speaks of you holding my image in your heart, a bright flame lighting the darkness of your life, an angel come down to earth.'

'A young man's nonsense. Easily forgotten,' he said lightly.

Emma leant back against his arms and he let her go. She smoothed her skirt and stared out at the silent building site. She had to say everything. She had to make sure there were no shadows between them. Tonight had taught her that, if no other lesson.

'I am about as far from a bright flame as I could be. We did not know each other very well then. Had I received that letter I would have refused you. My first duty was to my mother, and I could not have asked you to wait.'

'I understand.' His voice was tight and stiff.

Emma knew she was in danger of losing him, but she plunged on. 'Are you in love with the girl you thought I was seven years ago?'

His fingers closed around the ring. 'Does it matter?'

'Yes, it does.' She raised her chin and stared at his deep black eyes. 'It matters very much. I grew up. I changed. I found things out about myself that I never dreamt possible. I do not want to be a social butterfly. I want to be me, with all my faults, including taking an interest in building bridges and the like.'

'I don't consider that a fault.' Jack reached out and pulled her into his arms again, held her tightly. 'Emma Stanton, the boy that I was will always admire the girl Emma Harrison. When you refused me and did not answer my letter, I used it as a spur to make my fortune. No one would ever again have the opportunity to dismiss me.'

Emma gulped, but said nothing.

'When I came back here and found you unmarried, my first

thought was of revenge. But you piqued my interest. You would not stay in the box I had made for you. I tried to tell myself that I was only doing it to teach you a lesson in humility.'

'But you didn't.'

'It is you who have taught me. I knew at the ball that I did not want to administer a lesson. I wanted to protect you.'

'That night in the drawing room?'

'I took unfair advantage. I kissed you because I wanted to. I wanted to kiss the woman who was before me—who stands before me now.' His hand lifted her chin. 'It is you I want. It is you I made love to last night. I married you because I want you in my life.'

'But you are going away.'

'*We* are going away. We are taking my private railway car down to London, and then going on our wedding trip. Your father has agreed to look after the bridge with Mudge's help, to build it so the keep is saved. Stephenson will come up and help if needed. The bridge will be built to our design—yours and mine. And it will last. Mrs Newcomb will act as housekeeper, and it will give your father a chance to tutor young Davy.'

'You have thought of everything.'

'I told you, I like to get the details correct.' He dropped a kiss on her nose. 'It is part of my charm.'

'I have no gift for you except my love,' she said in a small voice. He loved her—her, and not some idealised dream. He had married her because he wanted to spend the rest of his life with her. 'I had no idea you felt this way. I wanted to hate you, to despise you. You threatened my whole world. But the more I tried, the more I grew to love you. I want to go with you, to be with you wherever you are.'

'Then accept the ring.' He slipped it on her finger. 'With this ring, I thee wed, Emma Stanton.'

'And with all my heart, I thee wed.' Somehow the vows

they exchanged felt far more real and permanent than the ones they had uttered in front of the vicar.

'Happy Christmas, Mrs Stanton,' he murmured against her lips as the bells of St Nicholas finished tolling the start of Christmas Day. 'You have shown me what Christmas is truly about.'

'No, it is you who have shown me, Jack Stanton.'

Turn the page for a sneak preview
of the first book in the new miniseries
DIAMONDS DOWN UNDER
from Silhouette Desire®,
VOWS & A VENGEFUL GROOM
by Bronwyn Jameson

Available January 2008

Silhouette Desire®
Always Powerful, Passionate and Provocative

Kimberley Blackstone didn't notice the waiting horde of media until it was too late. Flashbulbs exploded around her like a New Year's light show. She skidded to a halt, so abruptly her trailing suitcase all but overtook her.

This had to be a case of mistaken identity. Surely. Kimberley hadn't been on the paparazzi hit list for close to a decade, not since she'd estranged herself from her billionaire father and his headline-hungry diamond business.

But no, it was *her* name they called. *Her* face was the focus of a swarm of lenses that circled her like avid hornets. Her heart started to pound with fear-fueled adrenaline.

What did they want?

What was going on?

With a rising sense of bewilderment she scanned the crowd for a clue, and her gaze fastened on a tall, leonine figure forcing his way to the front. A tall, familiar figure. Her head came up in stunned recognition, and their gazes collided across the sea of heads before the cameras erupted with another barrage of flashes, this time right in her exposed face.

Blinded by the flashbulbs—and by the shock of that momentary eye-meet—Kimberley didn't realize his intent until he'd forged his way to her side, possibly by the sheer strength of his personality. She felt his arm wrap around her shoulder,

pulling her into the protective shelter of his body, allowing her
no time to object. No chance to lift her hands to ward him off.

In the space of a hastily drawn breath, she found herself
plastered knee-to-nose against six feet two inches of hard-
bodied male.

Ric Perrini.

Her lover for ten torrid weeks, her husband for ten tumul-
tuous days.

Her ex for ten tranquil years.

After all this time, he should not have felt so familiar but,
oh dear, he did. She knew the scent of that body and its lean,
muscular strength. She knew its heat and its slick power and
every response it could draw from hers.

She also recognized the ease with which he'd taken control
of the moment and the decisiveness of his deep voice when
it rumbled close to her ear. "I have a car waiting outside. Is
this your only luggage?"

Kimberley nodded. "I assume you will tell me," she said
tightly, "what this welcome party is all about."

"Not while the welcome party is within earshot. No."

Barking a request for the cameramen to stand aside, Perrini
took her hand and pulled her into step with his ground-eating
stride. Kimberley let him, because he was right, damn his
arrogant, Italian-suited hide. Despite the speed with which he
whisked her across the airport terminal, she could almost feel
the hot breath of the pursuing media on her back.

This was neither the time nor the place for explanations.
Inside his car, however, she would get answers.

Now that the initial shock had been blown away—by the
haste of their retreat, by the heat of her gathering indignation,
by the rush of adrenaline fired by Perrini's presence and the
looming verbal battle—her brain was starting to tick over.
This had to be her father's doing. And if it was a Howard

Blackstone publicity ploy, then it had to be about Blackstone Diamonds, the company that ruled his life.

The knowledge made her chest tighten with a familiar ache of disillusionment.

She'd known her father would be flying in from Sydney for today's opening of the newest in his chain of exclusive, high-end jewelry boutiques. The opulent shopfront sat adjacent to the rival business where Kimberley worked. No coincidence, she thought bitterly, just as it was no coincidence that Ric Perrini was here in Auckland ushering her to his car.

Perrini was Howard Blackstone's right-hand man, second in command at Blackstone Diamonds, a legacy of his short-lived marriage to the boss's daughter. No doubt her father had sent him to fetch her; the question was *why?*

* * * * *

Get swept away down under with the glitz and glamour of the Blackstone empire as Kimberley tries to determine the real reason behind her "reunion" with Ric….

Look for VOWS & A VENGEFUL GROOM
by Bronwyn Jameson,
in stores January 2008.

When Kimberley Blackstone's father is
presumed dead, Kimberley is required to take
over the helm of Blackstone Diamonds. She
has to work closely with her ex, Ric Perrini, to
battle not only the press, but also the fierce
attraction still sizzling between them. Does Ric
feel the same...or is it the power her share of
Blackstone Diamonds will provide him as he
battles for boardroom supremacy.

Look for

VOWS &
A VENGEFUL GROOM
by

BRONWYN
JAMESON

Available January wherever you buy books

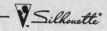

SPECIAL EDITION™

INTRODUCING A NEW 6-BOOK MINISERIES!

THE WILDER FAMILY
Healing Hearts in Walnut River

Walnut River's most prominent family,
the Wilders, are reunited in their struggle to
stop their small hospital from being taken over
by a medical conglomerate. Not only do they
find their family bonds again, they also find love.

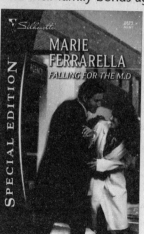

STARTING WITH

FALLING FOR THE M.D.

by *USA TODAY*
bestselling author

MARIE FERRARELLA

January 2008

*Look for a book from The Wilder Family
every month until June!*

REQUEST YOUR FREE BOOKS!

Harlequin® Historical
Historical Romantic Adventure!

2 FREE NOVELS PLUS 2 **FREE GIFTS!**

YES! Please send me 2 FREE Harlequin® Historical novels and my 2 FREE gifts. After receiving them, if I don't wish to receive any more books, I can return the shipping statement marked "cancel." If I don't cancel, I will receive 6 brand-new novels every month and be billed just $4.69 per book in the U.S., or $5.24 per book in Canada, plus 25¢ shipping and handling per book and applicable taxes, if any*. That's a savings of close to 15% off the cover price! I understand that accepting the 2 free books and gifts places me under no obligation to buy anything. I can always return a shipment and cancel at any time. Even if I never buy another book from Harlequin, the two free books and gifts are mine to keep forever.

246 HDN EEWW   349 HDN EEW9

Name _____ (PLEASE PRINT) _____

Address _____ Apt. # _____

City _____ State/Prov. _____ Zip/Postal Code _____

Signature (if under 18, a parent or guardian must sign)

Mail to the **Harlequin Reader Service®**:
IN U.S.A.: P.O. Box 1867, Buffalo, NY 14240-1867
IN CANADA: P.O. Box 609, Fort Erie, Ontario L2A 5X3

Not valid to current Harlequin Historical subscribers.

Want to try two free books from another line?
Call 1-800-873-8635 or visit www.morefreebooks.com.

* Terms and prices subject to change without notice. NY residents add applicable sales tax. Canadian residents will be charged applicable provincial taxes and GST. This offer is limited to one order per household. All orders subject to approval. Credit or debit balances in a customer's account(s) may be offset by any other outstanding balance owed by or to the customer. Please allow 4 to 6 weeks for delivery.

Your Privacy: Harlequin is committed to protecting your privacy. Our Privacy Policy is available online at www.eHarlequin.com or upon request from the Reader Service. From time to time we make our lists of customers available to reputable firms who may have a product or service of interest to you. If you would prefer we not share your name and address, please check here. ☐

HH07

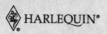

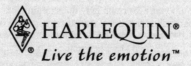

COMING NEXT MONTH FROM
HARLEQUIN®
HISTORICAL

- **THE VANISHING VISCOUNTESS**
  by **Diane Gaston**
  (Regency)
  When the Marquess of Tannerton rescues a beautiful stranger from
  a shipwreck, he has no idea that she is the notorious fugitive the
  Vanishing Viscountess! Can he prove her innocence—or will his fight
  to save her bring an English lord to the gallows?
  *RITA® Award winner Diane Gaston visits the gritty underworld of
  Regency life in this thrill-packed story!*

- **MAVERICK WILD**
  by **Stacey Kayne**
  (Western)
  The last thing war-hardened cowboy Chance Morgan needs is a
  reminder of the guilt and broken promises of his past. But when pretty
  Cora Mae arrives at his ranch, her sweetness soon begins to break down
  his defenses.
  *Warmly emotional, brilliantly evoking the Wild West, Stacey Kayne is an
  author to watch!*

- **ON THE WINGS OF LOVE**
  by **Elizabeth Lane**
  (Twentieth Century)
  Wealthy and spoiled, Alexandra Bromley wants an adventure. And
  when a handsome pilot crash-lands on her parents' lawn, she gets a lot
  more than she bargained for!
  *Join Elizabeth Lane as she explores America at the dawn of a new
  century!*

- **HER WARRIOR KING**
  by **Michelle Willingham**
  (Medieval)
  Behaving like a demure Norman lady does nothing except get Isabel
  married to a barbarian Irish king who steals her away on their wedding
  day. She refuses to be a proper wife to him—but Patrick MacEgan
  makes her blood race, and she's beginning to wonder how long she can
  hold out!
  *Don't miss this sexy Irish warrior—the third MacEgan brother to fight
  for the heart of his lady.*

HHCNM1207